BLACKSMITH'S TELLING

BOOKS BY FAY SAMPSON

A Casket of Earth
The Flight of the Sparrow
The Island Pilgrimmage
The Silent Fort
Star Dancer

Morgan le Fay
Wise Woman's Telling
Nun's Telling
Blacksmith's Telling
Taliesin's Telling
Herself

BLACKSMITH'S TELLING

Book Three of *Morgan le Fay*

FAY SAMPSON

COSMOS

To Alison and Arthur

Cosmos Books

an imprint of **Wildside Press**

www.cosmos-books.com

AUTHOR'S NOTE

In physics, Dark Matter forms an unseen world that is the inverse of the matter we observe. Matter and antimatter were created to exist in equal proportions. Together they hold the universe in balance. But when they come into contact the result is mutual destruction. Morgan's story is the Dark Matter of Britain.

Legend makes Morgan Le Fay half-sister to Arthur and also the wife of Urien and mother of Owain. The historical Urien Rheged and his son Owain flourished in North Britain in the late sixth century, some three generations after the probable dates for Arthur. Urien's kinsman and neighbour was Gwendoleu, whose bard was Myrddin. I have honoured a centuries-old tradition and telescoped the history of the sixth century to bring them all within the orbit of Morgan.

PROLOGUE

I make no excuses. It matters less than nothing to me what you think. I know what others have said of me, even young Taliesin, though I was kind to him.

I am what I am.

I am eternal. I am the shape-shifter. I am Morgan the Fay.

Yes, you may recoil. If you have heard of me at all, it will be nothing to my credit. I am the half-sister of good King Arthur, and his arch-enemy, am I not? The wicked witch, the embodiment of evil.

And yet . . .

Others call me Morgan the Goddess.

After the Battle of Camlann a silk-hung ship comes to fetch the mortally wounded king away to Avalon. I am the queen who takes Arthur in my arms for healing.

How could you understand?

You do not want to live with this ambiguity. Some editing of the story will clearly be necessary.

1

Of course, we knew whose side she was on the moment we clapped eyes on her. Well, she wasn't exactly making a secret of it, was she? I'm almost as much afraid of Morgan of Tintagel as I am of the Horned One himself, but, say what you will, she's never been underhand. Still, coming like that to her own wedding, in a Christian church! You could have blown me down with my own forge-bellows, at the time.

Yes, forge. You've guessed, haven't you? I've seen you staring. I've still got more stubble on my chin than a woman should have. Under this skirt, there's something there shouldn't be. And I've enough beer inside me now to tell you how I came to be shamed like this. For shame I call it to wear a woman's dress. Do you want to hear?

Morgan cursed me.

I was a smith. Do you know what that means? Smith! A wise man that knows the magic of fire and iron. And no common one, either. A king of the craft. They took me for Lord in all the Forest from the Wall to the Lakes. Gods! It hurts me every time I remember. Morgan finished that. She took my manhood and the best part of my magic with it.

It was here in Carlisle, on a May morning, like today.

I'd walked all the way from Lyvennet to feast at young King Urien's wedding. Carlisle didn't belong to him then. His Rheged was a smaller kingdom than it is now. But he was set on having the bishop and his grand church. Urien's always leaned that way. He gets it from his mother.

Not like Gwendoleu. He was the king here in those days, but he'd precious little patience with the Christians. He favoured the Ravens.

I'd tramped the road the old Romans built, with the dawn at my back, and glad to do it. I'd reason enough to be asked to his wedding. It was these hands forged the weapon he'd lifted when they'd made him a man this May Day. I wasn't court armourer. I was no man's hireling, not even the king's. But I had the craft. It was a secret handed down in my family. It was always us made the new king's sword. And I'd worked more in that weapon than a good steel blade and a fine-ground edge. My craft went deeper than that. It's served him true since then, too. There's never a sword will get past that guard, except by treachery.

Men, swords. That's a bitter thought, that is. I don't mind telling you it brings tears to my eyes when I think what I used to be, before I met Morgan. Urien's a big man now, and in all these years he's never recognised me for who I was, skulking about the women's quarters of his palace with a veil round my face. Sleeping in his own wife's bedroom, even. I'd give anything now for one look from him, man to man, even if he ran me through with the sword I made for him straight afterwards. If only, before I die, I could be looked up to for a blacksmith at my own forge, the way I was that day!

I was a strong man in those times, and I didn't begrudge tramping a score of miles if there was free food and beer to pledge the groom's health with at the end of it. There were plenty of others on the road besides me. It didn't feel like an evil day, standing there in the sunshine, with a great crowd of folk lining the street all the way through town to the big church opposite the palace.

There were three of them, waiting for her on the church steps. Young Urien, in a gold tunic. Gwendoleu, his cousin, that was king here in Solway, standing as stiff beside him as if he was the boy's own father. And Bishop Curran, decked out in his best feast-day robes as showy as the rest of them.

We were all waiting for our first sight of the bride. You don't need me to tell you what the women round me were chattering about. You can be sure their heads were full of the fine gowns and the silks and the jewels the ladies would be wearing. And had anyone heard what the Princess Morgan was like? Was she pretty? Was she kind? You know the way women prattle . . .

Morgan of Tintagel, kind! That shows how little we knew of her before she came to Rheged. They'd brought her up from the south-west, from Dumnonia. It might as well have been Gaul for all we knew about her. Some were putting it about that she was Uther Pendragon's daughter. But others said, no, it was only the Queen Ygerne's blood in her. Anyway, Uther

Pendragon was dead of poison years back, like his brother Ambrosius before him, that some call Kings of all the Britons. And neither of them with a son to follow them. We had kings a-plenty without them and were busier raiding each other these days than sending the Saxons packing out of Britain, but no great emperor over the lot of them. Well, it was all the same to me. There was plenty of work for smiths, either way. And it's the common folk who have to pay when you get some big, strong-armed warleader that thinks the bards will sing of him till the world ends if he gets a great army together and goes charging off down south to drive the Saxons back to their ships. And whose taxes go up so he can give his spear-host mead and gold before and after? And who goes hungry when they seize good corn to feed their war-horses on the march? Saxons? I'd never seen a Saxon, and I didn't think I ever should, High King or no High King. So what did it matter to me whose daughter Urien's bride was?

But there was a little cloud of dust coming at the end of the street, beyond the gate, and the women-folk were starting to stand on tiptoe. It was a fine May morning, with the roads dry and all the hawthorn in blossom along the Eden Valley. I'd a sprig of it stuck in my own cap, out of respect for the Lady. I dare say I was staring as hard as any of them at that old red arch through which our new queen would come.

And then we saw her. There was no mistaking which she was, for all the fine lords and ladies round her. And when I looked at her I thought the streets of Carlisle had disappeared. I might have been in our round that holds the nine stone dancers, at sunrise on the first of summer. I'm telling you, Morgan came to us like no queen on earth we'd ever thought to see. Imagine it. A stark, white gown. Plain as a nun's, I might have said at first sight, except that when she rode closer you could see that it was made of stuff so delicate you could almost see the colour of her flesh through it. Little sandals so fine they might have been made of catskin, that hardly hid her bare feet, and a circle of gold on her black hair stuck with fresh flowers. On a mare as white as the hawthorn blossom. Riding astride.

The May Maiden. Not another jewel, nor a golden tassel, nor a scarf of coloured silk anywhere. Just a green ribbon braided in her hair on one side, and a thread of scarlet on the other. She that had the right to wear six colours at once if she'd chosen, being a king's bride. But she'd cast her lot, and not in secret as plenty of the nobles do, crossing themselves for everyone to see and going to church to keep their bishop happy, never mind what they do with us in private. Oh, no! With Morgan it was out in the open, before the whole city, riding up to the door of the bishop's church on her wedding day. I could have kissed her for that, the proud fool that I was. I took her for my sort of queen. And if she was what she claimed to be that day . . . Well, then, she'd know what I was, too.

You should have seen the commotion when she rode through that gate. Like a great wind sweeping down a field of corn. I think every woman's hand flew to her mouth. Some were horror-struck, and some were laughing. And as for the men . . . Well, they were grinning all over their faces. The king's escort that had been sent to fetch her looked pretty grim-faced, I can tell you. So what could we all do but look round at the church door to see how the nobles there would take it?

From where I stood I couldn't see their faces. But there was no doubt which of them took her meaning quickest. I thought the old Bishop Curran was going to throw a fit. He banged his crozier down on the church steps, arguing the toss with Gwendoleu. Then he started off running like a hare. Going home, he was, sooner than give one like her his blessing in his Christian church. But Gwendoleu, that was a big king on both sides of the Wall then, and not a man to be crossed, he was too quick for the priest. He gripped Curran by the arm, just like an eagle snatching a lamb. What chance had the poor old bishop? He wasn't one of your tough hermits, man or woman, that live on berries and water and think themselves so holy they'll sit in judgement over any king in the land. Our Curran was a town man, with a taste for fine robes and palace food. He had to go softly. Where would he be if he crossed Gwendoleu? And the King of Carlisle had planned this match. He knew what he was about – or thought he did. Our little Urien came of the same royal kin as he did. Great-great-great-grandson to good old King Coel. He saw Urien might be top king in the North himself one day if he had powerful friends to back him. There were many useful men would have bedded him with a daughter or a sister to butter their own bread later on. They'd have had their eye on the good farmland in Solway. Tie the lad up quick to some Cornish princess that nobody's ever heard of, that's what Gwendoleu thought. Dumnonia's a mighty long way from Carlisle, and Pendragon's dead and half-forgotten, even if she was his daughter. A stranger from the south, that had no friends. You could see his line of thinking.

As for the bridegroom . . . Well, Morgan had startled us. But we'd a surprise in store for her too. Urien was a grand, well brought-up lad, and generous to us, like his father before him. But he was hardly old enough to use a razor yet. And when I saw what kind she was, I doubted if anyone had told the bride that.

The horses were almost on us by now. They'd strewn flowers and leaves, of course. Still, as the gentry rode by people were starting to cough with the dust and press back a bit. I stood my ground. It meant more to me, you see, than any of those standing there. You may laugh at me now, but I was Smith then. Damn you! Can't you understand? Teilo Smith of Way Bank, where the road runs down from Lyvennet to the Long Lake. Any smith's a man of magic, but I was a cut above all the rest. I was a king myself, in our craft. If she was truly the Lady I took her to be, she would know me for her equal.

She turned my head when she came. I'd never thought of a queen as a woman before. It had been years since we'd had one of our own in Rheged. Those that came visiting were always so dolled up in stiff linen and jewels and furs you couldn't imagine that underneath there was the sort of flesh that a man's hands might want to get hold of. But this one . . . With the sun shining clear through her white gown, and the shape of her thigh laid along the horse's flank, and her little white foot in its fur sandal hanging down. Black hair tumbling loose over her breasts, and pressing the thin stuff close. Eyes, when I got up my nerve to look at them, a truer green than ever I'd seen. A lady rode beside her, dressed all in green, with hair flaming like red gold and eyes as green as Morgan's own. Her sister, Queen Margawse, I found out afterwards. That one was chattering and laughing like a blackbird as they rode. Princess Morgan never answered a word. I could see a smile curving her mouth first, like a cat that's having pleasant dreams. But it told a lie. When she got close, it was her eyes that shocked me. I'd never thought I'd see a woman look so sad on her wedding day.

I thought she was going to ride straight by me. She was so close I could hear the horse's breath and smell the scent of her flowers. But her eyes turned away from her sister's and met mine. There was something quickened in them then. She looked full at me, till she seemed to suck the being out of me into herself, and all my secrets with it. The horse walked on. Her look stayed on me as she turned her head. Then, in front of all those kings and the lords and ladies, she bowed, very gravely. Yes, once, Morgan of Tintagel bowed to me.

That shook me, I can tell you. I don't know what I'd wanted from her. A lift of the eyebrows. A tiny smile. Just something to let me know we shared a secret. But you take your life in your hands when you start to play games with Morgan. I ducked out of that crowd like a fox from his back door, before any of the nobles behind her could have me seized and recognise me. As far as the nobility were concerned, I was a master blacksmith. The best, mind you. They could come to me for the finest edge to their weapons and the soundest harness, and the king's sword. But nothing more. Rheged's supposed to be a Christian kingdom. What I did after sunset, when their gates were barred and they were safe in their halls, and I was the only king that walked abroad, was none of their business. On feast-days, when the god's Servant dances in his mask and horns on the green, no one asks his name. I dare say they guessed, but it was never spoken out loud. She scared me properly.

So I was round a corner and never saw her face when she first set eyes on Urien of Rheged, that was to be her husband. But I could imagine it! Like a cat that sees a strange tom at her bowl. Well, Gwendoleu should never have done it, for all he was scared stiff the boy might be after his throne. Urien was only just come man enough to be a warrior, or a bridegroom. It was against the custom to match him with a woman her age. And what about her? Now that I came to think again of her face, it hit me between the eyes. Here's a full-grown woman, well into the prime of life. Not like my daughter Mair that was thirteen and ripe to be married next year. This Princess Morgan is old enough to be the mother of a whole family already. Where have they been keeping her all these years, that such a woman should come riding like a May Queen to her first husband now? And what sort of power is hers, that let them keep her maiden so long?

That was going to be a rum wedding night for both of them. Gwendoleu must have been laughing and rubbing his hands, to think how he'd fixed it. The old bishop was so scandalised I bet he drank himself silly at their feast, to get over the shock. But, for all that, Urien had an older head on his shoulders than you'd think for a lad his age. She could have done worse. Still, those two in bed! The boy wouldn't know what to do with a Maiden like that. Not like the Horny Lord.

I pulled myself up short. No, you're well out of this, Teilo Smith. Forget those green eyes and the white thighs and her signs of power. Forget the queen bowed to you. One step more and you'll be in over your head. When Urien rides back with his new bride to Lyvennet, you keep a safe distance away from them, and pray the Lord of the Forest no one remembers what happened today. Slip home safely to Way Bank, to your own wife and your daughter Mair. You want nothing from a woman like that.

2

I should have run while I had the chance. That was the second mistake I made that day. Only moments, it was, I stopped round the corner from the square to listen. I'd have given a week's beer to see that proud Lady's face when she saw which of those two her groom was. But Gwendoleu would have his way over her, as he had with the bishop. A woman her age couldn't afford to say no, could she? Oh, aye, she'd marry Urien. He was a king, when all's said and done. But, when it came to it, the folk were all shouting and pushing to get near the church steps, so I never heard what it was she said. They say Urien cried out when he got his first sight of Morgan, but he stood his ground and held out his hand to help her down from her horse, proud as they'd taught him. He's a brave one, that lad. He's got more than he ever bargained for in his marriage bed.

But it was high time for Teilo Smith to be getting away home and putting his wits together again. It's not every day of your life a queen bows to you. Still, we'd never seen a queen the likes of her before.

So I turned for the hills. But the street behind me wasn't as empty as it had been a moment ago. There was a man standing not a yard away from me. Tall, he was. Muffled up in a cloak and hood of whitish-grey, though it was as fair a May morning as you could wish to see.

There's nothing like having a secret for making you feel guilty. I started back as if he'd been a Saxon with a bloody axe. Then it came to me. I'm not stupid. And who's he, I thought, that watches King Urien's wedding round a corner too? I reckoned I wasn't the only one that had got something to hide. So we looked at each other, steady-like, to see which of us had the most to fear from the other.

He spoke first.

"You know this Cornishwoman?" I could tell he wasn't from round these parts himself.

I could have answered no. It was the truth. I'd never set eyes on her before. But that Cornish princess of his had already told half the world she knew something about me that I'd sooner they didn't know. The Christian nobles have got the power: Urien, Bishop Curran and their sort. What the rest of us do has to be done in the dark now. They'll clap and cheer when we come masked with the horns on the great feast-days. But only those that are sworn to us know what's done before and after. It wasn't a thing I wanted talked of, especially among the Christian gentry. I had my living to earn. There's craft and Craft. Even my own wife knew better than to mention it. It belonged to the dark. And I'd meant to keep it that way.

So I didn't answer him straight off. He brought his hands out from under his cloak and made the signs. That made me gasp a bit. I'd been wondering if he was one of their Christian saints, wrapped up in a pale cloak like that. Now we knew each other for what we were, as that queen had known me. Two of them, in the same day. It was a bit too much for me.

"I've never seen her before in my life!" I said, scared-like.

"So?" He considered that for a bit. "But you will again, be sure of that. She knows you now. And Morgan does not forget."

"Ah, but she still doesn't know who I am, does she? I mean, she knows *what* I am. She shouted that loud enough. But that won't tell her my name or where I live, will it?"

"You fool yourself if you think you can hide from Morgan. You were standing among a crowd of Urien's people, from Lyvennet way. And by your hands you are a smith. If I can tell that much, even here in the streets of Carlisle at our first meeting, how long will it take her, living among you in Lyvennet itself? Morgan is high in the ranks of wisdom. Even without those marks, the eyes of her soul would seek you out wherever you hid."

I'd feared that much already.

"What would a queen like her want with me? And will it do me any good?"

"That's a wise question. You do well to be wary of her, Lord of our Craft though you may be. Listen, Smith. I need a wise man. And one that is likely to gain the ear of Morgan, Queen of Rheged."

"Would I be right in thinking you're no friend of hers, wise or not?"

"Say, a friend of Britain."

"What's Britain? I'm a Rheged man. Urien's my king. And she's my queen, or will be in another hour when the bishop's done with them." We could hear their Latin chanting coming from the church now. "Do you want to set me against my own king's wife? What's your Britain to me, to take a risk like that?"

He grasped my wrist. Hard fingers, he had, and stronger than he looked. There was more power in him than just the muscle.

"The Cymry! The Kinfolk. Me, from Glevissig by the Severn Channel. You in Rheged. Morgan in Cornwall. And more than us. All the unfree of our blood, groaning under the heel of the Saxon's white Dragon. One land. One language. Britain."

"That's too big for me. It's all right for you. You're nobility. I can see that. And so's she. Your sort ride the length and breadth of the land and think no more of it than I did today walking from Lyvennet to Carlisle. But I'm a commoner. Rheged's broad enough for me. You leave me out of this."

"No ordinary commoner, Smith, and well you know it. You have much power. And Morgan covets the power of others for her own ends. You cannot escape her now she has picked you out. A child of nine years old, she was, when last I saw her. I feared her then. Yet not enough, it seems. I did not think that once she was free she would move this close to us so quickly."

"Who's we? And close to what?"

There was a crafty look came over his face then, though he kept it in the shadow of his hood. He didn't trust me. But I could tell he wanted something out of me. He stared at me for a fair while. Then those fingers locked round my wrist as hard as any slave-shackle I'd ever hammered.

"Dream bigger, man. No Romans, no Saxons, no Christians. *Our* gods, *our* language, *our* land. One Island of Britain, under the wise."

"Yes? You want a lot! You'll never shift the Saxons from down south. And even your Morgan's getting married in a Christian church."

"Pah! Moonshine. Their day has passed already. Rome's fallen. The Church will be next. Soon we shall drive the Saxons from these shores. The old ways will return."

When I listened to him I began to feel a thrill that seemed to start in the soles of my feet and run right through my body. I believed him, then.

He thought he'd got me. His eyes fairly sparkled.

"Listen, Smith! I could show you something . . . someone . . . that will gladden the hearts of all Britain before long. But we have come to the threshold of danger too soon. The fruit is not ripe yet. We must have no banshee shaking the orchard. I fear Morgan more than anything in the world, or out of it. I must learn what she says, what she plans, what she does. Above all, I must know what she knows. I am asking you to guard this harvest for us, Teilo. Befriend Morgan. Coil yourself near her like a dragon hidden in the grass. If you learn anything at all from her – and I am sure you will – send word to me.

"That sounds like dangerous talk. You just said as much yourself. She'd be my earthly queen by day and my Lady by night. You're asking me to be traitor to her twice over. I'd be a fool not to keep my mouth shut, wouldn't I? What's there in this for me?"

That iron bit into my wrist, cold as ice now. And yet I thought it burned me. I yelled as if I'd been branded for a runaway slave. That made him smile.

"Yes! It is not what you might gain if you agree; it is what might happen to you if you refuse. You would not wish to displease the god, would you?"

It was only half the sign he made, but it set me shuddering. I'd used that against others, but I'd never thought I'd have it turned on me.

"And if I did? Who is it that wants to know, and where do I send word?"

"My true naming is not for you to know yet. Ask for Silver-Tongue, Gwendoleu's bard."

That made me laugh. "Go on! Pull the other one. It's got bells on it. Gwendoleu's bard, and not harping at this wedding? A king's poet could earn himself a fortune on a day like this."

"Idiot! *I*, play for *Morgan*'s wedding! Do you think I'm mad? When she singled out you, whom she'd never met before, among a thousand? You spoke wisely when you said that this is a dangerous game we're playing. I should have had no need to feign sickness to Gwendoleu if she had seen me today. Morgan and I must dance different circles for a while longer. And listen, Smith! If you so much as breathe one word to anyone that you have met me here, I'll raise the Wild Hunt and have the spirit torn from your body by red-eared dogs, and hounded up every mountain in Rheged and down again, and drowned in the deepest lake and raised to life screaming, every night for a thousand years!"

If any other man in the world had threatened me like that I'd have struck him to the ground. And not with my fist either. But I'd met more than my match in power here. Those eyes went through me like a cold chisel through red-hot iron. I knew he could do what he meant. So he let me go, and I felt my wrist. A smith's used to scorch-marks. But he'd left a white scar on the flesh like nothing I'd ever seen before, and the blood wouldn't come back into it, no matter how I rubbed it.

"Remember well. One people. The Cymry. One land. Britain. One faith. The Old Way. It only waits for someone who can stop these petty kings tearing each other's throats out and lead us to glory again."

"All right," I told him. "So I don't get much choice, do I? I'm thinking it may be the worst road I ever took that brought me to Carlisle to drink at Urien Rheged's wedding."

He smiled at me then like a little boy, coaxing-like.

"Dream, Teilo! Drink to bigger things."

And then, blow me, the street was empty. They'd got me fairly trapped, the two of them. This magician and Morgan. I could see I was between his hammer and her anvil. And I was likely enough to be flattened before they'd finished. Well, look what I've come to. I wasn't wrong, was I? The only thing I wanted then was to be safe home in bed under the blankets and having it off with my wife Annis.

3

It's funny how soon you can forget the sweat of danger when you're tucked up safe in bed. I'd had what I wanted off Annis, but I was still wide awake. There were some thoughts I couldn't get my mind off, for all I'd been warned. It's not every day a queen looks at a smith as though there were just the two of them in the whole world, even if that man's no ordinary smith but known for a king in his own way in all the Forest south of the Wall.

So I lay beside my wife and let myself dream about a white thigh under a loose gown, and a crown of hawthorn blossom in blackbird hair. It would smell sweet, that hair. And then I started to think how I'd run my fingers lower down and there'd be warm flesh under that cool hair. Yes, you might well start and turn pale. I must have been bewitched already to imagine such a thing, mustn't I? I hadn't the sense I was born with. I should have clung to my own wife then, like a drowning man clutching on to an oar for dear life. She was a good woman, Annis. I swear I never meant her any harm. But she had feet as cold as frogs. Always had done. You show me a man that hasn't mounted his wife in the dark and dreamed she was someone else.

I'd known plenty of women's bodies. I had my fill of them when I played the part of the Horny One. All sorts, you wouldn't believe. Well, perhaps you would know. Old and shrivelled, some of them, smelly, but still eager for it. They thought themselves blessed if they had it from me. But there were young ones too. At the time they all seem the same. When the fire and the blood are up, and there's drink and drums, everything that comes under the god's hand is more power to him. Only sometimes there was a clean virgin. That's sweet, that is . . . was. You can't imagine. It makes a man feel like the king of stags and roar aloud. But it wasn't often. Well, it couldn't be, could it? It isn't every silly girl we let join us. They have to be old enough to know what they're swearing to. So there weren't many of them that were green.

And now this, come among us. Almost asking me for it. It made my heart pound so I hardly dared think about it. To have a fine noblewoman like that under my thighs. All that full, ripe, rich ladylikeness. Me, Teilo Smith. And a bride fit for a king.

She wouldn't be a virgin, of course. A woman her age, that had risen so high in our ways. You couldn't expect it. There's maidens and Maidens. But she'd know her art all the better for it. I rolled my Annis over to stop her snoring, and I lay in the hay on those old planks and I couldn't help dreaming of the king's bed back in Carlisle. Morgan of Cornwall and our boy-king Urien. And what was she teaching her husband now? It made my flesh creep. He was a brave lad. We knew he'd make a fine king, given time. But married to her! And him hardly out of the priests' school-house yet. What kind of a marriage night were they having, the two of them? She'd no father, by all accounts. It wasn't Uther Pendragon, after all. Someone must have had his knife into her, to have kept her unwed all these years and given her to a beardless boy now. If I was dead, I'd hate to think anyone would do a thing like that to my daughter Mair.

Mair.

I had to turn my thoughts away from that. Whatever I might have imagined in the dark, I never dreamed like that about Mair. We'd vowed her as a child, of course. But I'd never taken her into our circle to make her own sacrifice, not though I was High Chief and she was my only daughter. I don't know what it was that held me back. I just had this feeling that Mair belonged in the morning sunshine. I'd take her to our feasting and dances in the daytime, and she'd squeal with laughter and clap her hands. But I took good care she didn't even guess what her father did by night. I didn't want to think of her under any man, even myself. It wasn't a question of good or bad. There's strength and there's softness in this world. There's dark and there's light. You don't get daisies growing under a yew tree.

So I kept my magic for those that were ripe for it. And here's the joke. D'you know what folk round Way Bank said of me? The Christians, anyway. That Teilo Smith never looked at another woman, saving his

Annis! That was rich, that was. And I'm laughing away till my eyes smart, and I have to pretend it's the smoke from the fire making me cough. Well, I wouldn't look at them, would I? What would I need to for? There were only two sorts of women in the world, as far as I was concerned. Those that had vowed themselves to me, and those that hadn't. And, if you knew what it's like when that fire is lit and the power is in the blood, you wouldn't care to see them in broad daylight either, for all you can feel some of them making eyes at your back from the smithy door or see them squirming against the doorpost and scratching their skirts when you look at them. There's proper times and places for that.

And then there was the other kind, maids like my Mair, and a few good-wives too. Churchfolk, mostly. Well, they could be as bonny as an April day, but there was nothing in them for me. I wasn't going to waste my power on soil that couldn't grow me anything but trouble. I was a hot man, but it's not just the flesh that needs to be satisfied.

Still, for all that, I lay awake and I seemed to know every bit of that body of mine in the dark. I wasn't a young man, but I'd kept myself well. A smith's a man every woman looks twice at. It's the hard muscle, and the shoulders, and the strong hands that grip the hammer that gets them going. And I'd a fine red colour in my face from the forge. Even the dirt in our skin is a different colour. Black dirt, where an outdoor man's is brown. A smith is no common man. He can turn the head of any woman, high or low.

I was a smith! Curse the first one of you that laughs at me! I was a proper man!

. . . Yes, smile. Pity me. It's easy for you. You've always been women. You don't know what I'm missing.

You'll have to excuse me for a bit.

. . . Right. Well. Never till now had I turned a queen's head to mine. And I reckon it must have turned my own head. I lay in bed and hugged the thought of such riches as I'd never dreamed of. If Morgan came to me, under the moon, what kind of greater king would that make me?

Still, it's one thing to lie wrapped up warm in bed and dream. You think you could conquer the whole world. And then you get up in the morning, and your belly's empty and your feet are cold, and you're only half the size you felt you were last night. That grey bard, Silver-Tongue. He was afraid of Morgan. And by the power of his hands he was the greatest magician that I was ever likely to meet. I'd do well to lie low and tread softly. I'd be a fool to meddle with either of them. Him and his dream of Britain.

So I kicked the boy that minded the forge out of bed and shouted at him to rouse up the fire. All that day long I worked at the anvil and tried not to watch the road that ran past my smithy at Way Bank. A week went by, and we heard our king and queen had come home to their castle at Lyvennet. Well, not much more than a wooden fort, really, up there on the hill, looking down towards the foot of the Long Lake. It wasn't half as grand as this stone palace here that the Romans built. I worked with one eye on the road, and sweating from more than the fire. I was sure Morgan would send word for me, you see. Well, she could hardly come riding up to my door herself, could she? Though even that I wouldn't have put past her, come to think of it, bold as she'd acted on her way to the church.

Urien gave a great feast of his own the day he brought Morgan back from Carlisle. They said there was meat and ale enough for a whole army. And not just for the nobles, either. He was always generous, was Urien. Annis wanted to go. So did I. But I kept away. I hadn't quite lost my senses, even then.

But the sun went down that day, and a week of sunsets after that, and no word had come for me. I told myself they'd still be celebrating the wedding up in Lyvennet. They'd have feasting and singing and wrestling and racing, night and day. When it was over, and all the fine lords and ladies had ridden home in their chariots, then she'd remember Teilo Smith.

A month went by, and the meadows were going over to hay, and there was never a sign from her. Just one summer day following another. I couldn't have told you whether I was glad or sorry.

I should have known she wouldn't let me go that easily. It came to me that a woman like her had other ways of sending for me than human servants. As the moon got bigger I could feel her drawing me to her, just like my eyes had drawn hers down to mine on her wedding day.

So I walked to Morgan's dun at Lyvennet one evening in summer, when my work was done and I'd had my supper. I told myself I was her equal, even if I wasn't noble. I came like a man, with a dog at my heels and a stick in my hand, as I might be taking a stroll to cool the heat of my skin in the evening breeze. I kept my dignity.

I took the way that passes between the two rounds, and I couldn't help thinking how it would be to lead the dancing among the stones with one like her. Then I walked on and came to her dun.

I stopped at the edge of the trees, where the forest's been cut back and the grass runs clean up the hill to the walls. I stood there under the last big oak of the woods, as a stag might stand in the gloaming before he steps out to feed. I wasn't as afraid of her as all that. Not nearly as afraid as I should have been. I put my thought out towards her for the second time. I could feel the blood knocking louder and louder. She wasn't the only one that could send her soul out of her body. Mine would be flying soon.

But nothing happened. I came to myself and I found I'd stepped out into the open, like a fool. I could see the sentries up at the gate were looking my way. But I was only one man, with a stick and a dog, and I kept myself too far away for them to shout at me. I stood and watched the shadow of the walls creep down the hill towards me. Then they shut the gate.

I still didn't move. I just stared at the roofs over the top of the walls. Then I started to see strange things in the twilight. A white face, narrow like a half-moon. Hair glossy as it might have been a new-groomed mare's. Eyes . . . well, you've seen them. As much like the eyes of a black cat as a wolf was like my whippet! So I had my second sight of Morgan. But there was no sound. Her face didn't speak. Only those eyes grew till they filled the sky. I could feel them sucking the soul out of me.

They lit lamps up there in the dun and the stars pricked out. The dog started whining. I waited till the moon rose clear of the roofs and her face faded. She wouldn't come any nearer tonight.

After that, she never moved again in weeks or months. Twice the moon came full and my folk were waiting for me in the circle. It made me wild, the way they looked at me now. Some of them had been there that day in Carlisle. They knew too much. They'd have been whispering to the others behind my back. Fierce I was to the women those nights. I'd been keeping myself for better things than them. They twisted and yelled. But I wouldn't let them get away from me. She wasn't the only one that had power.

I took to watching the road all day. Many a time I'd carry a piece of work to the door. I'd be filing away and hardly looking at what I was doing. There was always plenty of coming and going past Way Bank. On the road from the north it was a different story. The Painted People were raiding closer these days. Sometimes it was a sorry sight, those that came from that side of the Wall, with whatever they'd managed to snatch up before they ran.

Our road was full of the king's men. His steward always knows when there's a shearing or harvesting afoot. He'll take his share. Open-handed or not, I reckon we pay several times over for the feasts they give us. But a smith's luckier than most. He gets respect. Likely one of Urien's men would stop off at the smithy for a bit of attention to weapon or harness and I'd have to tally it up on the wall against next quarter-day. But when I looked into their faces for a nod or a lift of the eyebrow or a word whispered, there was never anything but shouts and back-slapping and the sort of jokes you'd expect from king's men anywhere.

So I started to look out for another sort of messenger. We didn't get many ladies riding past Way Bank. But there were still a few, though the roads weren't so safe now as they say they used to be when Ambrosius Pendragon kept the peace. After all, wouldn't that be how Morgan would send for me? The men were Urien's, but the women were hers, and there would be more of them that followed the old craft. So every time I heard chariot wheels coming and dainty bells on the harness, I'd be at the door pretty fast. The neighbours could say what they liked about Teilo Smith and the women now. There were plenty of ladies smiled back at me, but none of them ever stopped, except in the way of business, and then I couldn't get rid of them fast enough, smiles or not. It was never Morgan's women, let alone the queen herself, riding up to my door.

She fought a battle with me that summer. Her weapon was silence. I lost. I was bound to, damn it. Once, she bowed her head to me. Morgan, Queen of Rheged, to Teilo Smith. But only once. And that was because she wanted my power when she saw it. I was right to be afraid.

4

Morgan dragged me to Lyvennet like a slave on the end of a chain. I didn't want to go, not for all the hot dreams I'd had of her. But I couldn't help myself. And anyway, it was Lugh's Day, and there was my account to settle. A good bit of work I'd done for Urien, one way and another. I was a free man, and master of my craft. I didn't work for nothing, not even for the king.

After I'd danced the god on the green, I scrubbed myself clean and put on my best, fair-day clothes. I didn't need Annis to tell me I looked a fine figure of a man. I took a sack, for I expected to come back richer than I went, and off we all set.

It's not far to Lyvennet. I left my wife and daughter outside the walls oohing and aahing over the pedlar's wares and I slipped off in the crowd. I thought I'd walk through the gate as easy as winking. I always had on quarter-day before. It was a man's place, was Lyvennet. Or had been in Urien's father's time. Plenty of ale and horses and weapons. A good place for a smith that knows his craft. And always open house on fair-days. Free drink for everybody, whether they came to pay or be paid.

But I pushed through the crowd around the tumblers that morning and everything had changed. The king's steward had set up his table outside the gate and there was a great mob around him of those that had come to pay and those that had come to get. He had soldiers guarding a great heap of stuff. Urien wasn't mean. I was glad to see there was still free beer and the steward looked pleasant enough. But I peeked through the gate and there wasn't a soul inside those walls except those that worked there. I knew now what it meant to have a queen in Rheged again. She'd want no common people inside her dun, only those that served her.

I felt sorry for young Urien then. A grand lad. We all liked him. Maybe he was a thought young to take his father's place. But he'd soon grow, and he'd the makings of fine man already. There were none of that family we'd have trusted more to be king over us. Poor lad. It wasn't his dun now. That was as plain as the nose on your face. It was no doing of his to keep his people out of his gate on fair-day. He'd have given a beggar a better welcome.

But I'll be honest. It wasn't more than a moment's thought I gave to Urien. It wasn't him I'd come to see, was it? I watched that open gateway like a green lad gazing at his first sweetheart's door. Years and years it had been since there were real ladies in Lyvennet, and every time a bright skirt went swinging past the gate my blood raced with the thought that it might be her. When it came to my turn to be paid, I still couldn't take my eyes off that gateway for fear I should miss the one moment she came. Four fleeces and two bars of iron. It should have been more than that. It was good work I'd done. But I hadn't the wit to drive a bargain that day.

It's a funny thing. Some of you may think it strange, me feeling sorry for Urien, and dreaming of doing what I was with his wife. But it's not like you think. What folk like us do in the circle, to honour the Lord of the Forest, is nothing to do with a man and his wife.

I stuffed my sack full and then I sat on the ground and waited, as if I might be expecting to meet a friend. She'd send for me, all right, in her own good time.

After a bit, I saw there was another table, on the opposite side of the gate. There were women there, and none that I knew, so I wondered I hadn't noticed them before. Fine lady's women too, by the look of their clothes. That set my blood racing. They had a store of bowls and flasks in front of them, and so many people crowding round you could hardly see what they were offering. But it didn't take long to work it out from the kind of sorry folk that shuffled up to them and the look on their faces when they came away clutching a bit of this or that they'd been given. It was healing medicine. Given? Half of those that came didn't seem to be handing anything over for it. I stared. I could see charms signed and stuff measured out, but as often as not those ladies were left empty-handed. I wasn't used to Morgan's ways then. They were busy all day, too. There were two of those ladies seemed to be in charge, turn and turn about. One was a tall woman, with a cold, bitter face, dressed in good stuff, but plainly. The other was a merry young lass, all yellow curls and ribbons and embroidery, and a bit plump in the face, as if she hadn't lost her puppy-fat yet. But she knew her job.

When I saw them, I knew for sure they were Morgan's women, though I didn't understand what her game was. And my nails were digging into the palms of my hands expecting any moment the queen herself would come walking out. I watched that gate as a cat watches a hedge-bank. She never came. All day I sat, with never a bite to eat, till the sun went down and they carried their tables inside and shut the gate. And here was a funny thing. The king's steward went in a sight richer than he'd come out that morning, for all the beer that was drunk. But the queen's women had hardly a basketful. Annis and Mair came looking for me then, and scolding me for missing all the fun.

I couldn't understand it. I'd been so sure Morgan would call me in. She wanted me. I knew she wanted my power. All this time, I'd felt her pulling me here.

I suppose there was dancing and more drinking and eating, while the light lasted. I don't remember. Then there was nothing to do but to walk home with them, down the road through the forest in the dark. The rest of the folk from Way Bank were laughing hard enough and staggering about. They made out they had to kick up such a noise to scare wild beasts away, but it wasn't that. I hadn't drunk so much. I sat and sulked in my smithy half the night. I didn't want to go to bed with Annis. Morgan must have known I'd come, all right.

It made me angry. She couldn't be such a very great queen, after all, or she'd never have let herself be married off late like this to a puppy. Somebody must have had power over her till now. Well, if she was too proud to go to her own gate to meet me, then I'd have to find a way to get inside and show her who was master. I wasn't going to be beaten by a woman, not if she was queen twice over. I was a king too, and I'd more cunning than most.

I let a moon go by. Then I went to Lyvennet again. If they wouldn't let honest craftsmen through the gate, I'd find another way to prove I was higher than Morgan. Only, to do it, I had to humble myself and dress in rags. I didn't have rags, let me tell you. I was a skilled man. I went dressed in stout leather and good wool. My work could buy the best. And I dressed my wife and daughter fairly too. I had to wait till the whole village was out harvesting and steal old clothes from empty cottages here and there. And then I had to foul and tear them, and rub peat into my skin and in my hair and beard, so my own wife wouldn't have known me.

I took a staff in my hand, and bent my shoulders a bit, and I trudged up the road to the queen's dun at Lyvennet as if it was the last city in the world.

I laughed in my dirty beard. They didn't recognise me. Not though Teilo Smith was a well known man for miles around. Near black, I was, as though I'd been years under hotter suns than we get in Rheged. But I kept my fingers crossed under the rags of my sleeves.

"The king," I quavered. "The young King Urien. They tell me the old king's dead and he's to be married. I'm a holy man. I come to bring him a blessing."

"Married!" Those sentries laughed at me. "Four months and more ago. Made king of Rheged in his father's place, and married to a princess from down south, out of Cornwall. Time enough now for her to be getting big in the belly. You're a bit late in the day, old man, if you've come to dance at their wedding!"

"All the way from Jerusalem I've come. Years and years I've been on pilgrimage. And when I heard the old king was dying I made all the haste I could. I've known young Urien since he was a bairn. And I've brought him a gift. A precious gift. The boy shall have it now. Look at this . . ." I drew a bundle of leather out of my pouch and unwrapped it. "A piece of the true Cross of Christ, from Jerusalem." And there it was, a piece of charred wood out of my smithy fire. But, for all that, I rubbed it with my sleeve and it seemed to shine in my hand as I held it up to the light. "There's not many that have seen the like of that."

They drew in their breath sharpish.

"Go on. It's not really, is it?"

"And come all that way to Britain . . .!"

You could see them reaching their hands out to touch it, and then stopping themselves in mid-air. I had to chuckle to myself. I was more used to mysteries. I put it away. I let them feel the leather it was wrapped in. That was enough good luck for them. They made the signs of blessing, touching it with their heads and eyes and lips.

"There's more. I can see the future. Let a man put his hand in mine and I can read it like a monk with a book. Sons, daughters, battles, wealth. It's all written there in the lines. Now if I could see the young king and queen . . ."

They looked sharp at each other when I named the queen. That's where it stuck, all right. It was always open house with Urien and his father. They'd have a welcome for any strolling poet or pilgrim. They loved a good story.

"Well," said one of the guards carefully. "Let's see how good you are first. Read my palm."

I'd a hard job not to laugh out loud. Read his palm? Dunnet of Lyvennet, whose wife was cousin to my Annis. Five sons and a crippled daughter. A broken leg that still troubled him in the winter. And likely to come into a little land at Woodend since his mother died at haymaking. It was too easy. They must be simple-minded not to know who I was.

But I impressed them. They sent word in to Urien, and pretty soon I was inside that gate.

It wasn't playing games now. It never had been really. After all, I was a holy man, in another fashion. And I could see further into the shadows than ordinary folk. It was just that bit about Jerusalem. Well, I knew they liked that, the lords and ladies. Travellers' tales. Rome's finished. Since old Vortigern brought the Saxons over and the traitors slew our Council, the chiefs that followed have had their hands too full to trouble about going abroad. They say it's the same tale all over the Empire. The whole world's on fire. Those old days won't come back. But our nobles still hanker after Rome and the East.

I'd been in that courtyard many a time before, but it felt different that day. I didn't know if I was welcome.

Urien was over by the kennels. There was a mastiff bitch there with a litter of new puppies. He motioned me to keep back. Then one of the guards went and muttered in his ear and he came and joined me. He'd grown taller, even since that May wedding. Tall and straight and a bit serious about the eyes. Aye, he'd make a king. Fair and blue-eyed to her black and green. They were a handsome pair, and in a few years the difference between them wouldn't show so much. I thought of their wedding night and of all the nights since. Had he . . .? Well, I suppose he must have, by now. A woman like that would know what to do, and he'd be a good pupil.

I'd guessed right. Of course he wanted to hear all about my pilgrimage. He sat down in the sun and called for ale. I had to make it up. It came easy enough. Oliphants and dragons, and the temples of Rome and one-eyed giants on the road over the Alps. I'd seen them all.

"And the holy mountain of Sinai? Did you see that too? And the river

Jordan where Christ was baptised? And the Church of the Star blessed Helena built at Bethlehem? Gethsemane? Olivet . . . ?"

He was getting carried away, and I was in deep water, for it seemed he knew more about such places than I did. But I reckoned neither of us had been there, so how was he to know if the pictures I painted for him weren't exactly true? I hadn't been to school like the bards, but I could have held my own with them for story-telling that day.

When I got out my little bit of blackened wood he touched it thoughtful-like, and I had an idea that he wasn't as easily taken in as those sentries had been. He thanked me courteously though, and gave me a golden buckle for it. That wasn't nearly enough, if it had been what I said it was, but a sight more than I deserved, seeing it wasn't. He's no fool, but he's generous. Maybe he thought he'd paid a fair price for a good story.

I read his palm too. I gave him the best future I could see. He'd be a great king. Greater than his father. Greater than Gwendoleu in Carlisle. I nearly said he'd be a greater king than Ambrosius, but I thought that might be going a bit far. But bards would sing of him as long as there were harps in Britain. Fine sons, good health, long years. And a noble death with his sword still in his hand. I was careful to praise that sword, you can be sure. I'd made it for him, hadn't I? But I praised the king more. You should have heard me. I did him proud.

There was only one thing I've been sorry for afterwards. When I told him he'd make a good death on the battlefield a shiver came over me, so I fear he'll die by treachery, after all.

But all the time the words were tripping off my tongue my mind was busy. The breath was struggling in my chest like a bird in a net, and I hoped that little crowd of men round me would think it was just from the journey and the talking. Where was she? They'd built a new house in the middle of the dun, with the thatch still yellow. A sunny-house for the women. I could see the flicker of skirts in and out of the doorway. But it was never her. I held her husband's hand in mine and thought how those fingers must have touched her white foot and her thigh and breast. Those breasts, full under black hair. I couldn't hold my own hand steady.

Well, when I'd done with him and got my reward I screwed up my courage and asked, "And the queen? Will I read her fortune too?"

He looked round quickly at the sunny-house, and I made out then he was scared of her too. I didn't blame him.

"Queen Morgan is busy. I do not think she is in the mood for such stories."

And what does a queen have to be so busy about? I thought.

I pushed my luck then. It was as if I couldn't help myself, though I saw the danger.

"Is it the true Cross you think will not be to her liking, sir? I have other stories better suited to one like her. Witches, mermaids, sorcerers' spells from Syria. I've seen them all."

"Morgan was schooled in a Christian nunnery. You presume too far."

I bowed and scraped to him as best I could, but it was too late.

"The queen sees no one today."

He turned away. I should never have come. I hadn't seen her, and I'd put myself properly in her power now. She'd know I was here, and why. It was a chill walk back to the gate alone, with every window of her sunny-house like eyes on my back. Morgan was watching me, I knew that. It would take more than peat-stain and rags to hide from her what I was. Even if she had forgotten me once, she'd be sure to remember now.

I got outside that gate and I vowed I'd never go back again. I'd done with that. I had to put her out of my mind. But it wasn't so easy. Way Bank lies much too close to Lyvennet for comfort.

5

'Teilo Smith! So this is the throne-room of your kingdom?"

I caught my thumb on the hot iron and I turned and swore. It was fear made me curse, more than the pain. A fear as if I would turn round and see death come for me. Months I'd waited to hear a voice I didn't know at the door and see a stranger standing there against the light. Now it had come. It was all I could do to keep a grip on the hammer I'd got in my hand.

I'd made up my mind it would be a woman. The figure was too tall for that. Hooded and cloaked in red, done up with tassels of fox-tails. But there was a grey gown showing under it. That jolted my memory. I called to mind where I'd heard that voice before. On Morgan's wedding day, in the streets of Carlisle. I can't tell you how sick I felt at that. Disappointed, and a different sort of fear to the one I'd felt at first.

"Oh, it's you, is it?" I said. I had a struggle to keep my voice steady.

He threw back his hood. He had white hair, but he carried himself like a young man. Grey eyes, and laughing at my face.

"I frightened you? That's good. You do well to be afraid. It's that that keeps a wise man's head on his shoulders."

I could see the boy's ears flapping for all he was worth, so I sent him off to chop firewood. I was mad with this magician. What did he want to come to Way Bank for, just when I'd put the pair of them out of my head? I could keep a secret better than he could, by the look of it. If I'm seen to be dealing with the nobility, it should be strictly in the way of business.

"You found out where I live, then."

"The King of Smiths is not difficult to find. Though it's a rough and icy road to here."

"I didn't ask you to come."

"Ah, but in all these months you haven't come to me. And I *did* ask *you*. If need be, I can be as patient as any man either side of the grave. But some affairs are too urgent. For safety's sake they will not wait."

"They will, when there's nothing happened."

"Morgan! Come, man, you must have seen her by now."

"No." I turned away. I'd done my best to put all that behind me since harvest-time. The queen didn't want to see me, and I didn't want to meddle with her. Or I tried not to.

"But she must have summoned you up. What else would she mean by that? The way she rode to her wedding. The way she bowed to you in the street. Power, Teilo Smith, power! Morgan needs what you hold. She can't have brought a full circle with her from Cornwall, can she?"

"There's a few new women up here, they say. Nothing like enough. I'd have heard if any of mine had gone over to her."

"Then certainly she still needs you and yours. This is your territory. The Horned One's country. Her Mare does not run here. She must respect the Stag."

"She's a funny way of showing it, then."

I wiped my hands on my apron to give myself time to think, and stole a look up at him. He wasn't watching. He was picking away at the wooden frame of the door, pulling splinters off it. He looked like a man with something nagging at his mind. Aye, I thought, there's more here. Maybe the queen needs my help, and maybe she doesn't. But this one hasn't come all the way from Carlisle just to wish me the time of day, either.

"She's not the only one," I said.

"Eh? What's that?"

"I may wear a sooty face, but I'm no man's fool. What's a fine gentleman like yourself doing here in my smithy? What Queen Morgan wants is anybody's guess. She hasn't told me, anyroad. But it's as plain as the nose on my face that you want something pretty bad. That's twice you've begged for my help now. She hasn't."

He made a face, half-mournful and half-laughing, like a boy that's been caught with his finger in the cream.

"There, I was right! I knew you for a wise man. But it's not I that need you, Teilo Smith. Remember? The Cymry. Look. Look at this!"

He got me by the shoulders and pushed me out of the door.

"There! Do you see that? Those hills?" He was facing me north. It was one of those pale blue winter skies, with the hills making a line across it, cold and clear. "There's the Wall running along them from sea to sea. And there" – spinning me round south – "the Pennines, like the long dragon's back. Once the roads on either side were thronged with warriors, lords and ladies, common men and women, coming and going freely from north to south, from east to west. Once our ships were free to sail the sea. Once there was one law from shore to shore, all the way from Lothian to the Land's End. One country of Britain. One Emperor. Don't you remember?"

"How could I remember? I wasn't born then. And nor were you."

He started a bit and gave that childish little smile he had.

"No! To be sure. I was dreaming."

"There have been Saxons in the east as long as I've lived. That's how it's always been as far as folks round here can remember. Uther Pendragon beat them a time or two, but he never drove them out entirely. They say even Ambrosius couldn't do that. It's Saxon land in the south and east, ours in the north and west. And just the hill country between us."

"The lowland the foreigners hold is ours. The soil of the Cymry. Ambrosius knew it. He drove his sword through the Saxons clear down to London town. We British hold that road still. But in other places the land is being eaten away. The Saxon Dragon is growing fatter every year."

"What's that to me? So long as they stay clear of Rheged. Ambrosius is dead and gone. There'll never be another one like him."

"Won't there, Smith? Won't there? What if I were to tell you that every road and river shall be ours again? What if the British held this island from the cliffs of Dumnonia and Gwynedd to the eastern sands? What if the Saxons went wading back to their keels for ever? What then?"

He was like a man drunk in the middle of the day, and as foolish.

"Oh, aye? That would make you a bigger man then, wouldn't it, Silver-Tongue? And what do you want me to do? Forge a sword of power for your little lad to fight them off with?"

That shook him. For a man that had such wisdom, he was mighty careless with his secrets. His hand shot out and gripped mine. I felt his strength again, and I remembered a bit late why I'd been afraid before.

"Be careful, Smith! Do not seek to know too much before your time. Secrets are power. And power can break a man. I warned you!"

That angered me. I was no ordinary workman. I had powerful secrets already, as well he knew.

"And who are you to threaten me about power? No true bard, I'll be bound, wherever you've sprung from."

His eyes went crafty, as a man's will do sometimes when he's in drink.

"Harps have their own magic too. A bard stands high as a Druid. I can play both. Gwendoleu will not regret the gold he gives me."

He dropped my arm.

"And why should I tell you who I am? You've told me nothing yet. My true name is one that Morgan of Cornwall knows too well. Twice seven years, I needed! I pleaded with Uther Pendragon to hold her penned up that long on Tintagel. Even fourteen years is young for the task that waits. But Uther is dead too soon and my aim has miscarried. I should not have trusted the Church to guard her. I fear Morgan has learned more in her nunnery than psalms and needlework. Now she is freed and wise and much too close. I must gain more time.

"I could use you in more than one way, King of Smiths. You are the High Chief over many circles. Your people could make a powerful ring of protection for us against her strength. Or, better still, I could set you to work as Morgan's false friend. Your King to her Queen. Let her join the circle with you, for her own foul purposes. You could tell me all she plots. And you alone, Smith, would know how to break her chain and let its power spill."

I turned pale at that.

"She'd know I'd done it! You couldn't hide that from the Lady. She'd smell who the traitor was."

"An earthly king takes his life in his hands when he rides into battle. What kind of king are you, to shrink back now when Britain needs you? War, Teilo Smith, is a dangerous business."

He turned to the door. And just then in came my daughter Mair, with ale and sweetmeeats.

She blushed. She wasn't used to gentlemen, and you could see this man was nobility in his foxy cape.

"Mother heard you had company. She's sent in some cakes . . ."

I never saw a man's face change so fast. He put his long hand under her chin and smiled, very wide and warm.

"Oh, excellent!" he said. And he was pressing one of her cakes through her lips and then swallowed the rest himself. "Delicious. This is one secret you've kept well, Teilo Smith."

When I saw that greedy shine in his eyes as he touched her I could have slugged him with my hammer, magician or no. I turned and thrust the cold horse-bit back into the fire. I was near to branding him with it. I was shaking with anger. What I did with the women of my own kind was between me and the god. But my daughter Mair was no part of it yet.

She laughed a fair bit and slipped away as soon as she could get free of him. She was a good girl. That bard wasn't long going then. He raised his hand first, as if he was blessing me.

"Wealth you shall have, if that is what you want. There will be spoils in plenty when we ride. The enemy's treasure for those who have helped us. Win me three years, Smith. Only three years."

6

There's nothing like knowing a secret for having it gnaw away at your insides till you can't think straight about anything else. And all the time there's more questions you wished you'd asked while you had the chance. A king that was going to better even Ambrosius? Top dog over all the other kings? A lad, and, by the sound of it, not yet full-grown? That took some believing. Whose son was he? Not Gwendoleu's, that's certain. And a man has to have more than royal blood to be made High King. He needs a host to shout his name, and war-horses, and forts, and a string of battles to his reputation. That's what the bards mean when they sing of a High King in these parts.

No, the great chiefs that followed the Romans were all dead, and left no new ones to come after them. They said Uther Pendragon was the last man of that house. As for what kings we'd got now, young Urien might still turn out the best of them, to my way of thinking. But that crafty bard Silver-Tongue couldn't mean him. He was Morgan's own husband! Gwendoleu? But he was a grown man, and he was more likely to make his kingdom bigger quarrelling with his own blood than by getting up a host to fight the Saxons. So who was there up here in the north to make such a stir about? What little prince? And why should he fear Morgan of Cornwall might learn where the lad was hiding and what his magician's real name was?

Fear Morgan? Aye. That's good advice, is that. Don't you forget it. You're well clear of her here. When I was inside her castle walls at Lyvennet I'd dreaded her like a fly caught in a web waiting for the spider.

Outside, I'd need to watch out for her sticky thread pulling me in. Curse that magician. Why couldn't they leave me in peace, the pair of them? Curse Morgan . . . Yes. Back at Way Bank I thought it! If she'd been old and ugly . . . If she hadn't smiled at me like that . . .

The nights were full of her face now. It was like the moon in winter, with her green eyes glowing as she looked down on me. A blacksmith, I was. I'd made do for twenty years on coarser meat. She made me twist and groan in bed. I wanted to have her and run a hundred miles from her at the same time.

It wasn't any better in daylight, either. Every time I stepped outside the smithy door I could feel her staring down from her castle walls, overlooking me. It was his hammer and her anvil closing in. I should have had more sense.

I did it for pride, and I've suffered for that ever since. But it was still a mighty lump of pride I had to swallow before I could do what I did. I'd show her I wouldn't take no for an answer. I was High Chief.

I'd seen how the wind blew. Lyvennet Castle was ruled by a woman now. I'd seen fighting-men looking shiftily over their shoulders. Up in the dun, men still bent the knee to Urien, because he was the king. But you can't have two rulers in one kingdom. Very well, then. I could play her game. It was a pity, though. I knew Urien could make us a fine chieftain, given half a chance. He's not so old, even now. She hasn't crushed him. Maybe the bards will sing of him yet.

Still, I'd handled power myself for too long not to have a nose for where it lay. I was used to masking for the god. When I put on his skin I was choosing which power I'd serve. This time I chose the side that was going to win.

I stole women's clothes, patched ones but clean. Not Annis's. I didn't fancy that, somehow. I hid them in a basket while I shaved all the hair off my face. I thought Annis was safely in the dairy-shed for an hour. But she came indoors and found me at it.

"Why, whatever are you doing?" she said.

"Nothing for you women to gossip over," I muttered. "It's a vow I've taken."

She was quiet at that. She'd lived with me long enough to know there was a part of my life that wasn't to be spoken of. She knew better than to ask me questions. She was a good woman, was Annis.

"I only came for a clean jug for the whey."

She took it down from the shelf and she stood by the fire, nursing it to her breast while she looked at me fondly-like.

"It must be all of twenty-five years since I've seen you without a beard. And you looked a fine lad, even then. Do you remember that day when I was sitting at my mother's loom weaving, and you were leading a horse along the road? And the king's soldiers came by, and your horse reared and bolted. We thought it would break clean through our pigsty. But there was you, hanging on to the creature's bridle for dear life and dragging it back to the road. And I thought to myself then, it might not be such a bad thing to be brought to bed by a lad with shoulders like that."

She was a good woman, my Annis. Not over-handsome, but comfortable. Another man might have been well content with her. It wasn't my fault if I was born to greater things than her, was it? I meant her no harm.

Still, I was glad I wasn't wearing the woman's gown when she found me . . . Yes. Make your sour faces if you like. I *am* ashamed of wearing this!

She said, "Well, this won't get the butter churned, will it? And you've work of your own to get on with, I dare say."

"I've got to go out. The boy can mind the smithy. I'll be back by supper."

I waited till I got to the forest, and then I dressed in the woman's clothes, with a big hood to hide my face. I stuffed my good leather things inside a hollow tree. That left me an empty basket. I'd seen what it was that Morgan's women were giving out on Lugh's Day. And it wasn't always "Queen Morgan" folk called her now. She was getting to have another title among them. I'd heard them name her "Morgan the Healer."

Well, that wasn't so strange. The women of our kind have always been known and valued for that. Of course Morgan would know such secrets. She could practise the women's art if she had a mind to.

I didn't use that side of the craft myself. I was the Black Smith. I had other ways, with fire and iron and stone. Things I wouldn't tell you of even now. But I'd had to learn that other wisdom, along with all the rest. There's not much the High Chief doesn't know. I had it all in my head. Still, it wasn't easy to fill that basket in the middle of winter, I can tell you. She'd have to respect me for it. She might be a grown woman, but I had ten years over her. And maybe we had things growing in Rheged they'd never heard of down in Cornwall. I could teach her a trick or two. I'd show her. I dug roots out of the hard ground with my knife. I searched about till I found leaves that were still green under pockets of snow. I picked the last shrivelled-up berries the birds hadn't stripped off the stalks. There's not many could have gathered such a rich harvest at that time of year.

When I stepped back on to the road I bent over double. Me, that had always carried myself so straight and strong. I clutched that cloak around me and let the hood fall over my face.

There were fresh men at the gate. They didn't know me. The look in their eyes was the same as those others when I spoke the queen's name.

"Herbs," I quavered, showing them my basket. "I'm a wise woman. I bring sweet herbs for Morgan the Healer. Can I see her?"

They looked at each other, none too easy.

"Best send them in," said one. "Let her women decide."

They called a boy to carry the basket into the sunny-house. I stood there waiting in the raw wind, and glad enough of the excuse to be wrapped up close inside the cloak. The blood was fairly hammering in my head. The guards saw me shivering. They offered me a seat in the gateway and gave me a beaker of hot ale. At last a woman came out, carrying my basket. They pointed me out to her. She came towards me. A tall woman, and dressed like a lady. I'd seen her before, on Lugh's Day. I didn't care to look her full in the face, but I stole a glance under the edge of my hood. She was older than Morgan. She had a long, hard face, with deep lines. It looked as if care had put scars on it worse than gashes from a sword.

"Queen Morgan thanks you. Those are dainty weapons that you have forged for her."

So I was right. She knew who it was that had sent them to her. I should have bolted then.

The woman held out the basket. It was empty, except for a silver button lying in the bottom.

"Doesn't she want to see me?"

"Why? What good would it do? She has your gift and you have hers."

"The wise should help each other," I mumbled.

"You? Help Morgan? She had no need of what you brought."

I started to go. My wits were in a muddle. I'd been so sure she was calling me here.

Then the woman caught my arm. And pretty quick she let it drop again. She couldn't stop herself shaking. I could see she had to say something to me and was afraid to ask.

"Old woman," her words came tumbling out fast now, "there is something more. There is light and there is dark. There is peace and there is war.

There is both dying and rising again. You have filled one side of her basket only. Could you provide the balance?"

Her hand flew to her mouth, as though she oughtn't to have let those words escape. But I had her now. I could hardly hold the man's triumph out of my voice and keep it womanish.

"Queen Morgan shall get what she wants. Trust me."

I saw what it was she expected at last. And I was the man who could give it to her.

7

King of Smiths I might be, but even I had to wait a while. The Horned God's a thrusting lad. He can dance a pretty quick step to the pipe. But behind him there's his Mother, and you can't hurry her. She'll give life too, but in her own time and seasons. So I had to wait for spring to come and crack the ground open, as if there was so much blood and sap inside the earth it would fairly burst apart. Sometimes I dream that'll happen, and we'll all be swallowed down in her darkness. Pretty, my Mair used to say it was, when all the little spring flowers came out. She didn't see the danger.

I'd let my beard grow, so I had to shave again. I took my basket into the forest a second time. Another man might have searched a lifetime and not found some of those things. For a while I sweated a bit and wondered if I should have brought one of my own wise women with me to point the way. Granny Sarran, maybe. But I cursed the thought. I was the god's Chief Man, and I wouldn't be bested by any woman.

I knew the forest, my part of it, anyroad. But I went deeper into it that day than I ordinarily cared to. It's an awful place. Black mud sucks at your boots and all of a sudden it'll grab your leg right up to the knee. There's huge tree-trunks lying across your path, and things like giant's faces growing out of them. You think they're staring up at you, till you see that even those faces are dead and rotting apart. I had to search their crawling innards for what I wanted. The trees that are living have got lichen and moss, like beards, hanging from them so long and grey they look as if they're hundreds of years old. Their fingers are knotted into each other over your head tight, so you can't get a glimpse of the sun to know which

43

way is home. I used my knife to mark the way with notches on the trunks, but after a bit it got so deep and dark I could hear every tree I cut scream out to the rest to warn them I was coming.

For years now, I'd been in charge of our rites. I knew how to make people afraid. I was the one with the horns, I was the one they bowed down to. I was afraid myself that day. I'd never felt so small and helpless in my own forest. Though that was nothing to what was coming. I said the charms and made the offerings for what I was taking. It didn't help me much.

But I found what I'd come for. Wolfsbane. Blackblood. The Sleeper, and all the rest of that crew. Under the lot I laid three caps of the Grey Lady. If Morgan was what I thought, she would know how rare a thing that was.

I was ready for her now. When I got back safe into the daylight and washed the mud off myself in the beck I felt pretty pleased with what I'd got. I didn't go home. I put on the same woman's clothes as before and I'd a job to shorten my stride to match as I set off to Lyvennet. All the same, when I came in sight of the walls I wasn't feeling so cocky.

I told the same story at the gate. I knew they'd let me through this time.

"I've brought some more herbs for the queen. She asked me to fetch these for her."

Herbs! A sweet name for the stuff I had in my basket today. Still, they'd be a certain cure for some things. To end a sickness that wouldn't heal. To rest a broken heart. To quieten a scolding wife . . . begging your pardon! Well, there's no sleep sounder than the one they bring, is there?

It was the same tall woman who came to fetch me. Today the colour kept coming and going in her face, like a fire that's not sure whether to take hold or not.

"Queen Morgan will see you."

She led me straight across the court to the sunny-house. The blood was fairly pounding in my chest. I felt that every man in the castle was looking at me. Not to mention those women.

Once, when I was a lad, I was taken out fishing in a boat on the lake. I looked down and I could see the stones close below me in the water. Then I turned away. It was only a few moments, but next time I looked overboard there was nothing beneath me, just darkness. Only then, deep down, a giant pike came drifting past. It was bigger than I was. I felt like that now. It was too late to turn back home.

I stumbled in over the threshold of the sunny-house, following the woman. I'd never been in such a place before. Fur rugs on the floor.

Pictures of animals and trees and flowers, all done in wool and hanging on the walls. Wood light as honey-wax and carved with birds' heads. The light from the windows was making bright patches on the floor. There was a little grey cat sitting in a pool of sunshine on a spotted deerskin.

The woman made me stand in the light. She moved to one side between two of the windows. Nobody said anything, and I turned to look that way.

Morgan was facing me, in the shadow between the windows. My eyes were so dazzled I had to blink before I could make her out plainly. She was sitting in a high carved chair like a throne. She had on a robe of blue so deep I thought at first it was black, with a great silver lune round her neck. Her hair was loose over her shoulders, like on her wedding day. Well, you know she can't bear to be bound. And her face was white in the shadow, just like the moon I'd been seeing all those nights.

She looked bigger than I'd remembered her.

The woman who had brought me was standing quietly by her side. More like a ghost than a flesh-and-blood woman, that Luned was. There was another of them on Morgan's other side. She was flesh and blood, all right. The young one I'd seen before. Pretty, and just a bit on the plump side. Another time I'd have been glad to have one like that among my own circle. But I hardly looked at her then.

Morgan fills any room where she sits. You don't need me to tell you. When she looks at you she draws you right inside herself. And the Mothers forbid you should think that I mean anything ill by that now. Whatever I may have dreamed when I was safe in my own cottage, that was all gone here. It would have been like death if I'd let my thoughts stray even one step in that direction. Catch a mouse dreaming of mating with the owl!

"So, you have come to offer me the other half of wisdom? The universe in balance. Put back your woman's hood, Teilo Smith. Let me see who is king in Rheged."

I let it fall to my shoulders. The three of them burst into peals of laughter. That fairly shocked me. It was no laughing matter, what I'd been through. Then I saw all of sudden how I must look to them. From the cheeks upwards I had a face scorched red at the smithy fire. But below, there was new, scraped skin that had barely seen the light of day in fifteen years.

That young one was laughing hardest of the lot. I saw her clearly now. She had bright blue eyes. Impudent, she was. Laughing fit to bust. At me, Teilo Smith.

Morgan held up her hand and they both went silent. She stood up, and I had a bigger shock then. I saw why she'd seemed a big woman, sitting in her chair. Her belly was swelling with child, so huge she must have been near her time. We'd heard the queen was expecting, of course. We were all hoping it would be a boy, and my people had worked a bit more for that than just hope. But somehow I hadn't pictured it. Not Morgan, with her belly sticking out like this, the same as any village woman. I can't explain it to you, but that sight shook me so much I nearly cried out loud. You see, to me, she was the young moon, the Maiden. That Lady can always come under the King and still be a virgin. She isn't the Mother. Can you understand that?

My basket was lying on the table where her woman Luned had left it. Morgan lifted the cover off and I saw her give a start. That made me feel pretty pleased with myself. I reckoned she was surprised at some of the things I'd found. She stared down at them for a mighty long time. Then she lifted her eyes to mine, and very wide and brilliant they looked. If it had been anyone else, I'd have thought she was scared by what she'd seen.

"Why have you brought me these?" Still staring hard at me.

"Because you asked me to!" I blustered. "Your woman said I had to fill both sides of your basket."

She swung round then, and the older woman turned paler still and shook in her shoes.

But Morgan never said anything to her, only looked hard from one to the other of us.

She turned back to the basket and picked out my treasures one by one. I could see her lips moving as she looked at them, but I never heard a word. Last of all she came to that rare toadstool that I call the Grey Lady. There's few enough folks, even of our sort, that know it, and some that do know it have worse names for it than that. But I always reckon it's best to be respectful. She stood, twisting and twisting it in her fingers, so I began to wonder if she knew its true power. I've known a man that only licked his fingers after picking it, and he sickened and died horribly before sunset. Someone must have ill-wished him pretty badly, to make him do that. He was a wise man. And how would I get up the courage to tell Morgan what she didn't know?

"So this is how you would choose to restore the balance. Why? You could have brought me the metals of the Black Smith's art, to match my woman's healing. Why these?"

I must have gasped sharp when she said that, and looked quick at her waiting-women. Morgan smiled a bit.

"We can speak freely in front of these two. They know what you are. They are high in the mysteries. Erith is young, but she is wise beyond her years. And Luned – would you believe that Luned was once a scholar-nun? She might have become abbess in her own nunnery one day. But the Christians don't like their white nuns to bear babies in the Mother's service, do they, Luned?"

Her older woman looked back at her with that harrowed face of hers. She had strange eyes. Dull, as if she'd used up all her feelings long since.

"I ask you again," Morgan said. "Why these?"

"Power!" I blurted out. It was the first word I thought of. I was a fool to tell her that was in my mind. But what was the use? No one could keep a secret from Morgan.

"You ask for power from me?"

"No! I'm High King in all these parts. I came to share my power with you. I thought you wanted it."

"You thought I wanted these? You come to offer power to me this way?"

She took the things up one by one and laid them out in front of her.

"Wolfsbane. Bitter on the tongue. A little can stir the dull spirit. More drives it mad. Blackblood, to rot the bowels. The Sleeper, that cools a fever but chills the healthy heart to death. And the Grey Lady, for which there is no cure."

So she did know.

She motioned to the younger girl. There was a silver casket on the other side of the table. Erith opened the lid and showed me what was inside. The things were shrivelled now, even more than when I'd picked them. But I recognised them. It was those healing herbs I'd gathered for Morgan in the middle of winter. The little grey cat jumped on the table and walked along, sniffing, till Erith snatched it off. I didn't say anything, and nor did Morgan. I couldn't think why she'd kept my gifts all this time if she didn't mean to use them.

"The kindly herbs. But did you know that excess of them can kill as surely as the others? While a little of the darker sort, used with great care, may sometimes save life?"

Of course I knew.

"Wounding and healing. Sword and scabbard. I have them both here under my hand. Perhaps you were right, after all, Smith, to leave your own art behind. I and mine suffered long ago through a wise man's magic. I have borne the pain ever since." She fell quiet then. None of us dared to say anything. At last she said, very low, "Are you teaching me that the cure is not to be sought from the men's side? That we must make it ourselves? That the balance lies . . . *here*?"

She raised her head to me then, and the look in her eyes nearly sent me staggering backwards. I swear to you there was terror in them. She might have been a woman pleading for her son's life. It was only a moment, and she was queen again.

"Things themselves are not power, Smith. While they lie on the table they are knowledge only. Power needs the will to use our knowledge, and the wisdom to know where."

"I am the Black Smith. I've used power. Both sides. When the price matched the need."

"And what price did you hope Morgan of Cornwall would pay you?"

"Nothing, your honour! Not to you. I brought these for a gift."

She knew I lied. I'd hoped to fatten my power on hers.

She gathered the herbs up, both sorts, and laid them back in the basket. Without a word spoken Luned brought her water and Morgan rinsed her hands very carefully. Luned wiped the table well too, I can tell you, and washed her own hands in clean water afterwards. "I did not need your gifts. I have had this knowledge long since. But it seems I lack something, after all. The will to act. The courage to hold both sides alone."

I straightened my shoulders. So she'd recognised my strength. I could feel the manhood rising in me.

"I'm your man!"

She smiled at that. "Exactly so. Take back both gifts . . . Smith. Show me how a wise . . . *woman* . . . should understand the use of power. How do you think I would use them?"

That black, bottomless lake was under me again. I could feel the cold water rocking my boat. The pike was swimming back.

"But . . . but who?" I stammered. "Who do you want me to use them on?"

She stroked the great curve of her belly with her narrow, white hands. "That is for you to choose. I shall watch where you think a woman's power should fall, and how it is used. And I shall learn from what I see. *Both sides.* You may go now."

They sounded soft enough words, but she gave me no chance to argue.

Her voice was like a hand, pushing me out of the fort. I pulled up my hood and turned to go. I was in deep now. Luned was holding out the basket to me, twice as full as it had been before. The sweet herbs and the bitter.

"Oh, and Smith!" Morgan called, very sweetly. "When you come back, wear those same clothes. They suit the lesson you are teaching me excellently. We have no need of men's craft, have we, you and I? I shall warn the guards."

I shuffled out of the door, with their laughs beating about my back. And that young Erith mocking loudest of all.

8

I must have been mad. Looking back on it now, I must have been bewitched to think I could match myself against Morgan. That's it. It was her doing. She'd put her spell on me, there in her castle. How else do you think a man of my wisdom would have done what I did, and in such a way? I was forced to do it.

My will to her power, that's what I thought it was. And I had that basket full of herbs she'd given back to me.

It's a chill thing to look around the circle of folk you know and say, "Which one of them shall I kill?"

It had to be right. There's always some who are old and sick. Their lives have got so bad they're a burden to themselves and other folk. It would have been a kindness for me to give the last sleep to one of those. But that was too easy. A woman like Morgan wasn't looking to me for kindness. It needed to be somebody strong, in the full prime of life. Power grows by feeding on blood, not slops. That's why those Christians'll never last.

Come to think of it, there wasn't a cottager in Way Bank she'd care about. What's one peasant more or less to a Lady like her? No. Let's come closer. There must be strong men in Lyvennet. Dunant, who guarded her own gate? Easy enough to swap a drink with him. Aye, there it came again. Too easy by half. She'd want more than that.

Morgan had laughed at me. Me. Smith. The king of smiths. She'd laughed me out of her door in my woman's clothes. Well, I'd show her. Yes, and I'd show that sneaking magician too. Common I might be, but I'd not be their tool. I'd show myself as great in the art as they were. They'd both bow down to me before I'd finished.

You want me to show you how I use power, do you, my lady? Right, then. You'll see. I'll come so close to you it'll make you shiver as if a goose had walked over your grave.

I thought I'd got it then. Kill Urien himself. Aye, I could have done even that if I'd wanted. But I still had sense enough to see that it was a daft idea. If Urien's dead, then Morgan's not Queen of Rheged. She wouldn't thank me for robbing her of her crown, would she?

There was a moment, madder than all the rest, when I thought of killing Morgan herself. And I couldn't stop shaking for the rest of that day, for fear she could read my thoughts, sitting up there in Lyvennet and looking down at my smithy door.

She'd made it a dun where the women ruled. The men were drones now. There hadn't been so much as a cattle-raid since Urien brought her back as his bride. All he'd done was get her with child. It was her women she looked to to feed her. She was like the queen-bee, sitting in her sunny-house, growing fatter and fatter on the power she sucked from them.

A women's castle. And then I had it. Those bright, blue eyes laughing over Morgan's shoulder. Impudent, she'd been. I could feel the smile spread over my own face when I thought about it. I could kill that one and enjoy it. That ought to make Queen Morgan gasp. A young witch, like herself. One step away from her elbow. She'd know better than to treat Teilo Smith with disrespect after that.

Since that second time I'd kept my chin shaved. I hadn't lied to Annis. It *was* a vow I'd taken. The folk in Way Bank might look queerly at my bare face, but there wasn't one of them dared to question me. Only my daughter Mair. She stroked my chin.

"You've shaved it again. There's fresh blood on it. Aren't you going to let it grow, this time?

Annis told her sharply, "Let your dad alone, girl. He has his reasons."

"I'm sorry, Da. But you look so strange these days. All the folk are saying so. Some of them are frightened to bring work to the smithy like they used to. And you're so often away now."

"Mair!"

She put her arms round my neck and kissed me. "It's all right. He doesn't mind. He's my Da, isn't he?"

I put her away from me. I couldn't bide still. I couldn't sleep or work. I'd have to get on with it, now that I knew what I had to do. And what if the boy did stare at me when I told him I'd be gone all day again, and he could smother the fire and take a holiday? Come to that, I'd kill him too if he didn't stop staring at me with those big brown eyes.

When he'd gone, I fetched that basket out and separated the plants, the right-hand from the left. I stewed the juice from the herbs of darkness while the forge was cooling. I wished I'd stuck to my own craft. It felt like women's work. I had to borrow some of Annis's pots and bowls while she was outdoors. Still, it's strange how the old chants come back to you from years ago, even though you've gone up a different road since you learned them. I had to do it right. It's not just the plants you need to make the spell stick. I don't have to tell you that.

When it was brewed, and rightly spoken over, I poured it out into a little flask. Then I stoppered it close with leather and wax. I stowed that away in my pouch, very careful. I didn't know what to do with the bowls. I couldn't hang about to wash them now. I could see Mair was outside the kitchen. If she found me at it, she'd ask questions, even if Annis wouldn't. I pushed the pots in a comer by the fire with a bit of sacking over them. I had the sense to tie the dog up so he wouldn't lick them.

Last of all, I stuffed my woman's disguise into a satchel, and strapped it on my back. I had to take that, even though I hated it. I knew I'd want to run to Lyvennet straight off to boast to the queen the thing was done.

When I stepped outside I had a bit of a shock to find some men of our village near the smithy door. I could tell they were muttering about me. I wondered how much they'd seen. They drew back a bit when they saw me come out. They didn't give me the time of day.

Behind the forge there's a green. My wife was there, and Mair now, with a basket of washing between them. They were spreading the clothes on the bushes to dry. They didn't see me. I had a terrible dryness in my throat. To this day it's a grief to me that I didn't call to them to say goodbye.

It was like a fever. I never stopped to think how I was going to come on Erith. I knew the Mothers would send her to me, just like a lamb to the eagle's claws. It had to happen. It was her name I'd spoken over the flames.

I hid myself at the edge of the wood outside Lyvennet. And it wasn't long before I saw them, Luned and Erith, coming out of the castle with baskets in their hands. They came down the hill towards me. Luned walked slow, but Erith was dancing about like a silly child. I drew back deeper under the hazels and let them go by me. It was *her* doing. She'd sent them out to me. She must have done.

I hadn't thought it would be quite so easy. That should have warned me.

I followed them into the shadow. I didn't need the path. This was my forest. I was at home here in my own kingdom. I was the stag. I could tread among dry leaves and twigs, and you'd never hear me. The women made little enough noise themselves, just a rustle of leaves and the twitter of their talking. I made none behind them.

They slowed down when they came to the spring. The moss is deep there and the mud's black and soft. It's a rare place for toadstools. The two of them bent down and started searching. Morgan had sent them to find something for her. When I saw what they passed over, I guessed what it was.

I could have told them where it grew. But I hid and waited. It was a slow business. Erith had stopped chattering now. I let the space get wider between them. Luned straightened her back and took a long look round. Then her yellow gown flickered away among the trees. That left Erith on her own.

I worked the stopper loose in the flask.

She found the toadstool. I heard her squeal for pleasure. And then I took her from behind. The flask was in my hand, ready. I got one arm round her and pressed her body to my chest. With the other hand I forced the juice into her mouth. One gasp was all it took. She'd gulped it in. Straight off, she tried to spit it back, but it was too late. She wrenched herself round and saw then who it was. Teilo Smith, with his face half-shaved, half-scorched. Lady Erith didn't laugh at me this time. Oh, no. She stared. Wide, blue eyes, with whites clear as a child's. Then the pain burned into her guts and her eyes turned bloodshot. I couldn't hold her body. She screamed horribly and fell kicking on the ground.

Don't look at me like that! I know. You wonder how I could stand by and see it. I tell you, I didn't feel anything then. Not triumph, not pity. Nothing. I just stood, and watched her die.

It was only a short time she lay there, writhing about, but for her it wasn't nearly short enough.

There was a crashing through the wood. Luned came running back. She'd heard the screaming. One look and she saw Erith's black face, and me with the flask in my hand. She stared at me, like Erith had. Then she clapped her hand to her mouth and went haring away out of the forest.

Silly woman. She didn't need to be afraid of me. You'd only to look at her face to see that Morgan had broken that one already. Where would have been the point in killing her?

So I was left with the corpse. I'd done what I swore I would. It should have made me feel more of a man.

I pulled out the woman's dress. I could feel myself coming over weak the moment I touched it. I hated the feel of it more every time I had to put it over my head. It's funny how clothes can add something to a man, or take it away. You don't know how it felt. You've always been women in your trailing gowns. It would have been different if I'd gone to her dressed in good smith's leather. I could have answered her then.

9

I had a feeling the sentries drew back as I came near. They didn't challenge me this time. They passed me through the gate before I spoke. Someone must have warned them I was coming. I wanted to hold my head up high as I crossed the yard. I'd earned the right now. Instead of that, I had to duck it under that floppy hood. It didn't seem to hide me as much as it had before. Men stopped working to watch me shuffle towards the queen's house. There wasn't one of them cracked a joke or called out a bit of bawdiness, like soldiers usually will to a woman. They knew something was wrong when they saw where I was headed.

There was a different girl waiting at the sunny-house door, a little scrap of a maid. She looked scared. She showed me in and shut the door on me as quick as she could.

Inside that room I felt as my whippet might, shut in a cage with some wild beast out of the forest. Morgan was not so much sitting on her chair as crouched, like a pole-cat on a branch. You could see her hands gripping the carving till they were white as bones. That stupid Luned was shivering behind her.

"So!" she hissed at me. "You dared to come and look me in the face. What is this you have done?"

I stood shaking in my shoes. The words wouldn't come out. I know I should have answered her back proudly, as king to her queen. I just couldn't.

"Only what you told me to," I got out at last.

"You fool!"

That wasn't a word I'd take from anyone. I was a wise man. It got my blood up.

"You challenged me! You gave me my herbs back and asked me to show you how I'd use them. Well, so I have."

"Fool!" she shouted again in a rage. "Have you understood nothing? To wound and not to heal? To curse and not to bless? To hate and not to love? Is this your wisdom? I challenged you to use both sides of that basket, Teilo Smith. Both sides!"

I suppose my mouth fell open at that. Did she mean those herbs of healing I'd brought her so proudly, first off? I'd taken those out and left them lying in the smithy. I thought she'd scorned them. I thought she'd passed them over as the sort of soft, soppy stuff any village wise woman uses in her trade. Of course I hadn't used them. They hadn't strength to match the other, had they?

And so I told her.

That shut her up. She stared at me for a long time, and all the fury drained out of her face. Queen though she was, she looked like a little girl that's lost her mother in the crowd

"Can it really be so? Is this the wisdom you are offering me, King of Smiths? Is this the truth of this world? The dark is stronger than the light?"

I felt a bit uneasy then, with her saying that.

"Of course there has to be both," I said. "I know that. There's dying and kindling again. Winter and summer. The world's a round. But one half's tougher than the other. It's only fit for the strong. That's common sense."

Morgan had got a grip of herself again. She was leaning forward now and there were two spots of colour starting to burn in her cheeks.

"Tell me," she said, in that sort of voice that's sweeter and softer than the way she's looking. "Tell me how the King of Smiths used this strength. Show me how you killed Erith."

It was awkward doing it in those woman's clothes. I'd just as soon not have had to go through it again.

"I brewed the spell in my forge. Then I tracked her down. I took her from behind. Like this. And held her till I'd made her swallow the juice. It only took a moment."

No more than a whisper from her now. And her green eyes fastened on me all the time. She never blinked. Like an adder.

"Then why did you not break her neck or throttle her, *Witch-King*?" Suddenly she screamed at me: "Strength? Is that the way of the wise? Brute force, Teilo Smith! Is that all you meant? Men's methods? Is this the wisdom I asked?"

She broke off with a cry and clutched at her belly. I'd forgotten that. She was so huge I thought it must be twins, though her face was thin enough above it. I feared she was going to drop her baby then. Luned came running to hold her. For a moment the two of them weren't bothered about me. Then Morgan pushed the woman away and drew herself up straight.

"I should have known better than to place my hope in a man of your craft. Any soldier in my castle, any slave in my fields, could have killed Erith more quickly than you did, and more mercifully, if that had been all I wanted. You understand nothing of our art. Nothing! Let me tell you this, Teilo Smith. If Erith had wished to kill you, it would not have been like that. You would have suspected nothing till the pain struck. You would have gone to your grave never knowing whose hand had shaped the spell, unless she chose to tell you at the end. I taught her!

"But that was not what I meant.

"You comprehend no more of the pattern of magic than Urien's wolf-hound. The only power you know about is in your muscles. A common blacksmith! Well, you will go from here. And you will never raise that smith's right arm again." Her own arm was stretched out pointing at me as she said it. "Your forge shall go cold, your hammer rusty. For what you have done I am taking away your manhood. When I know that you under-stand and your eyes are open, then come back to me and beg for mercy. You will get it from no one else. Only come dressed in women's clothes as you are now. I like to see you so. And women's clothes you will wear for the rest of your life. Two sides, Smith! You should have remembered. The universe in balance. Go now . . . *Woman*."

She sat down then, panting like someone who has run a race.

Those words stung me like a hailstorm in the face. Who was she to tell a man of my rank how to act? I felt like I used to as a boy when my mother beat me and I wanted to cry out against her but couldn't find the words. What right had Morgan to speak to me like that? No smith is common! I was as wise as she was, never mind that I wasn't a nobleman in a fine castle. A killing's a killing, isn't it? I'd only used what she dared me to. I could have shown her the other side of the art too, if I'd thought she'd wanted it.

She was holding her belly again and gasping a bit. Luned wanted to run for the midwife, but Morgan wouldn't let her. When the pain had gone again she smiled at me more sweetly than ever she'd done before. It made me shudder.

"Go! I have learned your lesson well. There is dawn, Woman, and there is nightfall. I can indeed use both sides."

So I found myself outside in the yard, shaking for shame and anger. I was a king. I was Smith. Both men and women feared me. They did what I told them. I danced the god. I didn't dress in women's clothes. I wasn't to be scolded like a naughty boy. What I did with my power was not for her to question. But to get out of her gate I had to bend my shoulders and let that hated woman's gown drag about me, and not raise my eyes beyond my hood to look a man in the face. Well, it would be the last time. I wasn't ever going to come back here to be insulted.

I stopped in the wood as soon as I could and tore the patched thing off my shoulders as though a cat had fouled it. Woman, she'd called me! I wasn't having that. I'd finished with her and her "two sides." Aye, and that grey magician with his wild talk of a new king. Let him whistle for his news. I certainly wasn't going to tell him about this. What did I care for the pair of them? I'd let the winter snow cover me naked before I'd drag that dress on again and go shuffling back through her gate. A common smith? I'd show her who's common. I'd call my circle again, folk that showed me proper respect. I'd done what she said, hadn't I? The girl was dead.

Still, it had upset me properly. I couldn't get the feel of her squirming body out of my hands. It was Morgan who made me do it. She laid it on me. It would never have happened if she hadn't taunted me. I'd never have needed to use my power against a girl like that.

So I stood in my man's clothes and I rolled up the dress and made to hurl it in the bog. But something stopped me. Morgan's voice chanting in my head. "Women's clothes you will wear for the rest of your life." It seemed like the strength went out of my arm and my hand dropped slack. Before I knew where I was, I found myself pushing that loathsome thing back into my satchel. I was shivering in the wind, even now I'd got my leather jerkin back.

There's not many cottages to pass on the road through the forest to Way Bank. The last was Granny Sarran's at Woodend. She was a good friend to me. One of my own. It was she that had taught me the use of the darker herbs and where to find them, when I was just a green lad. I'd grown a lot greater than her since then. But, all the same, she wasn't the woman to be afraid of me. And that was more than you could say for most of them.

She was in her garden, scratting among the kale. When she heard me coming she straightened her back to look. I gave her good-day. But when she saw who it was, she shook her fist and let out a screech. Then she rushed indoors, and the door banged fast behind her.

I stood and stared. I couldn't understand it. It seemed to me to be a chill thing, like a foreboding.

Hundreds of times I've thought about that day. If only I could have started it over again. If only I hadn't done what I did. If I didn't have to feel that girl struggling in my grip or hear her screaming for death. She must have been near the same age as my daughter, though scores of times older than Mair in knowledge. It hadn't been my idea to kill her.

I could see there was a knot of men outside the smithy. Men of Way Bank, with cudgels in their fists, barring the road.

They'd seen me. They were snarling like a dog at a stranger. But you could tell they were afraid. Look at them shifting from one foot to the other. So I think, if I stand my ground now . . . I've only got to stretch out my finger and speak the words of power.

But what's up with them all?

Then I see women crying, behind them. And I go cold. Oh, holy Mothers! She wouldn't do that would she? Not my own daughter! Not *Mair*!

But here's my sweetheart. Breaking out from between the apple trees. Running in front of the men to throw herself at my feet. Clawing my ankles. Her pretty face all streaked and ugly with tears.

"Why did you do it? Oh, Da, why did you do it? What made you kill her?"

Why should she care about it? She didn't even know Erith.

"I had to do it, Mair. The queen laid it on me. She made me strike her down."

Mair flung herself away from me with a great scream.

"Then it is true! You did poison her! My own mother and you murdered her! And she always loved you so dearly! And to curse her like *that*. I watched her die. It was horrible. Horrible!"

With her scream there was a stone came flying out of the crowd past my ear. I think it was the boy that threw it. And then they were all running at me with their cudgels up.

The breath seemed caught in my throat. I couldn't get the strength to raise my right arm and point at them. My mind was spinning. I couldn't remember the words of power I ought to shout. Annis? My Annis? Ill-wished like Erith? And they were still coming for me.

I knew then she'd done it. Crouched up there in her castle she'd thrown her spell. When Morgan stretched out her hand towards me she'd been willing this.

I ran for my life. Without saying another word I turned my back on Mair and ran. I never told her that I hadn't killed her mother. My only daughter, and I've never seen her since. She left Way Bank. She doesn't know. To this day she still believes I cursed her mother.

10

I went crashing into the forest like a wild boar when the hounds are after it. I was a strong man and I'd always looked after myself. But the blood was knocking in my head and I had pains in my lungs. I couldn't have told you where I was going. I just knew I had to get away from there.

I don't reckon they wanted to catch me. They were afraid of me. And they had the sense to be scared of coming too deep into the forest. More sense than me. I still ran as if the Black Hunt was after me. I daren't stop to listen if they were still there.

Somewhere in every forest there's a line. You can't see it. You can run right over it without even noticing. Then, a few steps later, you know you've come too far. Miles too far, that's how it seems. You look back, and you can see that other part of the wood. It's a homely sort of place, where the sun comes through the branches here and there, and there are blackberries for picking, and you can herd the pigs to root for acorns. But where you are it's damp and dark and still, and even then you feel it's not as still as you wish it was, and the hair starts to rise on the back of your neck. You want to run back into the sunny side, but there's something here that didn't want you to come and it's not sure now it's going to let you go.

I'd been in there, of course, and at night too, for rites I wouldn't dream of telling you of even now. But not without a full month of preparing and a strong guard forged about me and my circle. And here I'd come blundering into the black heart of it without one word of strengthening, without strong drink, without a drop of blood offered . . . unless you count . . . Oh, no! Not that! That wouldn't shield me. I was like a baby naked in a blizzard.

I didn't stop till I fell into a dark stream and hauled myself up the rocks the other side. I looked round. It was all strange to me. My forest, my own kingdom, but I didn't recognise it. I was the stag. I'd worn the god's horns. But when I looked round and saw that old black wood rotting away and feeding on its own flesh, I knew I wasn't king here any more. I wasn't even a man. I was sobbing with fright like a baby, and with good reason. I was starting to see faces of demons and spirits in the trees. There was a ring of them now. Greyish-white, or green. They were closing in on me. I knew that if I once looked over my shoulder, I'd see that horrible purple mouth of Erith coming up behind me. I tried to run again. It's awful stuff, that leaf-mud, with black water underneath. In the end I was crawling through it on my belly, like a whipped dog.

You may wonder why a wise man like me didn't stop and say a few spells to help myself. I had the knowledge, didn't I? I couldn't. I can't find the words to tell you the terror I felt then. It drove everything out of my head, and that black fear came in that wouldn't let me think of anything else. I only had one thing in my mind. She's done this. Morgan's made me kill Erith, and then she's punished me by cursing my Annis and putting the guilt of it on me. She's snatched my power away and left me naked here. Even now, she's coming after me. I'll run till my heart bursts, but I can't escape her. If I die, she'll have my shade.

That was an awful time . . . an awful time . . . Better for your peace of mind that you don't know. There are nights I wake up screaming, remembering it. And sometimes I've opened my eyes and found Morgan standing over me, watching. There aren't words to tell you the worst horrors of it.

At times I'd come to, and wonder how long I'd been lost and wandering like that. I might be down by the water, far on from Way Bank, no part I knew. I'd never known the lake was so big or so twisting. It was like a serpent coiling its head into the mountains. More than once there was a great storm whipping up the waves and hurling them on the stones, and I was drenched to the skin. Another time I woke to find myself up in the branch of a tree face-to-face with a lynx, staring at me with yellow eyes, and all that was keeping it from springing at me was that I was singing to it in a high, cracked voice. I didn't recognise that voice for my own, first off. The most terrible of all was when I'd lost the forest entirely. It was night on the mountain, so high up and sheer I couldn't imagine how I'd got there or how I'd ever get off again. There was snow settling on the scree and an icy cloud dropping lower to wrap me round. I lost sight of the precipice in the dark, but I could hear demons screaming underneath the drop.

I should have died then. I don't know why I'd lived so long, or how. Do you suppose I grubbed in the dirt for acorns and toadstools and raw worms, like a wild pig? I've no recollection of where I slept, or how long I was lost. But when I found myself on the bare mountain with the banshees howling for me . . .

. . . What?

Oh, yes . . . Well, I lived through that winter. That's obvious, isn't it? I had help. And not from where I expected it.

I came round, as if I'd woken up from a deep sleep after a fever. I was so weak I couldn't lift my head, and didn't want to. But I wasn't fretted. All the frights and horrors had gone, sweated out of me, you might say, and it had left me weak, but clean. I just lay there resting, looking at the sunlight, and not troubling about anything. And then it came to me that I hadn't seen sunlight for a long time. It didn't touch me where I lay but it looked good and wholesome. I saw I was lying in a cave, quite near the door, and there was a little stretch of grass in front of it. Across the tops of the bushes I got a glimpse of a lake, smaller than the one I knew, and as green as grass. There were hills beyond. Grim, dark mountains that still made me shudder, though I couldn't remember then why.

"Christ is risen! Good morning."

He had a harsh voice. I don't think he talked much. Not to another human being, anyroad. I turned my eyes a bit. I hadn't the strength to move my head. He wasn't a big man, but he was so lean and bony he looked taller than he was. He had on a cream-coloured gown that was none too clean, and he had an apron of hareskin over it. I wondered at that afterwards, when I found he didn't eat meat. He laughed a bit wild and said he saved what the fox left or the eagle dropped. But that came later.

I felt my skin go stiff when I saw him. I hadn't come on many of his kind in my life before. I'd kept well clear of them. But I knew what he was. What I'd taken Silver-Tongue for, first off. A Christian hermit. Not like your house-priests, that play politics and live like gentry and shut their eyes to half of what goes on. This lot are tougher. There's no half measures with them. Sworn enemies we were, our sort and his. So I'd jumped out of the cauldron into the fire.

Brogan, his name was. When he saw that I'd got my wits back he asked me questions. Who was I? Where had I come from? What was I doing, wandering on the mountain where he'd found me lying blue with the cold in the snow? I suppose he must have carried me all by himself down to his cave. I didn't think of that then. Or who told him he'd find me on the peak.

I wouldn't answer him. I don't know that I could even remember it all myself, straight off. I just wanted to go on lying there, like a newborn baby, and not be bothered.

He wouldn't let me. He made me sit up and drink some herb soup. Soon he had me starting to walk, though my legs were as shaky as a couple of reeds. But not that first day.

It took me some while watching that sunshine before I realised from the little new leaves on the bushes that it was spring. I couldn't believe that. That the winter had passed me by, out here in the hills, and I couldn't remember any of it. Only the snow starting to fall on that bare scree, and the cloud coming down. And the screaming.

That hermit Brogan had saved my life. But he was expecting something in return. I could tell that. All the time he was nursing me back to health I could feel him watching me, biding his time.

He'd make me a bed of bracken out of doors and sit beside me for hours telling me stories about his Christ. I hadn't the strength to curse him. I needed his food. But he wasn't satisfied yet.

"The body is healing," he said. "But the soul is still troubled. Repent! Admit me as your soul-friend. If you unburden your load to me, I can lead you to him who will lift it from you."

Well, I couldn't tell him, could I? The death-spell? Poison? He'd never forgive that, would he, a Christian like him? So I put him off with tales of this and that and bided my time. I was getting stronger, but I couldn't shift for myself yet. I didn't think I could bear it if he threw me out on my own now.

He thought he'd got me. He thought I'd taken his bait. He taught me their catechism. It was no trouble to me. Hundreds of chants I've had to get by heart in our own business. I said the words, and crossed my fingers behind my back.

One day he watched me carry a skin of water up from the spring and swing it down from my shoulder. It felt heavier than it would have done once, but I could manage it now.

When he saw that, there was a gleam came in his eye. "It is almost Pentecost. The body is whole again and I've instructed your soul. On Sunday Bishop Curran will come to Lyvennet to receive the catechumens into the Church and give them their new robes of white. Will you come down with me and accept baptism too?"

So that was his game! I saw the danger I'd walked into, straight off. I was a fool to trust a hermit. They may live wild on prayer and hymn-singing where nobody can see them, except some pious folk who'll climb miles out of the way to get their blessing. But they keep their own feast-days, the same as we do ours. That's when you see them coming down from the hills and out of the woods to the big churches. Those times when the towns are full of converts in white after one of their baptisms. The Christians have their own High Lords. Brogan would have to report to his bishop what he'd been doing. Did he think I'd go trotting off down the mountain beside him so he could boast to all the world he'd converted a pagan? And there I'd stand, the murderer, Teilo Smith!

Smith! Suddenly it came back to me.

The feel of my hammer in my hand, a smell of oak chips on the forge, my daughter.

I nearly brained him then, but he jumped aside. I snarled at him like a dog.

"You little white stoat! You thought you'd tricked me. One soft word from me and you'd have put a noose round my neck. I should kill you now. How much did she pay you to find me out?"

And more such nonsense. He just stared at me with his great hollow eyes. Then he pulled himself together and shot up his hand.

"*In nomine Patris, et Filii, et Spiritus Sancti . . .'*

I didn't know what it meant then. I thought he was putting a curse on me. I tried to fend it off with one of my own. But my head was empty. There wasn't a word would come to my tongue. I grabbed up a stick, but I couldn't hit him with it. I started to run and then I stopped at the edge of the bushes and let out a yell.

"My satchel! What have you done with my satchel?"

I didn't know what made me say that. I'd never given it a thought till then. But suddenly it seemed as if it was the most important thing in the world to me. I couldn't go without it.

He said, very harsh and sorrowful, "Unhappy man! It has been your pillow these many months. It is lying there."

And so it was. All scuffed and stained, but laid safe inside the cave where I'd slept. Then I began to see the awful truth in front of me. Not the whole, by a long way. I might have let him hang me if I had. All these months I'd been out of my wits. Summer and winter, I'd lived like a beast or a madman. And in all that time I'd kept it with me, that satchel of old women's clothes. I'd lost my bearings, my reason, near enough my life, but never that. I shouldn't ever be rid of it.

I had to have it. I snatched it up and made to dash past Brogan. He was in the cave door.

"Kneel! Repent!" he thundered.

He could have stopped me. I've never got my full strength back, even now. But when he saw how I'd made my mind up, he just groaned. He picked up the blanket he'd used to cover me with, and I saw then what it was. A whitish cloak, the same stuff as his gown. His own mantle, that he must have given me in the middle of winter. He ripped it in two with his knife and held out half to me.

"At least take this to remember him who saved you."

I threw it back at him. I'd keep nothing from him and his kind.

"If you breathe one word to your bishop you've seen me . . ."

But I couldn't remember the words of the curse I'd meant to put on him. My tongue tripped up on it, and I was left staring at him with my mouth gaping open like a fool.

Only then a crafty thought came over me. I was getting my wits together now. I grabbed his torn cloak back and ran.

He shouted after me, "The peace of the Spirit go with you and give you..."

But I couldn't hear the rest of it for the clattering of stones on the path.

I stopped when I got down to the lake. Very dark, it was, cold but sunny. I leaned over a rock to get my breath back, for the run had tired me out.

I thought I was looking down at a water-bogle. A gaunt bag of bones with rags of clothes hanging from its hunched shoulders under the water. Elf-locks of white hair draggled over its neck. And a horrible face dark reddish and blotched above the mouth, and deathly pale below, with a few sprouts of white whiskers on the chin.

I made to cry out, and that creature down in the water opened its own ghastly mouth as if it was going to swallow me. I backed away, and I must have kicked a stone. It splashed into that thing's face and the horrid picture broke up in waves and bubbles. The stone fell through it to the bottom. And then I knew I'd been looking at my own reflection. I don't know which was worse: the horror of that goblin thing from under the lake, or the sight of what I'd been turned into. I began to shake till I thought the madness was coming back on me. She'd done this. Morgan. She'd put her mark on me, so I was fixed the way I was the day she cursed me. My beard wouldn't ever grow back. The forge fire was never going to redden my chin to match my cheeks and nose. The big blacksmith's muscles had shrivelled on my arms. I looked like some hag in the rags of a man's clothes.

And so my face is still. Wait while I unwind the linen. There! You may wonder at it. But nothing will change it now. No matter what I do, the winter's never going to fade the red or the summer burn the white. The full beard won't grow again. I'm caught like this. I'm neither one thing nor the other.

Well, I looked up and my heart gave a sort of leap. There was a dark speck at the far end of the lake, that I took for a boat. Men fishing, most likely. My first thought was that I'd shout to them. Call and ask them to take me home with them. Home. A warm house, a fireside, hot stew. I'd drawn in a great breath and I was waving my hand. And then there was a splash on the water and that speck took off. Only a cormorant, flying off up the beck.

I tell you, I felt so lonely at that I could have wept, till I caught sight of myself in the lake again. Then I knew I couldn't have called, even if it had been men. I saw what they'd see.

Teilo Smith, who'd shaved his face for a vow. Teilo Smith, with his hair white and his leathers in shreds from the thorns, but still the same clothes he'd dressed in the day he killed Morgan's young lady. Teilo Smith, who'd poisoned his wife. Morgan had put her brand on my face like a runaway slave.

I saw I had no home, and never would have now. I'd never dare to brag myself Smith any more. Morgan had robbed me of all I'd ever had: my wife, my daughter, house, forge, kingship, tribe. I'd lost the lot, between one day and the next.

There was only one way I could hide what I had been. I took up that hermit's cloak. It was good, thick stuff, and there was a fair bit of it. I found my knife and cut holes for my arms. I took off what I was wearing. Then I pinned the sides of the other together with thorns to make a rough shot at a gown like Brogan's. There was a deep hood on the half he'd thrown me. I hid my face in it as well as I could.

It made me feel queer, looking down in the lake again. I didn't know what I was now. I'd sworn I wouldn't ever wear woman's clothes as Morgan had told me, but I wasn't a real man either. Not as I understood it, anyroad. I screwed up my leather tunic and breeches in my hand. I thought about flinging them in the lake for safety. Only . . . I knew, if I did that, it would mean Teilo Smith was finished. I'd never be a proper man again. I stuffed them into the satchel with the woman's gear.

11

I'd gone past terror. I didn't feel that any more. But I couldn't bear the dark and loneliness a second time, not though I'd been wandering alone a powerful long while before Brogan found me. It was different now. I'd reclaimed my wits again. I started along that lake-shore, weeping like a lost child for pitying myself.

Repent, he'd said, that hermit. Of course I repented! It cut me inside like an open wound. I'd poisoned my wife. My plump and loving Annis. I'd killed her horribly with pride and cunning. Erith? Annis? It had sounded the same to Mair. It had got so they were both one in my mind too. Every time I thought about that day it made me writhe with the agony of it, like a snake on the end of a spear.

I suppose I could have changed my mind. Gone back to that harsh hermit, Brogan. Made a clean breast of it. Begged him to keep me safe. But how could he? Teilo Smith, that had shaved his face for his god. A witch and a poisoner. I'd be a known man for miles around.

I hadn't got a razor, but I hacked off half my hair, so that I was as near bald in front as the saint himself. I didn't look so much like Teilo Smith now, save for that chin.

I daren't stop there. I had no way of knowing how near I might still be to Lyvennet. I had to leave that behind. I had to hide Teilo Smith away as secret as his leathers.

It was going on dark when I started to climb up the hills at the head of the lake. I was mortally afraid of the night.

The gods let me live, though. They'd had their vengeance another way, and there was more to come. I should have known I wouldn't escape her, no matter what I did. Yet at the time, I thought I'd walked out of a nightmare into Fairyland.

I came off the hills just as it was growing first light. I hadn't dared lie down and close my eyes, so I was almost sleep-walking. There wasn't a scrap of colour anywhere yet, the fells black as charcoal, and the sky grey. I caught a glimpse of another little lake below me, like an eye opening, and then the mist rose up, white and thick, so I wondered if I'd dreamed it.

I kept on going down the slope, stumbling a bit for tiredness. I wasn't used to that long hermit's gown either. And all the time the mist was rising up to meet me.

I couldn't hear a thing. There wasn't a bird singing anywhere. And all I could see was that clammy white wall around me. I knew I'd found the soft brim of the lake when I felt water slopping over my shoes. I couldn't make out any more than the edge of it, very still, a little space of wet pebbles and a few ripples round a clump of reeds. I drank a few handfuls, and the sound of my splashing seemed too loud in the silence. I was afraid to go on. I found a rock and sat down till I could see where I'd come to.

It was a thrush started to sing first, everything twice. And then I heard cattle lowing, far away and hollow-sounding in the mist. A flock of swans came swimming past me and vanished again. I felt the air was starting to thin. When I looked up, the sky was blue over my head. I sat and watched that world come into view, and it was the prettiest place I'd ever seen.

Every lake has its own colour. There's black or silver or a chilly green. This one was red-gold with bits of blue sky flashing in it like jewels. And the hills all round it, not black grim mountains like I'd seen before but low and gentle, with tops like little running waves. The mist was clearing all the time, just wisps of it curling up, like they might have been lily-flowers. Everything round me was gold. The greeny-gold of the little new leaves on the trees, the red-gold of the lake and the old bracken on the fells, and the daffodils the truest gold of all along that shore. Just for a moment I forgot to think about myself and how I must have been the only ugly thing in all that dale.

I couldn't hear any cattle now, just the birdsong and a few ducks taking off from the water. And that was better than if I had, for a quiet herd means they're contented. But I knew that somewhere near-to there must be a farm. And that dale seemed such a peaceful, pretty place, I suddenly longed to be back with my own kind again. I was still afraid, even dressed in the saint's cloak. But I told myself they'd have to be kindly folk, that lived in a spot like this.

I remembered how Brogan's face was burned nearly black, praying out in the sun and wind all day. So I stooped down and rubbed brown peat into my chin and over my shaved head as well.

There wasn't a path I could see, and I was glad of that. It meant it was some out-of-the-way farm, hidden in this hollow in the hills. I wasn't ready for crowds. I picked my way along the shore, stooping under branches and trying to mind my hood snagging on the twigs. For a while I was too busy to look up ahead.

Then I heard a horse neighing. That quickened something in my blood. I'd been a smith, remember. Bridle-bits, buckles, harness-charms, that was all my work. I looked up quick, and found I'd come almost to the end of that little lake, and just then I tripped over a bolt of wood. I went sprawling, but not into soft black mud this time. There were timbers, sawn logs, lashed together to make a causeway over the marsh where the river came into the lake. A proper road.

I can't say what it meant to me, that first solid, built thing I'd come to since I ran from Way Bank. I could feel the heart racing in my chest. I was back among humans. I didn't count that mad hermit. He was half-wild himself, living in a cave like the beasts.

This road might mean danger, but I couldn't part from it now I'd found it. I turned and followed up the causeway. It felt good and solid under my feet. There was a little wood of willows on either side of it, all yellow with catkins. It stopped me seeing far. Then all of a sudden I was on firm ground and there were stones under me. Not cobbles, mind you. Huge slabs of stone, shaped to fit each other with hammer and chisel. Such a road as the Romans had left behind, between Lyvennet and Carlisle. Here, in this little dale with not a town in sight! That made me feel pretty queer, and I began to wonder if this road was as solid as it seemed or if my wits had turned again. The trees were thinning ahead. I'd be coming out on to a meadow pretty soon.

There were the cows I'd heard, red and white speckled. And horses.

Horses? Dozens of them. That shook me. They were fine horses, too, well fed and groomed. Fine horses mean fine men. This was no common farm I'd stumbled on. And then I saw it. The house at the top of the meadow. Well, I tell you, till then I'd never seen a house like that outside Carlisle, and half of them are falling down. Two storeys high, it was, and as long as a street, with two arms reaching towards the lake at either end. It had porches on columns, open to the air. And the whole of it of plastered stone. Red tiles on the roof. Not a bit of thatch anywhere, except for some huts at the back. It looked as grand a house as ever the Romans built. Just like the road I was standing on.

I just stood gaping and wondering where I'd come to. Next thing, there was a great shout from the house, and a crowd of lads came racing out with saddles and hunting gear over their arms. There were women laughing behind them too, but I hardly noticed them. Those boys were whooping and yelling, and some of them had hounds on leashes, that were yapping round their legs. Well, that set off the horses. Some of them trotted forward as if they wanted to be saddled, and the rest went dashing off in circles round the meadow. But those lads were smart. Before long they'd harnessed and mounted, except for the ones that were running on foot, and the whole lot of them were coming my way at a fair old pace. I heard a horn blow, and seeing those boys' heads go up I turned to look over my shoulder. There was a red deer standing high up on the fellside. The lads let slip the hounds and the dogs and horses broke into a gallop. The runners were pelting after them as hard as they could go. I just stood like a fool staring at the brave sight they made, with their chequered cloaks flying and the metal flashing on lads and horses. I never thought that they were going to ride me down.

They were almost on me when one golden lad at the front saw me. He yelled, "Clear the way, you fool!" Then he wheeled his horse round hard left in front of my nose and the whole shock of dogs and horses and hunters went rushing past me up the side of the fell. The hounds belled on the summit and I saw those horsemen against the sunrise. Then they vanished over the top like a fairy-rade.

You look too long at the sun and it scorches your eyes so you can't see the world clear after that, just a dark shadow of what was bright before. I was like that for a long while afterwards. I'd seen that boy, a young man almost. Blue fire in his eyes, like sparks struck from steel. Hair gold with just a touch of the red about it, blown back in the wind, strong limbs the sun had turned the colour of copper, and sitting his chestnut horse as though the two of them had been cast by a master-craftsman out of the same bar of metal. I'd seen warriors, princes, kings. I'd had their horses and weapons in my smithy. There wasn't one looked like that lad. And never mind that he had just shouted at me for a fool.

Well, you've seen Arthur. I'm not surprised so many have fallen in love with him, women and men, and given their bodies for him, one way or the other.

71

12

That lad had dazzled my sight. I didn't even know who he was, then. But the moment he'd gone I saw he'd first set eyes on me too late. If only I could have been dressed as a smith when I met him. If he could have recognised me for what I was!

Not a ragged hermit, in a draggled skirt. White hair, and muscles wasted away. I'd been a blacksmith. I'd served fighting men. I was a great Smith.

I felt such a hurt I didn't think about my own danger, even after I'd lost sight of them. My hands felt empty of tools, as if I'd been robbed. I think I had tears in my eyes. I walked on up that road as if I'd been drunk, or in a dream.

I came to with a nasty shock. There was a sudden rush and I found a sword held to my throat and a spear pointing at my guts and a ring of blades all round me.

I let out such a screech, and they all burst out laughing. One of those guards tipped back my hood and looked me full in the face.

A woman. That shook me properly, you can imagine. There was a score of them. All sizes and ages. Hair braided, wearing tunics and boots and a heap of jewellery and not much else. They meant business. They knew what they were doing with those swords, and some of them had spears and clubs. I stood mighty still, only the blood was hammering in my head so hard I thought it would knock my skull apart. But it seemed I'd startled them too.

"Are you a Druid or a Christian saint?"

She wasn't a beauty, that one in front, and not so young as some of the others. Square face, square shoulders. She wouldn't have looked out of place as one of those centurion statues they have here in Carlisle.

I could see their Roman mansion and I was standing on a Roman road. I knew which was the safest answer. The Romans were never any friends of the Druids.

"A Christian hermit, lady."

Though, come to think of it, the Romans never put women in fighting gear. That was a British thing. I began to wonder if I'd said the right answer after all.

"Who sent you to us?"

"Nobody sent me. I came into the hills to seek my god."

I made the Christian sign. I'd seen Brogan do it often enough.

She looked me up and down. She wasn't satisfied. "Where have you come from?"

I waved my hand back down their lake. I didn't need to lie. I'd no notion where I'd been these last few months.

"I cannot tell you, daughter. I was caught up by the Spirit, lost to all humankind. I can no more tell you where I've come from than where I am now."

She looked at me shrewdly. "Even the longest wandering has a beginning."

Well, I gave a bit of a shudder, as if it wasn't a thing I wanted to remember. "The east end of the Wall . . . Darkness now . . . Our little family . . ."

It wasn't play-acting that made me catch a sob then, thinking of Mair and Annis. That softened them a bit.

"The Saxons?"

I nodded.

"So you crossed into Rheged to escape them? Urien's kingdom?"

"Morgan's now," said another of the young ones, pretty sharp.

So they knew. I hadn't run far enough. She'd cast her long shadow, even on this dale.

"And in all of Britain you stumbled upon us. By accident?"

I'd told them a pack of lies. But the one thing that was true they didn't want to believe.

I must have staggered then. I know I had spots before my eyes. I'd walked all night and I hadn't got my full strength back.

Two of them caught me. The rest had lowered their weapons now, but they hadn't sheathed them. They started to lead me to the house. And suddenly it was like a tangle of reins slipping loose. All the others began to fall away from me, joking and sparring with each other, till I found there was just the two lasses leading me pretty firmly by the arm. I heard the shriek of metal behind me, and when I turned my head there were pairs of women spread out all over the field, feet splayed, arms up, going at each other with sword or spear, and skilfully too, from what I could make out. They'd forgotten about me. They were playing at war, if you could call it playing. They laughed pretty loud, but they knew how to use those weapons if they had to.

If I'd been lost before I was fairly bewildered here. I couldn't make sense of anything I'd seen.

The lasses led me through one door and out of another into a courtyard. There was a porch all round it, and a little fountain. They left me sitting on a bench. There were a few servants coming and going along the corridors. Slaves, by the look of them, with their hair shorn and wearing colourless clothes. Too like me, I thought.

One of the men brought me food and drink. Milk that was thick with cream, bread hot from the oven, a handful of sweet dried plums. When he gave them to me I nearly grabbed his hand, just to feel the grip of a proper man again. And then I thought, a slave? I'm no proper man myself now. A bloodless saint. Next thing to a woman. So I mumbled my thanks as though my wits were wandering. Pretty soon he left me quiet and went back to his work.

I could have sat there for hours, out of the wind in the sunshine. I was watching the servants going about their jobs. They were not over-hurrying but busy. Everything I could see inside that house was well found and seemly, and so different to Urien's fort it could have been in another country. But then those girls outside, with tunics up to their thighs and muscles like racehorses.

I was half-asleep when another young lady came tripping along to fetch me. I don't know if she'd been out in the meadow with a sword too. But, whether she had or not, she was dressed like a proper maiden now, mostly in white. There was gold embroidery round the hem of her gown and her underskirt was fine and delicate, almost like silk. So was her skin. And then I couldn't stop the thing between my legs from leaping up, and I knew I was getting better. I saw the danger. A bit of food and rest, and Teilo Smith was coming to life again, wanting to jump up out of that satchel where I'd strapped him down. Watch your step, I told myself in a bit of a sweat. You're supposed to be a Christian holy man.

I tried to keep my eyes off her, but the sun from the windows in the corridor was turning all the little hairs on her bare arms to spun gold.

She showed me into a room, a hall, you might call it, almost. There was a lady sitting on a chair at the end in the full sunlight, with a lot more gathered round her. Morgan had faced me in a chair like that. But where Morgan was dark, and sat in shadow, this one was all white and gold. Gold curls tumbling over her shoulders, all prettily braided with flowers made out of gold and coral. A white silk dress, and a gown over it, shining like water, and shifting from blue to green. She had white skin too, just touched with pink and gold like the dog rose. I looked at the ladies round her. I tried to square them with those guards that had stopped me in the meadow. But these might have been fairy women, dressed almost as fine as the one on her gilded chair. Only then one of the older ones lifted her arm and I saw the white scar where her sleeve fell back. That made me shudder. So they were mortal flesh and blood that could be wounded, but not like any mortals I'd ever come across. I didn't know what I'd happened on.

There was a pool in front of the steps to the lady's chair, like a little lake indoors. And there must have been a spring at the bottom of it, because the water was bubbling up so the whole surface was moving, and there were fish darting in and out of the sun and the shadows. All round it there were flowering cresses growing among the stones. Stones! Wherever I looked there were little coloured stones set into pictures and patterns. The floors, the walls; they'd even got them on the ceiling over my head. Pictures of grapes and palms, men hunting and women dancing, dragons, dolphins, and even, yes, I was pretty certain those must be pictures of somebody's gods. Not mine, but I wanted to make the signs to protect myself just in case. Only I couldn't do that, dressed as I was, with all of them watching me. I had to make the Christian sign instead, like Brogan had.

When I took my eyes away that lady was watching me with a curious look.

"I see you are a holy man. Valeria tells me you chanced upon us by accident. You are the first for a long time to find your way here uninvited. None of those who did have returned."

That made me stop, all right. I cursed myself for a fool. There had I been, taking my ease, enjoying her food and drink, and not thinking I might have been eating my last meal.

"You wouldn't kill a saint of God, lady!" I gabbled. "Not even if you worship a different set of them to mine. It's ill luck on anyone to slay a holy man."

She looked a bit contemptuous at that.

"Say the Lord's prayer."

That startled me. Which Lord did she mean? I thought I'd better stay with the one whose dress I'd taken. The fewer lies she caught me in, the better. It wasn't hard. Brogan had made me say it over with him three times a day.

"*Kyrie eleison*," she said, looking at me hard as if it was some sort of pass-word.

"*Christe eleison*," I answered.

I wasn't going to let her best me, whatever it meant.

"What signifies baptism?"

So she was a Christian, after all. I thanked my stars I'd learned that cate-chism to keep Brogan sweet. She tried a few more after that, but I was ready for her. All my life I've lived by words of power. Thousands of them I've had to get by heart. It hadn't been hard to stow his sort away in my head along with all the rest. You never know when knowledge will come in handy.

That lady leaned forward and studied me, very thoughtful.

"Who may wear the horns?"

I answered her straight off. She couldn't catch me out, so why were they all laughing?

Too late I saw she had. It was no Christian's catechism that wisdom came from. It was an answer I shouldn't have known, dressed as I was. It was a thing not so many of our own kind should know. I stared back at her, my mouth hung open and the blood burned in my cheeks and then ran cold. I thought I was done for sure then.

But the lady wasn't angry with me. She burst out into a sweet sort of laughter, like little bells. All of a sudden, she jumped up and ran down the steps towards me, skipping round that pretty pool in her gold sandals. She took my hand and rushed me out of the hall, with two of her women running after us. In and out of the sun and shadow we went. Round corners, down steps, till I was out of breath with the hurry and the queer-ness of it. And her little soft hand held tight round mine and setting my body on fire.

Down over the grass we went. There was a narrow stony beach at the edge of the lake and a boat pulled up out of the water. Her women pushed it out and the lady jumped on board. She beckoned to me to follow her. I couldn't guess what she meant to do with me. Her two maidens got in after us and rowed us away.

There were little islands in that lake, mostly covered in trees. The one we were headed for had a small white building on it, like a sort of temple, with steps going down from it into the water. We landed there and the lady led me inside, making the signs I knew.

It was a plainer sort of place than her great house. Marble pillars holding up a dome for the roof. The walls were mostly white, with a bit of a pattern in blue, but no pictures. Inside the door there was a small room with a stone pool. No plants or fish this time. Just plain, with more steps going down into it. At the far end of the inner room there was a table with two candles standing on it. That was plain too. It wasn't much to look at, but it had a holy feel. The lady gave a sort of breathless little laugh and led me into that sanctuary.

I'd been wrong about the pictures. They were there, all right. Someone had drawn them on the floor with charcoal. A twelve-pointed star. There were twelve signs marked, and a different stone laid at each point. It was like another life coming back to me. I felt her watching me.

She led me right into that circle. I didn't want to go. As I passed through that ring I was even more afraid. I wondered if she'd felt the cold sweat break out on my hand.

She stood and faced me. Eyes as bluey-green as her lake. "Who are you? Tell me the truth this time? Did he send you?"

I shook my head. I didn't know who she meant.

She signed to one of her maidens. The girl lit a fire in a brazier in the middle of the circle. She set a little cauldron to boil. It wasn't long before the fumes made my head swim. The Lady stood across the flames from me. She was rippling like water in the heat.

"Secret for secret. Name for name. I am Nimue, Guardian of the Lake. I do not play games. By the power of the twelve houses you will reveal what you are."

I couldn't help myself. She didn't curse or threaten me. And she had a prettier smile than Morgan's. I had to tell her.

"Gillie Kernun – Servant of the Horned One." Yes! You're right. I hadn't even spoken that to my own daughter. It came out pretty hoarse.

"I thought so. Valeria did well to spare you! It is a strange pair of holy men I have now."

She picked up one of the stones. Her white arms held it so I could see it through the steam.

"What is this good for?"

I looked at her, pretty startled. That's men's magic. There's only the highest Ladies of our craft are allowed to learn those secrets. Stone-lore, fire-lore, metals. Likewise you women have your own mysteries, with blood and earth. There's very few of us know the whole truth of that.

And so I warned her. But she just laughed.

She was coming round the fire to me now. She pressed the thing into my hand. It was a shaft of polished greenstone, that fitted snugly in the palm like a tool. Only you'd never have used a beauty like that for rough work.

I shook my head. Her hand stayed round mine.

"Which would you use to bring thunder?"

"I don't know."

"I think you do."

The water in her cauldron was bubbling. I was terrified. I told her. She clapped her hands. She was like a little girl now, playing a game, for all she'd said she wasn't.

"To make one wealthy?"

Well, why not, now? I might have been drunk.

"To turn someone to stone?"

I should have stuck there. I'd put us both in more than enough danger already. But she stood very close and put her arms round my neck. I was drowning. I had to stop her somehow.

We were in that temple a good long time, and she got out of me more at that first meeting than I'd ever told another woman in my life. It scared me senseless when I thought about it afterwards. But at the time there was something else that was frightening me even more. There was one secret I never told Lady Nimue. I doubted that she'd have kept me alive if she'd guessed.

I'd taken every one of those stones of power in my hands, and I hadn't felt a thing. Just a lump of rock, cold and heavy on my palm. There wasn't any thrill ran through me, like there should have done. Those stones didn't speak to me, the way they always had since I was a boy. I'd known what was wrong the moment I'd stepped through that ring. I'd lost my power.

13

The Lady left me. Her maidens washed the marks from the floor and rowed her back to the shore. It wasn't a big lake, but I felt like a prisoner on that island, watching them go. I saw then something I hadn't noticed, rowing out. Straight across the water, on a little grassy slope, there was another temple just like the one I was standing by. I thought it was some trick of the lake, and it was my own reflection I was looking at. There was a man in white standing beside that one too.

I wondered if I had to sleep there alone, like the hermit I'd said I was. I knew Lady Nimue hadn't finished with me yet. But I wasn't sure how long I'd last. Was I like a cow she'd come to milk daily and feed well between? Or a carcass she'd strip bare of flesh and leave just the dead skin and bones? I watched the light go off the meadows as the sun went down and everyone going indoors for supper. I felt pretty sorry for myself.

Her boat came back, though. They'd sent a slave to fetch me. A dour sort of man. He looked me up and down as if I was a mangy dog. It wasn't full dark yet, and a warm evening. The windows were open, and I could hear music and voices coming from the women's hall. The man led me past there and round to the back of the house. There were two rooms the like of which I'd never seen before. In the first one we passed there were two slave-girls. They had their dresses down round their waists, scraping the sweat off each other's backs and looking for vermin. They shrieked with laughter when they saw us coming and made to hide their breasts, only not so quick as they could have done, if they'd wanted. It made me go hot in that hermit's gown. I followed the man through a second door.

"You're to put these on when you've washed," he said, throwing me a bundle of clean clothes. I picked them up. It was stuff much like I was wearing, only better made. Plain creamy wool, white linen. So she was another like Morgan. She'd make me live the lie I'd tried on her. I started to pull them on.

"Aren't you going to bathe first? We're not short of water," he snapped. I heard him mutter under his breath, "Filthy fanatic!" Then he must have seen me looking. He made a holy sign. "Begging your pardon, sir. You're not used to Roman ways. This is the wash-room."

They had tiles on that floor too. Stone basins, and water running all the time through the place, like a stream in a pipe. The man stood and watched, with that sneer on his face. I wasn't sure what I was meant to do. I had to scrub the black mud off my skin the best I could, but there was plenty of it on the towels afterwards. I got those fresh clothes on and that made me carry myself a bit straighter and prouder, milksop weeds though I thought them.

He was staring at me. I realised too late that I'd washed my chin white. He gave me a sour sort of grin. "That looks better for my lady. Smells sweeter too, if you don't mind my saying so. You won't be wanting this again, sir?"

He picked up the thing I'd hacked out of Brogan's cloak. I shook my head. It was good stuff spoiled. Then I saw that he'd got my old satchel under his arm. Inside there were my own smith's leather tunic and those women's clothes Morgan had ill-wished on me. I don't know how it was, but I let out such a screech. I couldn't have screamed louder if I'd been a mother and it was my baby he was snatching away. I grabbed it out of his arms and clutched it to my chest. He backed off quick and gave me a funny look.

"All right, all right, sir. I don't want the smelly things. I was going to burn them."

But I jabbered at him some more and hugged my satchel tight. I couldn't part from those clothes no matter what happened. Not though I hated what they meant.

He showed me then where I was going to sleep. It was one of a row of rooms at the back of a courtyard. The room was small. Just the one big bed. I wondered who I was sleeping with. I didn't know what I was here. Not noble, nor servant. Not man, nor woman. I glared at that long-faced slave till he went away. Then I hid my satchel under a corner of the bed. A girl came with some food.

I found out later who I was sharing that bed with. Bytwini. Her Christian chaplain. The one in white I'd seen across the lake. She had a fine sense of humour, that Lady. He didn't look pleased, though he was polite enough, that first night.

I had to sleep beside him. I had to hear him snoring, the same as Annis snored. That was torment to me. I don't mean his body. We never touched each other. Not that way, anyroad. You can't share a bed on a cold night and not lie close to a man sometimes. But I'd wake in the night thinking I was back at Way Bank, with Annis cuddled up to me and Mair just behind the curtain. And then I'd come fully to and know I was in Nimue's house with a Christian priest lying alongside me, and I'd never see Annis again.

In the morning I had to join in his prayers. I knew he was listening to me.

That day Nimue called me to her in a room full of sunshine. There were cupboards in the walls, with locked doors. When she opened them they were stuffed with books. I didn't think there had been so many written in the world. She showed me one special shelf. There were some rolls on it, yellowed and spotted with damp, and a row of big fat books. Beautiful covers, some of those had, thick, soft leather stamped with gold, or dark wood carved with patterns that seemed as if they'd have meanings, and one or two of the bindings just old and brown, half rotted away. She opened some. The old ones were full of words to the end, but the new ones half empty, pages cut and ready for writing. I'm no scholar, but it gave me a queer sort of feeling, wondering what they were waiting for.

"Well, Gillie Kernun, will you help me fill my books?"

The room swayed a bit.

"Me, my lady? I can't read or write." Though I could a little, enough to tally the count of what was owed me and mark a sign for the name. But not a whole book, line after line, like this. "What could I put in them?"

"Magic!" she said, raising her pretty eyebrows. "Why else should I keep you alive here?"

I was feeling pretty bad already. I'd thought when I saw this dale I'd found myself rest and safety, and here I was already in deeper than I wanted. When she smiled at me like that, so charming, I could feel the water lapping all around me, like the lake opening its mouth to suck me down.

"Just a bit of stone-lore, lady. Good craftsman's stuff. That's all I know. Not the high magic your ladyship's sort would want."

It was a lie. For all her pretty looks I was terrified of her, and of her books too. What I knew shouldn't be written down. There isn't a language invented by any scribe that's fit to hold those things and put them on a page for the unwise to pick them up and read them. That's too dangerous. They should be chanted in our secret places, or whispered from father to son and mother to daughter. Years you have to serve before you're fit to be told some of them. How did I know how deep she'd been taken or who else she might show them to?

"That is not true, Gillie Kernun. You could teach me much more."

She touched my wrist. I felt a thrill from that, all right.

"Do not be afraid, White-Chin. You are among friends here. There is not one of my maidens that has not taken her vows. The Saxons are growing stronger in the east. And in the west the white Christians are spreading, even without the army of Rome to shield them. I guard the wisdom of Britain, that it be not forgotten."

But she was standing in this fine house the Romans had built, in her pretty white dress and sandals, with a Latin book in her hand. And she kept a Christian priest. What was I to believe? Well, it didn't matter what I thought, did it? She'd gone too far. She'd shown me what she had and what she wanted. I could say yes, or I could say no, but either way I wouldn't leave her dale alive, that I did know.

"Wisdom is for the wise," I said. "I'll share what scraps I have with you, my lady."

Well, she hugged and kissed me. She was always a great one for that. Then she pulled away from me, laughing like a little girl.

"Is there no strength left in your arms, White-Chin? I cannot tell if I am kissing a man or a saint."

She'd got me by the short hairs, saying that. I cursed the day I'd put on the hermit's guise. Dressed like that I didn't know who I was, myself. She was near driving me mad, but if she'd taken off her clothes there and then in front of me I don't think I could have kept it up.

After that first evening I ate with the gentry. I was their curiosity. The holy man out of the wilderness. Those ladies lay on marble couches strewn with cushions. They ate off silver and drank out of goblets of green glass. I felt a pig in front of them, scared stiff of dropping things or using my knife the wrong way. But they hid their smiles behind their hands.

Bytwini never smiled when he looked my way. He didn't eat much either. No meat, except on Sundays. Water in his wine. And not a quarter the bread and cheese I'd put away when I'd worked in the sweat of my own forge. I tried to copy him. I don't know why. He was the only one that didn't know I was a sham. Or did he? I went to bed hungry.

I had to pray whenever he did. I'd got the words by heart already, Latin or not. The worst was when he made the Offering on Sunday. We all went to his white chapel by the lake-shore. Those women were dressed as modest now as any Roman matron. Servants who hadn't been baptised yet stood in the anteroom. Dressed as I was, I had to follow into the church with all the rest. When we knelt in front of him he picked up the dish of bread.

"If there is any cause why you cannot receive this holy sacrament of your Saviour's flesh and blood, confess it now. Else you will eat and drink to your own damnation."

I didn't flinch. I'd been damned by both sides already, mine and his.

But when he got to me he stopped and looked me hard in the eyes.

"Brother, what is done here when the bread is broken?"

That hermit had cheated me! There must have been secrets they won't tell you till after you're baptised. I floundered out something, but it wasn't right.

Bytwini ordered me out of his church, in front of all those ladies. Even her slaves were welcome where I wasn't. And never mind that every one of her maidens had taken their vows to someone who wasn't his god. He still fed them his sacrament. Didn't he know? But I saw him look pretty angry at Nimue before I went.

Nimue tried to make it up to me. She stroked my cheek next time she had me alone.

"Power, White-Chin. The Church is power, of another sort. I need every tool in my hand."

It was two days before the hunt came back. I'd looked for that troop of lads the first evening, but nobody seemed to be worried when they didn't show up.

When they did come home at last there was such a hullabaloo we all went rushing out to look.

There were cattle pouring into the meadow, with a great brown bull in front of them that had horns as wide as the branches on a hundred-year oak. He came roaring and stamping, with his cows after him. But that wasn't all the noise. Those boys were yelling and hallooing and blowing their horns, and the dogs were barking fit to make themselves hoarse. A secret dale! I reckon you could have heard the row from the top of Helvellyn.

The Lady had come running out before anyone else. That golden-haired lad at the front jumped down from his horse and threw his muddy arms round her neck. "Well, Nimue? Is this not well done?" And he threw back his head and laughed to make the hills ring, like iron on anvil. You couldn't help but smile with him.

She laughed and kissed him, so I wondered if she might be his mother, though she didn't look old enough.

"Reckless, but brave. Did you lose many men?"

He moved away for her to see. I hadn't bothered with his friends till now. They were a motley lot. Some his age, some a bit older. Short fat ones and tall lanky ones, the way boys are when they're still growing. Fair-skinned, brown, red-freckled, and two as black as charcoal. Only one didn't get down. He was hung over the neck of his mare, so his mantle fell over his face.

"Poor Cathno," Lady Nimue said. She lifted the cloak and touched his grey face with just the tips of her fingers. "He comes to me too late."

Some of the other lads were nursing gashes, too. I had a chilly sort of feeling she might be looking to her new holy man to salve them. I didn't know what to do. I could tell her the herbs. I knew which chants I had to speak. But what use was any of that if the power had gone out of my hands?

The field-slaves were herding those stolen cattle in for milking. By the look of their udders they were good and ready for it. It was small wonder they were bellowing. When I looked round, the Lady's maidens were leading off the wounded and I could see the women were pretty used to this sort of thing. It didn't look as if I'd be needed, after all.

When they'd gone, that Nimue stood with her arm round her golden lad's shoulders and the two of them were looking mighty pleased with themselves. And I don't mean he was pleased with himself and she was just proud of him, mind you. They were both laughing in each other's eyes as though it was as much her doing as his. She played her fingers up his back and through his curls in a way that made me go hot and tight. And him too, from the way he grabbed her to him.

But she wriggled clear and pulled the horn out of his belt. She blew a little haunting call, just four notes. There was a bit of a silence round about, for the beasts were settled now and most of the folk had gone indoors. Then there was a call answered far off on the hills, then another, and another, thin and high, like the horns of Elfland. I spun round to look where they were coming from. They were spaced out all along the hilltop. Little black figures standing up against that gold evening sky. It was too far off to see them plainly. But by the way they were standing, feet apart, heads up, spear in one hand and horn in the other, they looked to me like fighting men. I'd no idea they were there before. So it was more than the women down here guarding this dale.

Nimue touched the horn to her lips and then the boy's, with a bit of a laugh.

"You are not quite ready yet for the spoils of manhood. Be careful, Arthur!"

"But I soon will be."

And the two of them came up the steps with his arm round her waist.

Arthur . . . That name meant nothing to me then. But when I saw them together like that I knew I'd stumbled on more than I'd guessed.

The lad himself never even looked my way. I might have been one of the slaves. But as the Lady passed she caught sight of me, left standing all by myself staring at him. She stopped smiling. Her pretty blue eyes looked into mine so keen then I nearly fainted.

14

We feasted in the old British way that night, trestles down the hall and great cauldrons of meat and drinking-horns. There was only a marble table and couches for Arthur and Nimue and their pet friends. That caused some trouble. Pretty soon there was an argument broke out over who was to be sat at the top. In less time than you could crack a nut it turned to fighting, and more than half those boys were at it. They'd all changed into handsome house clothes with as much gold and jewellery as they could hang on them, and some of them had washed the mud and blood off themselves pretty carefully and others hadn't. But there was more blood spilled now, and split noses and black eyes. The dogs were going mad under the tables, and the servants hopping out of the way and trying to save the food and drink from going over.

Some of the women jumped up, and for all they were nicely dressed up for that feast I saw them look at their lady, and their hands went to their belts as though they were wishing they'd got weapons. If she'd given them the word I could see they'd have sorted those boys out, even so. But she put out her hand to stop them and looked at young Arthur, who hadn't done much up till then save yell at his lads. He had two stout friends either side of him. Cei, that was the tallest man in the room and a black brow on him like a raven in a bad temper. Cei the Fair, they called him! And Bedwyr, that looked as pretty as a girl, but could run or fight or drink with anyone in that hall till he was the only one left standing. The three of them looked at each other and went into the thick of it. Arthur had a tough job of it at first, and he took some pretty hard knocks himself before he'd got them round to his way of thinking. Cei didn't bother with arguing: he just walloped anyone who wouldn't stand still. Bedwyr got their arms behind their backs and twisted them round so they had to listen.

"Shame on you!" cried Arthur. "There's a fine feast here going to waste. Meat we've raided. Grease your knives on that and enjoy it, before the wine's all spilt. We're blood-brothers, heh? Settle your rank of honour on the field tomorrow."

There were some of them still growling, and there'd be more quarrels to settle now than there had been before the fight. Arthur put his arm round Dillus, who'd started it all by shouting loudest because he'd been put lower than Custennin. He took a great gold chain off his own neck and hung it round Dillus's and kissed him. But he led him back to the bench and made him sit down in the very same place he'd been put in before. The rest of them watched pretty tense and the hall went mighty quiet then, but Dillus only growled something about the morning. The meat was carried on to the table double-quick and Arthur raised his drinking horn. He'd carried it off.

I was nothing. I wasn't a servant. I didn't wait at table, but I wasn't sat with the gentry either, not like Bytwini on the end of Arthur's table. The priest was trying to talk pretty seriously to Arthur, but the lad just clapped him on the shoulder and laughed in his face. I was tucked almost out of sight at a table near the bottom of the hall. I'd seemed pretty important to Lady Nimue these last few days, but she'd no time for me now Arthur had come.

A lad with a raiding party. And I was a smith. I'd managed to keep that quiet from Nimue and her women, weapons or not. But this was different. I gripped my beaker so hard it might have been a bar of hot iron I was bending.

I watched them drinking and feasting. They weren't very old, those boys. Half of them not full-grown men. They couldn't hold much liquor. He'd stopped them fighting. But after a bit there was vomit and cups knocked over and boys sprawled on the table or under it. The Lady sat and smiled at it, chatting away to Arthur and Cei and Bedwyr. Her women did what they could to hold things steady and call the slaves to clean the mess and set things straight.

There was a harper, and a good bit of song and story-telling, and that quieted them, till they cheered him at the end. It was all new to me, the way the gentry lived, Roman or British. I'd never heard harping like that, though I knew some of the stories. He sang about the blessed head of Bran that was carried about, and Queen Rhiannon that was made to go like a horse, and Pwyll that changed places with Arawn, King of Faery, and a lot more besides. I remember there was one about how Uther Pendragon beat the Saxons. They liked that. Then he sang a new song telling how Arthur had stolen the brown bull of Crec and brought it home. And those that were still awake roared and stamped at that like the old bull himself.

Well, by that time I'd had my fill of meat and beer like everyone else. I didn't bother now about picking at my food like Bytwini did. That one meal was better than all the feasts I'd had in my life put together.

Still, I was sat pulling the gristle out of my teeth when I saw another of Arthur's lads pissing before he could get to the door. I felt so sad when I watched him the tears were rolling down my cheeks. And not just for myself this time. For all this fine house and their clothes and jewels, Arthur wasn't the prince of Elfland, the way I thought he might have been when I first saw him. That only happens in songs and tales. This lot were mortal. Boys. Dirty and bloody, with black eyes and grease down their tunics. Not fairy warriors at all. Just boasting and brawling and getting drunk and making themselves sick, as boys will everywhere. That made me weep. I was pretty drunk myself.

\#

It was a brisker sight in the morning. Never mind what sore heads those boys might have had, they were all out on the field before the mist was off the lake. The women were there too, instructing them, and pretty stern teachers they were. They knew their business, though how they had come by it themselves still beats me. It was all strange, that place. I sometimes wonder if I dreamed it.

I looked for those sentries on the hill, but I couldn't see them now. And never did unless the Lady signalled. I had a cold thought then. They must have been there in the heather the night I came. Had I wandered between two of them in the dark? Or did they see me? Why would they let me pass?

I didn't have long to worry about that. Lady Nimue had work for me. Every day she'd take me to the library, or her store-room of herbs, or that temple on the lake. Or we'd just walk out of doors. Wherever it was, she'd make me recite to her some more of what I knew. She was going to milk me of magic till her buckets ran over. Greedy, she was, for power. You could see it in her eyes. If I'd been Smith, if I'd been King in the Forest still, I'd have smelt the danger. I'd have been pretty careful how much I spilt to that one. But I wasn't king any more, was I? The god had left me. Morgan had robbed me of that. So what did it matter to me what I told the Lady? That's how I thought then.

This particular morning she took a bundle of things wrapped up in a cloth, and a little writing tablet, and led me into a sort of garden at the back of the house. It had stone walls around it, high, so you couldn't see over. And even here, where it was just grass and trees and flowers, the stones of the wall were all cut and squared, not lumps of rock such as you'd put round a sheepfold. Weeks it must have taken, just to make that garden wall. Even the grass was cut into straight edges or circles, with little walks between. There were marble steps and seats. But it wasn't that that took my breath away first off. When I clapped eyes on them I thought I'd seen the gods. They were like the ones in the oak . . . No. I was forgetting. There's only a few of you have seen them, and there are still some things I'm not speaking of, even now.

Only these weren't wood but stone, all shining in the sun. And gods they should have been, by rights. There was a lady with an owl on her shoulder. And a chap with a club, wearing a lion-skin. There was even, begging the Horned One's pardon, one a bit like our own sort, with hairy legs and little horns corning out of his hair. And lots more besides, that had a fishing-spear, or grapes, or breasts to suckle two babies, so that between them they covered just about everything that needs looking after. I should have fallen down flat on my face and howled for safety. But I didn't, not once I'd pulled myself together and got over the shock. I didn't need to.

They weren't gods, though they had the shapes of them. All my life I'd lived by the things of power, even as a lad. My father was king before me. It wasn't just the great ones in the holy place. We brought little ones of that kind away with us too. Wood, clay. Small enough to slip into your pocket. But you wouldn't. You'd carry them carefully, and you'd set them on a shelf in the house and light candles to them. They were the god too, or a bit of him. They were holy. When you spoke to them you were talking to the god himself. So I don't know how it was I could look face-to-face at these figures, and some of them bigger than I was, and not feel afeared of them.

Something changed that day. I felt like a river was sweeping the firm ground from under my feet. I didn't know where I might be carried next, or if I'd ever fetch up safe again. Only one thing I did know: those things had the shape of power, but that was all. They weren't gods. They were nothing but human beings in fancy dress.

My mind was pretty near reeling, taking in all this. The Lady made me sit down on one of her marble benches and unwrapped her things on the seat between us. I had another start. It wasn't stones this time, or herbs, or dead animals, though there were hundreds yet we hadn't talked about. It was a set of weapons, and no common ones either. I recognised the markings on them. The knife. The spear. The bow. Not so richly jewelled as some I'd seen hanging in her hall. But rarer, for all that. It was a bright day. The metal was polished up and winking, so it dazzled my eyes. And she was bright too, looking up into my face with her little-girl smile.

"Tell me, White-Chin, what do you know of these?"

And she stroked my hand, as though she didn't know she was doing it. Like a little wave lapping.

"I'm just a poor seer. I told you, my lady. Only a handful of stone-lore and fire-lore. A few charms for mending. Well, maybe the odd one for cursing too. These weapons are the high magic. You need a king of the craft for that."

"Do I, Gillie Kernun? You know, don't you? You could tell me their secrets if you wanted to?"

And her little hand went creeping up my arm.

I had to save myself.

15

That Nimue was no fool. She made them drive that bull and his cows, those we hadn't eaten, back over the hill and turn them loose in a bog the other side. If those that had lost them came tracking the herd, let them try and get them out of there without being sucked under. There'd be precious few hoofprints to follow over those peat hags, and suppose anyone did come scouting round our side to pick up their tracks again and see where they came from, well, she had those who would make sure they never got back to tell of it.

I don't think Arthur minded losing his bull. He'd got his glory. He'd proved he could do it. He'd led his troop and taken what he wanted, before those he robbed got wind of what they'd lost. Those lads killed everybody in sight of that herd who might have told what they'd seen, or so they bragged. They'd come away with only one man lost and a tale to boast of.

She made him be careful after that, though. Only not as careful as he would have been if she'd been his proper mother. She'd make a warrior of him. They still went raiding, and pretty far from home, from the tales they brought back with them. But now it was just killing and looting stuff they could easily carry. No more cattle raids. And she taught him to cover his tracks, make a big circle, ford rivers, scatter and group again to fox the enemy. There would have been some queer tales told round those parts. This troop that rode up out of Annwn, all young and handsome like the Fair Folk, who took what they pleased and vanished into the hollow hills at daybreak or dived into the bogs and were never seen again.

They were learning their lessons well. There was never a horn blew alarm on the hills. Just once or twice when I was with her, my lady lifted her head quick at a hawk's scream. But it wasn't ever a troop of angry horsemen coming over our skyline. As I said, it was like being in Fairyland down there in that dale. And just as dangerous to mortal men.

I stayed too long. They say that humans always do in Fairyland. But where else could I go? I had shelter. I was wanted there. Lady Nimue made a fuss of me. She gave me a room of my own to stop Bytwini from ranting at her. You can imagine how queer that felt. I'd never lain by myself before. I don't count that awful time after Morgan cursed me . . . For a long time I was so scared I couldn't sleep. It was a fine grand house in daytime, but I wasn't too sure what might be abroad at night.

We'd got into a kind of pattern. I'd spend an hour or two with my lady every morning. I'd forgotten I even knew so much till she plucked it out of me, like finding thorns long after you've fallen into a bramble-patch. Then the rest of the time was my own. Sometimes I'd hang around the back quarters and help the servants a bit. It felt more wholesome than you might think to be fetching a sack of flour or polishing up a bit of harness. I'd like to have done more of the men's work. But they looked sideways at me in my holy man's gown. They never talked free when I was around. They wouldn't share a joke with me. That hurt, seeing real men that didn't have to hide what they were. And it seemed as if I didn't have to try so hard to hide it now. I looked older than I was, with my hair turned white, and I hadn't the muscles I used to. I've never got my full strength back since Morgan blighted me. When I'd outstayed my welcome I'd go off on my own. I could wander anywhere I wanted. I might watch the lads training, and hurt myself some more, aching to get my hands on their harness and body-armour. It never entered their heads what I was, of course. Just a white seer, hanging about the field. They'd have taken more notice of me if I'd been a ghost. There wasn't any of them had a use for me, only Nimue.

The time slipped by, and they brought in the harvest. It was a pretty house, but it was built on poor soil. It put more meat than bread on our table.

I was walking round the lake, taking it easy in the sun and picking up little feathers the birds had dropped by the water's edge. You never know when you'll have a use for things like that. I'd done the full circle and I was nearly back to where I'd hit on that causeway the first day, when I heard a sound that made me stop. Horse's hooves and a loud old jangling, coming along that old stone road through the wood. Well, you may say, what's a road for if not for horses to travel? I'll tell you, this road only led to one house and it seemed as if it came out of nowhere. There was nobody came to that house by it and nobody went out on it. When Arthur and his mates went raiding over the moor, they'd take the back way over the fells, any path for them but the one that looked plain and easy. So I stopped where I was, under a holly tree, and I wouldn't have been surprised to see some Roman ghost come riding by.

He was stranger than that. And it wasn't a horse but a black mule that came into sight, hung about with huge panniers that clattered a bit. Full of pans and dishes, poking out at the top. Not over-fancy stuff, but worth a fortune just for the metal in them. I should know. And perched on top of the lot, with his legs stuck out on either side, was the queerest sort of fellow you ever saw. He had a cloth of speckled yellow and black tossed over one shoulder, and a skirt of the same that didn't cover his knees, and the rest was bare, and so thin and scrawny you could see the shapes of gristle and bone under his skin. He didn't need covering for his head. He had hair that spread down over his shoulders as thick and white as a lamb's fleece. My elf-locks were cobwebs to his. You never saw so much hair, and so full and curly, on an old man. Old? Well, he was and he wasn't. He had a face scored with lines as deep as the cracks in a piece of driftwood that's been left out years for the rain to leach and the sun to dry, and as grey too. You couldn't ever have forgotten if you'd seen that face before. And yet I felt I had.

I thought the sun went in as he passed me. I hadn't moved to hide; I just stood still in the shadow. He didn't look, and the mule went clattering on, only the sound of her hooves changed when she struck the causeway. The pedlar was humming a little song under his breath and he peered ahead pretty eagerly as he got near the meadow. I reckon I must have been the ghost, not him, slipping along after him through the trees. There weren't many left out on the field by that time. The lads whipped round and stared, and some of them went for their weapons, but the women-guard looked up at the hills and then at each other. They signed to the boys to let him pass. But they all stared at him riding up to the house.

Then out of the doorway comes the Lady Nimue herself, and she's running down the steps with her arms stretched wide. She fairly threw herself at that pedlar and his mule, and he hopped off, quick as a frog, and hugged her to him. The two of them were dancing each other round, laughing and singing as merry as you please.

The boys seemed to come to, then, and put up a great shout. "It's Merlyn!" "He's back!" "Merlyn!" And they all came pelting up to greet him.

Well! I felt as if three spears had run me through from different directions. I didn't know which of them was going to be the one that finished me off.

This crazy-looking pedlar was Lord to this Lady and she'd never spoken a word about him all this while.

And then his name. Those boys had shouted it out as careless as if he could have been anybody's uncle. Merlyn. There'd be more than one that had that handle. But I didn't need telling twice which this one was, not here. Merlyn, the high magician the tales tell of. The one we wise talked of in whispers. The one that steered the boat of Uther Pendragon and then vanished. And I had stumbled on his Lady's house by chance. Or had I?

And at the back of all this, one thought colder than all the rest. I remembered now where I'd seen that face before, in a very different disguise. That grey bard in the street of Carlisle. Silver-Tongue. In his foxy red cloak, darkening the door of my smithy and flirting with my daughter. So it had been Merlyn all along, binding me to be a traitor to Morgan for the sake of his secret little king.

16

Merlyn. Morgan and Merlyn. So that's what it was. They'd got me caught properly, hadn't they? They'd driven me from one to the other of them across those mountains, like hounds turning a boar on to the spears. I should have known I hadn't escaped. I should have seen where I'd come to. He'd as good as told me, hadn't he? A boy king to rule over all Britain. To drive the Saxons out and make the land one. All summer I'd watched those lads playing at soldiers, and it had never once crossed my head what that enchanter had said to me. That had happened in another life. The day Morgan cursed me was a black pit in my mind. All that other business had been on the far side of it. I daren't let myself remember back so far. Well, I'd had my eyes opened now, and I could see I was in far worse danger than I'd thought. Merlyn had set me to worm out Morgan's secrets, and instead I had found out his.

Arthur. So this was the lad that had to be kept hidden from Morgan, though Silver-Tongue had never let on why.

You can be sure the first thing I thought of was that I'd cut and run before the magician saw me. I'd got the wood at the back of me, and that old lost road. Then I remembered the men in the bracken, and I went a bit cold and I thought that maybe the only escape I was likely to find would be on the end of a spear.

I didn't have a chance to try for it. I wasn't as well hidden as I thought I was. Nimue must have seen me over Merlyn's shoulder as they hugged. She broke off then and whispered to one of her women. That one came running over the grass towards me, while the Lady took Merlyn indoors.

Valeria, it was. The square-faced fighter that had held her blade to my throat the first day. She was a sort of captain among them, so I knew it was serious what she'd come to say. She hurried me back into the wood a bit, where we couldn't be seen.

"My lady counsels that you use discretion, for your safety and hers. Her visitor doesn't know of your coming, and it is better that he does not. We do not ordinarily welcome strangers."

"I could see that for myself," I told her.

She grinned a bit at that. "You were lucky. You had something that my lady wants. You bought your life with wisdom."

"And Merlyn's got more than I have."

She looked a bit shrewdly at me then. "You know him?"

I was a fool not to be careful.

"I'm a wise man. Which of us hasn't heard of Merlyn?"

"Yes."

She still looked at me hard. Then she started leading me through the wood, off the road. We came out by the lake edge. She made me keep back while she slipped out and looked. I saw her wave her arm, and another of them signalled back from the house. Valeria hustled me into a coracle pretty fast and rowed me across to the island. I kept my head hidden close. He might have taken me for Bytwini if he'd seen.

"My lady desires you will stay here. Food will be brought to you. Merlyn sees beneath too many hoods. It is better that you do not cross his path. Do not worry. He never stays long."

"Don't fret," I told her. "I've no more wish to be shrivelled into a toad or turned to a block of stone than she has. I'll keep close till he's gone."

"Good. And, White-Chin, one thing more. Use no charms or spells while Merlyn is in this dale. A great magician like him could sense it."

Make magic? I hadn't been able to cast one single spell since the day I killed Erith. I'd talked of magic. Charms, recipes, conjurations, signs. All that and more. But I hadn't used any of it. I hadn't put the bits together and made them work. I didn't know if Nimue had tried.

So I kept close, in that little white temple looking out over the lake. One thing scared me more than anything. Would Bytwini tell him a stranger had come in the false get-up of a Christian hermit? The priest was no friend of mine. I needn't have worried. I wasn't the only one who'd left the house. I saw Bytwini walking by his own little chapel across the water from me. I found out afterwards he'd never stay in the house when Merlyn was there.

He tried what he could to be soul-friend to Arthur, and the lad looked up to him. He taught him reading and writing and a lot more besides. But there were some things in this house he couldn't shut his eyes to.

Merlyn came and went pretty often that autumn. I was never easy. There'd be a lass come running up to me where I was singing chants to Nimue in her library or walking down by the lake, and I'd be hustled off into hiding for days or maybe a couple of weeks. The worst was when he came so sudden they couldn't get me down to the water without him seeing, and then I'd have to lie close in my room till it was dark. That made me sweat, being so near to him, only a few walls away, and wondering what would happen if he discovered me. He has a mighty loud laugh.

I saw him close to, once. It was night, but almost as bright as day, with a big golden moon coming up over the roofs of the stables and washing that courtyard outside my window silver. The sort of night that made me think of Morgan. I heard laughter, and when I looked out there were the two of them, Nimue and Merlyn. They were coming out of that garden, the one I told you about, with the old statues. They looked a bit like a pair of statues themselves in the moonlight, her in her white Roman dress and him in a toga, with wreaths of leaves in their hair. They'd stopped still now, very close together, and he was holding a bunch of grapes over her mouth. When I saw the way his hands were going over her I thought of the look he'd had in his eyes the day he'd fondled my daughter. When I'd dashed the tears off and I could see straight again, they'd gone. I thought he'd have to feel the curse I sent after his back then. But I didn't care, and nothing came of it. It seemed not even black anger could put the strength back in my spirit.

Still, I was sure I couldn't hide from him for long. I'd lost the cunning to put a mist between us. He'd find me out.

I saw Nimue's game. She was feeding on both of us. She'd gobble up Merlyn's high magic while she had him with her, and leave my crusts for other days. And she wouldn't want him knowing she had another larder. When I realised what she was up to I wondered that Merlyn could be such a fool as to share his wisdom with her. I know he'd an eye, aye and plenty more besides, for a pretty woman. But he was supposed to be the wisest enchanter we'd ever had in Britain, wasn't he? And who was she to learn what he knew? There's ranks and grades and ceremonies to go through, year upon year, and even then you wouldn't come anywhere near where Merlyn was, by all accounts. I began to wonder then if there mightn't be more to this Lady of the Lake than I'd thought. Maybe she wasn't as young and silly as she liked to act with him. Or maybe she's always been young ... Always?

Now what did I mean by that?

Those times were bad for me, sitting alone in that temple, night and day. It was a plain enough place, but it frightened me. Things were coming back now. I knew it wasn't only the moon that looked down on the lake over the tops of the hills. Once Morgan had watched over me in my forge at Way Bank. She was watching me here. I could feel it now. I was a fool not to have seen it before. She had driven me here, and for a reason. I could still put her out of my mind when the lads were on the field and you'd got the clash of sword on shield and the noise of horses' hooves. But sat there in the silence, and especially in the dark, with the water lapping all round me, that was a different story. I'd get back to my room again when he'd gone and I'd find myself pulling that filthy old satchel out from under the bed. I'd sit nursing it on my knee, like a wise woman with her toad. I'd feel inside it. Smith's leathers and woman's skirts. I wasn't safe from her, not here. I'd shudder then. I could tell for sure now, it was Morgan's doing that had put me in this house. For her good, not mine.

I noticed the lads hadn't been raiding for a while. The place seemed to have gone more grim and serious. They still trained on the meadow, harder than ever. There were men giving them lessons now. Hard, hefty soldiers, with muscles like iron bands and scarred faces, in leather battle-dress and dark-red cloaks. I didn't know where they'd sprung from, unless it was off the hills. And there were more noblemen coming in every week. Older warriors, too. The lads were going on men themselves now. By day they didn't laugh as much when they practised, and they fought sterner. Over the wine at night they'd laugh wilder and fight less.

Arthur had lessons of another sort in Bytwini's chapel now. They'd spend hours there alone, the two of them. And sometimes Bytwini would call the whole lot of them round him and make them sit very quiet on the grass while he talked to them.

But other days it was Nimue's turn. Arthur would row across and she'd be waiting for him on the steps of that little temple in the lake. She'd take his hand and lead him inside. They'd be in there a mighty long time and they'd come out looking grave. And then as like as not they'd burst out laughing and go racing each other down to the boat, as if he couldn't wait to be back in the saddle and she was no older than he was.

I should have seen what all this was leading up to. I'd been Smith. That was my craft. Didn't I forge the sword that made Urien a man? But I walked into it as blind as a hare slipping her head through a noose.

It was Midwinter's dawn. I'd never missed that sunrise. I hadn't got the wise around me, or not my own sort. I've no doubt those women had their ceremony, but they didn't call me to join them. But that year there was a bidding on me stronger than I'd ever felt before at that season. I knew it wasn't right to be doing what I had to do on my own. I was awfully scared. I hadn't made the preparations. I hadn't tried to use my craft in all the time I'd taken that saint's gown. I didn't think I still had the power. And, if I hadn't, I'd be putting myself in worse danger. But it had to be done, somehow. Up at the house we'd had a great fire, with feasting and dancing half the night. Arthur had gone off early. Bedwyr said he'd taken himself to the chapel, and nobody was to follow. And then the ladies disappeared. Most of the men had dropped off to sleep before it got morning. I slipped away in the dark and howled a bit to myself that I hadn't got the guise of a big he-stag as I used to do. Yet go I must, no matter how wrongly I was dressed.

It was freezing outside. There was ice cracking under my boots and then I was crunching frost on the grass. It wasn't light and it wasn't dark out there in the open. There was just a bit of a glimmer from the water and then black fells all around with snow on the tops. I couldn't see the island in the middle of the lake, no matter how hard I strained. But I knew it was there, so I kept my eyes on where it should be. I chanted the words and made the passes I had to, to bring the sun back and turn the world right side over again. I couldn't feel it working. It wasn't doing any good. All the same, there must have been others at work besides me. The water was getting paler and there was that island, getting more solid now, black first off, then grey and green, and at last I could make out the little white temple, so I knew it must be coming on day. I kept trying, harder.

There was a mist beginning to smoke up off the lake, and the sky above it was turning a cold sort of blue. Then I got a shock. A stone moved on the beach quite close to me. I heard feet walking down to the water's edge. Two men. I couldn't see plainly. Just tall grey shadows in the fog. I stayed stock still as the bushes behind me and shut up. I don't know why, but I daren't move.

The lake looked smooth as brown marble in between the curls of mist. It wasn't deep. You could see weed when you looked down. But I'd lost sight of the rocks between me and the island now. The men had stopped walking. They must be watching, like me. Those wisps of fog seemed as if they were walking on the water. Then I swear they started to dance. White ladies circling in rings, with their hands joined together, and their little bare feet skimming the surface. The light got stronger, and I saw the Lady of the Lake. You won't believe this, but I tell you she was standing straight up out of the water. She had her golden hair loose all around her and her white arm lifted high. She was holding up something and it caught the first of the dawn and brought it down to the lake, like lightning.

A man spoke close beside me. His voice rang deep and strong, as if he'd waited all his life to say these words.

"Well, Arthur, your day has come. Will you go out and take it?"

Merlyn! Standing next to me. And I hadn't had one word of warning.

"By God, I will!"

There was the scrape of a coracle on the shingle and a bit of splashing. Then Arthur settled to the oars. He rowed away, in and out of those dancing women. It wasn't so far. I saw clear enough how he took the bright thing from the Lady's hand where she was holding it up to him. Then the sun rose up over the fells in a ball of red fire and all the ice round the lake and the frost on the hills was flashing bright as jewels to dazzle us. There was a shout from the boat. Young Arthur was kneeling up and raising his man's sword high to show us. I could see him laughing.

Red, that lake was, with the sunrise full on it now.

17

With Arthur's shout there was a roar from behind me. I whipped round and there they all were, standing clear above the mist on the porches of the great house. The young warriors and the old ones, the Lady's maidens, house-servants and field-slaves, all waving and cheering to see Arthur made man. And over the top of it all the horns from the sentries up on the hills blew for the kill. That was a brave sight, and a sound to make me pull my back up straight even though I'd got tears standing in my eyes and I was wearing that unmanly gown.

It's always that way with Arthur. I don't know what gift Merlyn gave him at his birthing, but there's that fire in him that makes you feel he carries the sun about with him. You'd follow him anywhere. And, yes, I know some of the things he's done afterwards. That wouldn't have made any difference, if you'd been there. When he smiled at you, you could forgive him anything.

Arthur came rowing back to us with his face fairly flushed and his eyes shining. Merlyn hugged him. The man had got tears running down over his cheeks.

Then out of nowhere Nimue was there with us. She had a thick soft cloak, purple as heather, wrapped close around her, so I couldn't tell if she was wet or no. Her hair was dark with damp, but that might have been the mist. There was a glow about her and she was laughing, a bit breathless. I moved back a bit. She'd scared me before. It came to me now that this one at least might not be a mortal woman.

Well, there was a deal of kissing and hugging between the three of them and all the folk from the house were rushing down to the shore shouting.

Nimue raised her hand and they stopped were they were, in a big circle round her. She made Arthur kneel down at her feet, holding his new sword. Then from under her cloak she drew out a sword-belt with a scabbard hanging from it. She held it up high in her left hand to show us all. And with her right she took Arthur's hand and made him lift his sword. They were a strange pair. The sword had a hilt that was as grand as any I'd ever seen. Two gold dragons, with rubies for eyes and tongues of red enamel shooting out of their mouths and licking along the guard. You can be sure I'd an eye for that blade too. It was true and deadly, bluish steel, cold, where the haft was hot gold. But the scabbard in her left hand was a different matter altogether. Plain black wood, old and a bit cracked, bound with leather that was scuffed and worn, and fixed with just a few curls of silver. You'd never think to keep a fine weapon like that in such a shabby case. Yet when she brought her hands close those two slipped together as though they'd been made for each other.

The Lady buckled the sword-belt round Arthur's side. Her maidens handed her the rest of the arms. She set the spear in his right hand and the shield on his other arm, and slipped the dagger into his belt. Then, very serious for her, she kissed him on the forehead.

"Rise, Arthur, who shall be Pendragon. In the strength of the names your father and your mother named, go out and win."

She raised him up.

"Who follows Arthur?"

The crowd went wild. The men were all shouting at the tops of their voices, "I!" "I!" And I reckon I must have been yelling and cheering as loud as any of them.

"See, Arthur, how you can rouse the blood of all Britain. Here's a Christian saint would ride to war behind you!"

I turned my head to find Merlyn himself, laughing at me. I was looking straight into his eyes. Me, Teilo, that had been called Smith, with my nose and cheeks still burned red by the forge and a few poor white bristles sprouting on my chin, standing face-to-face with the wisest of the wise. But he went on slapping Arthur on the back and laughing and dancing about at the joke of it all. He didn't know me. Arthur was grinning at me too now. He reached into his pouch and tossed me something.

"Here, White-Chin. Say a prayer for me!"

I think his smile meant more to me. I nearly missed what he threw me. It was a coin. Money. Not a thing I had any use for. I rubbed my thumb over it. Old words. Somebody's face. It had the feel of silver.

I stammered out some thanks. I didn't feel like cheering and waving any more. For, if Merlyn couldn't recognise me, it meant only one thing. It was what I'd feared all along. There wasn't a drop of magic left in me, and never would be again. I was like those statues in her garden. I might hold the things of magic in my hand. But I'd lost all my power to use them. I didn't count.

I got a look at Nimue. I knew she'd have her heart in her mouth and be waiting for him to strip her secret bare. She'd gone a bit pale, but she was no fool. She turned the talk away from me pretty quickly.

"Tell me, Arthur," she says, with that pretty little laugh of hers, "which do you prize the most? The scabbard or the sword?"

"My sword, of course," he cries, waving it about in front of her nose.

Well, a man would say that, wouldn't he?

She shook her head at him. "Caliburn is a mighty weapon. As long as it sits in your hand you will win every battle. Yet the scabbard is older far. She who trusted it to my keeping swore that its virtue was worth ten times the sword. It holds the power to heal all wounds. I have kept them till this day and armed you with both, as I was charged to do. Do you in your turn guard them well. Sword and scabbard. I have trained you here to use both the one and the other. Cherish that wisdom, for your own sake and Britain's."

"Trust me. I have had the fairest of teachers. Thanks, Nimue! There'll be plenty of work for both your beauties now. Old Caliburn has slept in his scabbard far too long. Now I'm a man at last he'll be unsheathed and there'll be rivers of blood for your scabbard to stop!"

She laughed, only not so merry as she usually did.

Well, they moved off to the house and there was such a feast that day as beat all the rest. I hung back by the lake to the last. I could have slipped off with the crowd. It was almost as if I was wanting Merlyn to uncover me. He disappointed me. I don't know what I'd started to hope. That Merlyn could save me from Morgan? Give me back the manhood I'd lost?

But the magician never looked my way again. He walked straight past me with his arm round Nimue, fondling her, and the two of them were smiling in each other's faces, as if they'd been the lad's own father and mother. I felt a bit sick then. All right, he hadn't spotted power in me because I'd lost it. But it seemed he couldn't sense an untruth either. And he was Merlyn, wasn't he? The greatest enchanter we ever had in Britain.

You can be the wisest of the wise and still be a great fool.

It hadn't escaped Nimue, either. As they were passing me I saw her eyes go quick to Merlyn's face and I thought she held her breath. And then, when nothing happened, she turned her head and stared back hard at me. There was a nasty sort of doubt in her face I hadn't seen before.

She called me to her chamber next day. It seemed it didn't matter now whether Merlyn saw me or not. He thought no more of me in my white skirts than he did of Bytwini. Well, there on her couch was that sword, Caliburn, and the old black scabbard lying beside it.

"White-Chin," she said, "is it true? Can the scabbard really be as powerful as she says? Could this keep someone safe, against more than Saxons?"

You'd have thought she was pleading with me for something.

I had to pick it up. I never wanted to touch it. I knew it would say my hands were dead to magic now. I was right. I didn't get any sort of thrill from it, first off. Then, as I held it, there was a heat began to creep through my fingers and up my arms and spread right through my body till it warmed my heart. I hadn't felt such comfort since . . . Well, I hadn't, ever. It wasn't any magic in me that was speaking; it was the thing itself. Anybody would have felt the same.

She watched my face, and let out a sigh.

"Ah! So you feel it too! I'm glad of that. Our hopes hang on such a slender thread." A little smile of triumph crept into her face then. "Arthur cannot win all his victories with Caliburn, though men he can rouse in plenty to fight his battles. But a sheath will still be needed to clothe his blade. In the end, the scabbard will be more powerful than the sword."

I kept quiet at that. I wasn't sure what she was talking about. It wasn't just the weapons, I knew that much. It came into my head again how Merlyn had feared Morgan, though I'd no notion why. But I wasn't going to name Morgan in this house.

The Lady was still watching my face. But whatever she hoped to get out of me, she didn't press it.

I don't mind admitting I'd been sneaking a look at the sword too. That was more my style, never mind the dress I wore. But she didn't offer to let me have a hold of that.

Those lads didn't stay long with us afterwards. They were all made warriors now, those of them that hadn't got man's weapons up to that day. The Lady's maidens armed them, and very prettily they did it too. Merlyn was hopping about all over the place, ordering stores and pack-mules and picking what servants would follow them. He didn't want many, he said. They'd need to ride quick and light. I thought of that elf-troop that had galloped off in the dawn. Well, there'd be flesh and blood Saxons on the end of their spears this time. I never felt so helpless. I was a blacksmith. I had the secret of armouring. Warriors would need me. I hadn't thought what it was like till then, to be a powerless woman and have to see your own blood ride off to the wars and not know if it would be a hero or a bloody corpse that came home again. When I saw them mustering on the meadow to ride away, Bedwyr with a great horn at his side and Cei shouting the baggage-train into line, and Arthur sitting on his chestnut mare with his head in the air and a shine in his eyes as though he was seeing clear into Heaven, and that sword Caliburn already half out of its sheath, well, I couldn't help myself. I didn't even think. I ran forward and gripped hold of his leg.

"Take me with you, sir!" I begged. "I can do fine work for you. You'll need my craft."

I'd been Smith. I'd furnish his horses rarely, put a fine edge on his weapons, rebuild his body-harness so no Saxon would dent it. But how could he tell that was what I meant, dressed like I was?

He laughed so hard at me his horse reared up in my face and threw me back.

"There's no need for your sort where we're going, White-Chin! This is men's work. Pray for my army, if you like. But I bear a scabbard that says I can never be harmed and a sword that can vanquish every enemy. I can kill and not be hurt!"

He waved Caliburn. Then Bedwyr blew a great blast on his horn and all the swords flashed out, and the lads cheered and the ladies waved their scarves and clapped and called good luck. And off they trotted, that whole brave troop of horsemen, with Merlyn riding beside his golden boy. They rode out of the dale by the old Roman road this time, off to call the kings of Britain to young Arthur's banner.

It was pretty chill on the field when they'd gone. The ground was all churned to black mud and dirtying the hems of the ladies' dresses, and the lake had gone a dull, stormy sort of red. The women trooped indoors and called for hot wine and pretty soon my Lady was sobbing into her cup and some of her women were fingering their own scars mighty thoughtfully.

After a bit Nimue lifted her head and called me to her across the hall. I was shaking before I got there. I think I knew there was something up. Those sweet blue eyes of hers were wet with the tears she'd been crying for Arthur. But she'd forgotten him. She stared at me as if she hated me.

"Get out! I release you. Go back and tell Morgan she has lost."

18

I must have stood and gawped. Nimue had known! Near on two years she'd given me a bed and fed me from her table, and all the time she'd known just who I was.

I don't know why she hadn't killed me. It would have been no trouble to her women. And then it came to me that maybe this Lady of the Lake likes power more than is good for her, or her little Arthur either. I'd been useful to her, even without the power in my fingers, And so she'd taken a risk. Morgan's creature here in her camp. Or did she just want to show Morgan which of them had the upper hand?

"I'm no servant of Queen Morgan!" I shouted out. "She murdered my wife by witchcraft and then put the blame on me."

"She chose you. No one escapes Morgan that easily. She sent you to spy on us."

I'd known myself all along that's what it must have been.

However it was, Nimue let out a great sigh. You'd have thought she'd just put down a heavy burden.

"You have lost. You cannot hurt him now. Arthur is a man, with Merlyn beside him. And neither of them guesses how well I have served them. Morgan sent you here for evil, yet here I have bound you. Your side is too late to stop Arthur raising his banner. I have armed him with Caliburn that will win every battle and with the scabbard that heals every hurt. None of you can defeat him. Not Saxons, not Christians, not Morgan."

My thoughts were in a whirl. Merlyn against Morgan, that's what I'd thought it was. Those were the two I'd feared. And now she was saying the enchanter was nothing. It was the women, Nimue and Morgan against each other, all along. And I'd let her stroke my leg, and put her arms round my neck, and . . . There wasn't a word I could trust myself to say to her.

She raised her head to me, and her voice too. She was pretty drunk.

"Go back to Morgan. Tell Arthur's sister she has failed a second time."

"His *sister*?"

"You didn't know! She hasn't told you?" She pealed with laughter. "And Merlyn did not either? No, he wouldn't. Even our little changeling has yet to learn his father's name."

It was all tumbling back now. Bits I'd picked up on the street in Carlisle. Morgan of Tintagel. The last Pendragon's daughter. No, stepdaughter only, out of Ygerne the Wise. I hadn't bothered with it then. Tales of old Cornwall, dead kings. It was nothing to do with me.

"Then it was true, what the songs say? Uther Pendragon had a son, and lost him?"

"It is true. And there will be greater songs sung of that boy yet, now he is found."

"Let me stay here," I begged. I believed her. "Let me serve Arthur. I'll never go back to Morgan."

"You must. You can serve Arthur best in Morgan's hall. Tell her she deals with a wiser enemy than Merlyn now. Frighten her."

Well, she had to be drunk, with power as well as wine.

Even so, she must have seen she'd gone too far. She laughed a bit, as if she was flirting with me. "Woman-talk, you understand. We shall not say so in front of Merlyn, shall we?"

I could promise that. I'd just as soon not speak with Merlyn again as long as I lived. Morgan still less. But I wasn't going to stop and argue the toss. Now Arthur had gone, it would be good enough for me if she'd let me out of that dale alive.

"Go then! Take up again that bag you keep under your bed. The burden Morgan laid on you."

Was there nothing secret she couldn't winkle out of a man? I felt a bit sorry for Merlyn, after all. High Lord of the wise he might be, but she wasn't human.

It made me pull a sour face. Even then I couldn't bear to think of how I'd come by those clothes, or what they meant and what they'd cost me.

"Put on that other dress. Your passport back to Morgan. Your usefulness here is finished . . . Smith."

So she'd known that too. From the look she gave, I think she meant to wound me, calling me that. She'd never let me be a proper man. Only near enough to torment me. She could use a sword herself. She'd trained Arthur for war. She knew what mattered to men. Just that once she called me by my man's name. And the sound of that was better to me than if she'd kissed me ten times over. It had been true, once. I hadn't made it up.

Still, I left in that holy man's gown Nimue had made me keep. I'd got the satchel strapped on my back, but I'd made up my mind I wasn't going to wear the clothes Morgan had willed on me ever again. Oh no! I wasn't going back anywhere near Lyvennet.

I was mighty scared when I set off up that old stone road. I didn't know what sort of a world I might find. To tell you the truth, I didn't really know where I'd been. I thought the world might have changed, hundreds of years gone by, like in the old stories you hear of folk coming back after a day in Fairyland.

I wish it had. The world hadn't changed enough as far as I was concerned.

I came up over the lip of the hills and looked down the other side. It was going on the end of winter. There were pockets of snow lying by the road, grey where it had started to melt and frozen again. And the leaves that should have been green were all black and sodden with frost. No sun overhead. I got a glimpse of the sea in the distance, grey and cold. I stood looking at that plain below me and I knew Nimue's sentries were watching me. Down there at my feet there were houses. Villages, odd farms, even a town or two. There wasn't enough sun to show them clearly, just huddles of brown thatch in the winter mud. But you could see the smoke creeping out of the roof-holes and hanging in clouds. It made you think of fire, a dog in front of the hearth, hot meat. I'd be a man in a man's world again.

Nobody stopped me and you can bet I was hardly over the pass before I had that white gown off my back, and never mind if the wind did blow raw round me. I opened my satchel. But it was my smith's clothes I pulled out of it. The leather had a bit of a slimy feel to it, being wrapped up so long. There was mildew on it. I shook the things out. Rags. I hadn't remembered just how badly I'd torn them, running through the woods like a wild man when I'd lost my wits. Still, they were all I had left. I had to put them on. I'd never worn rags before, only when I went disguised.

I left the saint's garb behind in the heather, though it was good stuff, clean and warm.

I marched off down the hill. I tried to walk like a man and whistle like a man again. It didn't come easy after all this time. I was sorry I'd never been able to grow a proper beard since that black day. Just these few white whiskers.

They were an unfriendly lot at the first village. The dogs came barking and the children ran indoors when they saw me. A couple of men looked round the corner of a wood pile. They had axes in their hands.

"Who are you? What do you want?"

"I'm a smith," I said. The word felt pretty dry on my tongue. "If you've got tools to mend, blades to sharpen, I'm your man." Smith? I sounded more like a tinker.

"Oh, yes? Let's see your own tools. Got a forge on your back, have you?"

I felt my feet go cold and my heart sink down to meet them. I'd left too much of myself behind at Way Bank. They didn't give me a chance to argue. They set the dogs on me. At the next village they stoned me. Third time round a woman screamed when she saw my queer face. I didn't wait for any more. I turned and ran.

I didn't call myself a smith after that. I bent my back and let the hair hang over my cheeks and took to begging my bread. I'd have done better for that to have stuck to that holy man's gown and not left it behind in the heather. Without it, they might throw me a crust or a turnip, but they'd turn me away afterwards. I was no use to anybody. They wouldn't let me stay. I'd be lucky enough if I could find a hayrick for the night.

I'd no notion where I was going, only that it was south, as far away from Rheged as I could get. There were times when I was so cold and lonely I thought I might just lie down and die. But I didn't dare. I was a murderer. I'd killed my wife, or Erith. It was all mixed up. I was afraid to die before I'd paid the blood-price.

Then it started. Folk coming the other way, pulling carts, or carrying what they could. They had a beaten look, but they were hurrying too. They stared at me, seeing me going the opposite way. One woman called out, "Are you mad, you old fool? Do you want to march straight on to a Saxon battle-axe?"

There were more of them, after that. Some of them had bloody bandages.

I left the road. I knew which I was frightened of most. It wasn't the foreigners in front of me; it was those enchanters behind. I went more carefully. But I carried on. I can't say what I thought would happen. That there'd be just a band of Saxons, and I'd get past somehow and find good British folk again beyond?

I was coming off the hills now. There was a great forest down to the east, and bits of farmland and rivers and lakes. It looked a richer, softer land than what I'd come through. Then I saw smoke. Too much of it. Black and rolling where they'd fired the farms. I thought I heard screaming. I didn't know if it was beasts or Britons. I'd gone too far.

I heard a crashing through the bushes and I made sure my end had come. But it was a ewe came struggling out in the open, bleating as if it was slaughter-time. I saw straight off what was wrong. She hadn't been milked in a good long while and she could hardly walk for the great udder between her legs. Well, we could help each other. I put her teat to my mouth and had a good squirt of warm milk.

I turned back then. Only it wasn't soon enough. I heard voices, and no language I'd ever heard before. A nasty harsh sound, like breaking stones. They were behind me.

I held my breath, and I'd have stopped my blood beating too if I could. I tried to tiptoe round. The ground was getting boggy. There was a clump of silver birches right ahead of me. I had my head turned sideways, listening to those evil voices, so I didn't see him till I almost bumped into him.

He was standing with his breeches down, having a piss. He turned his head towards me. He had a helmet on and he looked more like a statue than a man. He had holes for eyes. But I'd seen something worse. There was an axe at his feet. And not like any wood-chopper you've ever seen. He hadn't even bothered to wipe the blood and mess off it yet. The moment he saw me he made one grab at his breeches and another at his axe. I shot out a foot and kicked it into a pool. Then I was off, with him shouting and the rest of them running and yelling to see what was up. They came after me. I couldn't think at first how they didn't catch me. I wasn't fit. They might have tired themselves with killing and burning and stealing already.

Later on, I knew it wasn't that that spared me. It was Morgan's hand over me. She'd put her mark on me for her own. There isn't anybody but herself she'll let destroy me.

But I didn't know that then. I just ran. I kept on going too, long after I'd lost sight of those Saxon butchers. You don't know how fear can weary a man. I was driven. I couldn't stop and rest. Every time I closed my eyes I'd see the blood on that axe. I'd thought I wanted to die, but now I was fighting to live. I'd lost all sense of where I was going. Even if I struck a road I was too afraid to follow it. When I saw another human being I was sure it was a Saxon.

I wept for Arthur then. For that little lad riding off into the early morning to try and save us all from what I'd seen. Power or not, I sang what charms I knew for him.

I lost count of the forests I crossed. I was half-starved by now. So when I saw another village through the trees I didn't turn and run, but crept up quiet. Then I heard children calling, and it was our own British tongue. I thought that was the sweetest sound I'd ever heard. I stumbled up to the gate and set up my whine.

"In the name of the gods your fathers named, pity. Do not refuse the stranger at your door. Food and drink will bring a blessing on her who gives it."

A woman came to her door. Quite young, she was, and a kind face. She had a bowl in her hand that was giving off a bit of steam in the cold air. Not much smell. It might be a dish of porridge. She smiled a bit.

"Here, granddad," she said. "It's not much, but it will line your stomach for a few more miles. Give me your blessing." Then her hand flew to her mouth and she dropped the bowl on the ground. She let out a screech.

"It's him! Half-Face! The witch from Way Bank. Poisoner! Wife-killer!"

Well, that brought the ugliest crowd I'd ever seen in my life. From nowhere they came. I'd sooner have been chased by a pack of wolves. Howling and snarling they were too, and hurling whatever they could get their hands on at me.

There's one thing I'll say. Nobody really wants to catch a witch. I'd never have got clear else. I couldn't run fast. I wasn't the man I used to be.

But I knew where I was now, the moment she'd called out what I'd done. I'd come full circle. I was back in Morgan's country. I wasn't Teilo Smith any more, but I still had the marks of Teilo Smith branded on me. Morgan had seen to that. When I thought of all I'd suffered to get away from her and where I'd come to, I sat down and wept. I'd been a fool to think I could ever escape from her. If Arthur wouldn't have me, then Morgan must. I was finished now.

I knew what I had to do. I'd been fighting it two long years. I took out the woman's clothes I'd worn for Morgan and they felt heavy as lead as I laid them down on the ground. They weren't rotten and mildewed like my own leathers. Oh, no. The colours looked as fresh as when I'd stolen them. I dragged them on. I stood there then, holding that handful of smelly rags that had once been Teilo Smith. I thought of stuffing them back in my satchel. Just in case. But Morgan had put an end to that. Like she'd seen my beard would never grow again. I was a marked man for the rest of my life. There was only one way I had left to hide my chin: under a woman's veil.

I've made sacrifices in a bog before. They're supposed to cost us. There wasn't ever an offering I made that tore the heart out of me as much as that one did. I never said a chant or made a sign. I just pushed the last of my smith's leather clothes down under the black swamp and watched the water creep back over.

I hadn't noticed just what part of the forest I was in, but I knew it didn't matter. I wasn't a bit surprised when I came out of the trees and found myself standing under the walls of Lyvennet again. Those red banks of stone and earth, the walls of her castle. The buildings looked a bit grander than the way I remembered it. She'd been busy up there.

Three years it had taken her. Three years since the first evening I'd stood here like a man, with my dog at my feet, looking up at her house. But she'd had her way.

I wondered if the guards would remember my dress, if they still had the same orders to let me through. It wouldn't matter. She didn't mean to keep me outside her door this time.

There was just one thing startled me when I stepped out of the wood. I suddenly saw that we'd turned from winter to spring. I hadn't expected that I'd come back to Morgan with violets and bluebells and primroses all up the path. That was a bitter joke.

19

Things had changed more than a bit. I found a rare old bustle going on at Lyvennet. I told them at the gate I wanted to see the queen. I had a bit of difficulty when they asked what name they should tell her.

"Say . . . the woman with the basket." I kept my chin tucked well out of sight.

I was glad the gate-men were none of them that knew me. All the same I thought they peered a bit strangely under my hood. It might have been my fancy.

She kept me waiting a long time at the gate, so long that I started to wonder if she'd got my message. The whole dun was in an uproar. Urien's men were going about in a brisker way than I'd seen for a long time. Their gear was polished and they were walking smartly. They were handling their weapons as though they expected they'd be using them before long. There were more servants about than ever I'd seen. Pretty young women. And young warriors, too, casting an eye over Urien's horses and trappings as though they'd seen better. I began to think that Morgan must have visitors.

"What's to do?" I said at last. I didn't want to call attention to myself, but curiosity had got the better of me. "Who are all these folk?"

"Where have you been, granny? Asleep with the fairies?" they joshed. "Gwendoleu's called the kings of the north to a council. He's giving a big feast in Carlisle for them and their queens. There's some say he'll try and sweet-talk them into a war. King Lot's ridden down from Din Eidyn to get Urien's ear first."

"Carlisle's going to take on the Saxons?"

They roared with laughter at that.

"Saxons? Gwendoleu? Not him! It's his own crown he's worried about, and it's a young Briton he fears could take the shine off it. It'll be ourselves at each other's throats next, Cymry against Cymry, if he has his way. You can bet he won't let that upstart boy steal a march on him and get all the glory. If the lad did beat the Saxons, folk might cry him High King of all Britain."

"Unless he gets a spear in his throat first," said the other with a wink.

"What boy would that be?" I croaked, just as if I hadn't felt the hard muscles of his leg under my hand and heard his breath come quick for impatience. I can see the shine in his eyes still, looking up over Nimue's lake to what was coming.

"Looks like the queen's got an answer for you at last," the gatekeeper said suddenly. There was a young woman crossing the yard to us.

I was almost gone past fear after all that waiting. I just had a dread and a sort of numb hopelessness. Men, war, it couldn't ever be my business now. When the girl let me in, Morgan was not in the sunny-house. Only Luned. She recognised me, all right. She looked scared to see me again. I felt a bit better for that. At least there was somebody who still showed me respect. She didn't speak to me. She was busy packing silken ribbons into a box. But all the time her eyes were watching me. I turned my back on her and stood in front of last night's fire. I poked at the burnt logs with my boot. Somewhere there might be a spark of light left. Only the wood fell away into white ash. The fire in my smithy would be cold these two years now. Or would it? I didn't even know if another man had taken my place and kindled it.

Then the door burst open and the room was full of women. One taller than all the rest, with flaming hair, dressed all in green and gold. And Morgan herself, behind her. Beautiful, she looked, dressed in blue and silver. Radiant, somehow. I'd never thought she could look so young and happy. Then I saw why. She was a mother now. She had a fine boy toddling at her skirts and the loveliest little girl I'd ever seen, saving my Mair.

So I'd been right. That huge belly giving her pains the day she cursed me – she'd borne Urien twins. And for all the harm she'd done to me, when I saw her like that, so bright and rosy and womanly, I couldn't help myself. Under that sagging gown my thing rose up to meet her.

Morgan started when she saw me. And that flock of pretty, giggling girls turned my way. Yes! Go on, smile again. Some of you older ones were there, weren't you?

I saw that flash in Morgan's eyes, and I knew that they hadn't warned her. It must have been Luned's doing to let me in.

She changed like a thunderstorm in April. Where she'd been laughing as merry as you please before, she was scowling now.

"So, Woman, you have come back at last! Has it taken you so long to learn my lesson? Put back your hood. White hair befits you. I am glad to see that the time has not been kind to you."

She stroked her little son's head and took her daughter's hand as she said it. Time hadn't spoiled her. She was queen and the mother of a prince now.

That brought the blood to my face. It was all right for her! But I had been Teilo Smith, in the prime of manhood. Listening to her laughing at me I could feel the muscles withering on my bones. My man's pride, what there was left of it, shrivelled up and collapsed. Those girls tittered behind their hands. But not like Erith. Not so knowingly. There wasn't one of them had half her wisdom.

The red-haired woman spoke, and I knew her now for Morgan's tall sister, Queen Margawse, that had ridden beside her to her wedding in Carlisle.

"That's a sick fancy you have there, Morgan, to want a hag like that about you. She's worse than that stone-faced nun. Why, she almost has a beard! Are you so ugly that you need goblins like these to stand you comparison? Even your cat is scarred for life."

"It pleases me to care for those that are marred. They are a sign. We are all hurt and unlovely in some parts. You will excuse us."

She signed for me to follow her into her inner chamber. Only Luned came with us. It was a smaller room than the other one, and her marriage bed took up most of it. That grey cat was curled up in the middle of the bedspread. Morgan lay down and stroked it and the sweat broke out on me under the veil. I wouldn't have stood so close as that to such a woman if I'd had the choice. She told me to kneel on the floor, so that I was lower than she was. She rested her eyes a long while on me before she spoke.

"Well, Woman." She's never called me anything but that. I've never had a proper name from her. "Have you indeed learned my lesson? What have you come to tell me?"

"My wife is murdered!"

116

I hadn't known I was going to say that. But it was the only thought I had just then. Seeing Morgan's face in front of me again like that, it was as if the two years I'd been away had disappeared and it was still the same black day she'd cursed me, in this very house. It still stung like a fresh burn. Erith? Annis? They were all one woman in my mind. I could hardly tell now which of them I'd killed.

I swear I didn't mean to keep anything back from her. Nimue. Merlyn. Arthur. I'd forgotten clean about them. Annis is dead. And I'm here dressed like a woman, in her place. That was the only thing I could think just then.

Morgan wasn't mocking now.

"*Erith* was murdered! And even that was not enough brutality for you! Did you need to kill your own wife as well? Why? Could you have supposed that would please me? Two women poisoned instead of one, and neither healed?"

"I?" I must have jumped up then and shouted out in a man's voice, because Luned ran to stop me. "*You* killed her! You cursed me, here in this very castle. You said you'd show me how a wise woman ought to work. And I found Annis bewitched to death!"

Morgan had sprung up on her bed and was kneeling facing me. There was a wild light in her eyes, almost as if she was frightened.

"I did not do that! How could you think it? Are you so cunning you would put your wickedness on me? Do you not know what they call me? I am Morgan the Healer. Why should I want to kill Annis, your wife?"

"Because she *was* my wife. Because I killed your waiting-woman. You had to show me you were stronger than me."

"Hurt for hurt? Morgan the Wise to prove herself to you?"

"How else did she die? You cursed me!"

"I did not! I did not! I did not kill your wife!"

To my horror she started sobbing like a little girl. Luned went to comfort her and both those women looked at me as if they hated me.

"Tell him I did not, Luned! Tell him I did not do it."

The woman drew her mouth down, very prim and severe.

"It was a stern curse you laid on him, for Erith's death."

"You think that too? I . . . killed . . . Annis! No! Do not say that! How could my anger poison her without my will?"

"A great wise woman only needs to lift a finger. None of our circle left Cornwall. But Uther died. And you are greater than Gwennol and all her circle ever were. Hate was enough."

Morgan shuddered. She'd stopped weeping now. But she rolled over and buried her face and lay still as death. I could have fallen where I stood. I don't know which had shaken me most. That Morgan, for all she made herself out to be such a wise enchantress, hadn't seen till then which of us had killed poor Annis. Or that someone like her could do such a terrible thing without even meaning to. She had so much power in her that the ill wish must have been enough without even the name spoken or the hand pointed.

It was an uncomfortable time, standing there waiting. She got the better of herself in a bit.

"However that other happened, Erith is dead. And that was your doing. I have gathered many others now. But her place I have kept empty. Now you must fill it . . . Woman."

I couldn't grasp quite what she meant. Or didn't want to.

"You need to make your circle? And you still haven't found enough of the higher grades to play the chief parts?"

She smiled mockingly then.

"I am Chief Lady. Erith was our Maiden. Did you think you could play that role? No, that was not what I meant. If the rumours are right . . ." The colour was coming and going in her face now. "If this boy who has raised his banner is who I think he may be . . . I am the daughter of Uther Pendragon's queen. That has brought me much hurt, and may do me more harm yet, if there are others who remember it. I shall need a wise woman who can guard my back by day and lie in my room at night."

It took a few moments for her words to sink in, and, when they did, the hairs stood up on my neck.

"Erith was . . . ?"

"You'd make *that* thing into your tiring woman?" said Luned.

"Erith is dead. What he has taken away he must restore, for the balance of the world. You took life but you did not give it. From henceforward you shall be the one who keeps off death. Two sides, Woman. That was my lesson."

I was going cold and hot by turns. How long before I was discovered for what I was . . . what I had been? In her bedchamber! What if Urien . . . ?

Morgan was beginning to enjoy herself now. She'd got herself and me reined in. Even the cat was purring.

"Kneel."

She whispered to Luned. The woman fetched a bowl, a towel and a little ivory razor.

"I shall make you Woman, by my own hand."

Well, I almost screamed at that. When she picked up that razor I had only one thought in my mind of what she was going to do with it. It was all I had. The only thing I'd got that still had manhood in it. She was going to cut it off.

There was more blood than there should have been. I was shivering so much I couldn't keep still and Luned had to hold me. But it was only my chin that Morgan shaved. Those last poor tufts of hair that would keep growing, where before I'd had a thick bush of beard. She has smooth white hands. She didn't mean to hurt me. But she did.

20

They gave me fresh linen to bind my face. I hadn't thought till then how shameful a thing it's reckoned to be a woman, and have to hide so much of yourself from the world.

That other queen, Margawse, she raised her red eyebrows and gave a teasing sort of laugh when Morgan came out of her room, with me trying to hide my stained wimple behind Luned's back.

"Your tiring-woman now, is it? You're surely not taking that thing to Gwendoleu's feast in Carlisle? Why, you will make the Pendragon's daughters the laughing-stock of Britain."

"I am not Uther Pendragon's child!" Morgan flashed out at her. "And nor are you. We are daughters of Gorlois of Cornwall, that Uther killed!"

"Still," said Margawse, smoothing her fine green skirt. "The Pendragon was a bonny king while he lived, and got a good husband for me. It was better to be on the winning side. So Mother reckoned."

The colour flew to Morgan's cheeks at that and she breathed pretty fast. "That false man is dead. There shall be no High King of his sort again to ride roughshod over Britain, grabbing what he wants."

"They say that if Gwendoleu goes, your Urien could be king over Rheged and Solway joined. He might rule both sides of the Wall from sea to sea, as his forefather Coel did long ago."

"Those that say that talk dangerously. Urien is little more than a boy yet."

"It was no boy got these two on you," smiled Margawse, patting little Owain on the head.

Morgan seized the bairn by the shoulders and made to pull him to her. But Margawse let him go and swung her feet up on to the couch. Morgan was left standing stiff as a she-wolf with her two cubs on either side of her, son and daughter.

"If I thought Urien would grow like Uther I would kill him now with my own hands."

Margawse pealed with laughter. "Morgan! Morgan! You never change. Who was it snatched our little brother Arthur? Who was it almost destroyed him in the sea? Who got herself imprisoned in a nunnery till the years had cooled her temper and the Pendragon was dead?"

"I . . . did . . . not . . . kill . . . Arthur." She seemed to have trouble spitting the words out.

"He might as well have been dead. Our mother has not seen her only son these fourteen years. Well, it seems she may have her chance soon."

"You think it possible? This Arthur they are talking of could be our brother?"

There was a sly sort of smile on Margawse's face. "Elaine says he is."

"Elaine! You have seen her? And she . . ."

"Yes. I thought that would bring a spark to your eyes. Of the three of us, it is Elaine that has the seeing. Our little Arthur is a man and comes into the light at last. Oh, silly, headstrong Morgan! So all your anger was wasted and your punishment for nothing. Could you not have smiled and tricked and waited your chance, like me?"

"I do not trick!"

"And so you scared our dragonlet away into Merlyn's secret lair. Now he has come out full-grown and with a warband at his back. Well, never mind. I know how to deal with warriors!"

"What do you mean?"

"You know very well what I mean. I can see it in your face. Why not admit it? Poor Morgan. The mother of twins and still a virgin at heart!"

Morgan let go of her children and made to strike her. The red queen's maidens rushed in to shield her, but Margawse put up an arm, quite lazy, and turned the blow away.

"He would rather choose my death than yours, if he's the true son of Uther, that bedded Ygerne the same night he widowed her."

"He shall not fall to you! He shall not!"

"Then which of Gorlois's daughters do you think will make an end of him . . . Elaine?"

And Margawse laughed, as if that would be a great joke. Morgan was prowling the room, with her little girl Morfudd clinging on to her hand, though she hardly noticed her.

"I knew he was still alive!"

"You? You said Merlyn was less to be trusted than any man living."

"I trusted him to keep Arthur safe. Why else was the boy got by high magic? Not for Uther's lust, but for Merlyn's."

"*Merlyn's*? For Mother!"

"Oh, it was not Ygerne's flesh he desired, but her blood. That old and powerful blood. A wise woman, of a true line of kings. That blood we share. Our mother Ygerne has given Arthur twice the power that Uther ever could."

"And whoever raises Arthur rules Britain?"

"Unless *we* take that power."

#

When Margawse had gone to bed Morgan sent all of her women away but Luned and me. It was worse than I'd dreaded. She put me in Erith's place, oh yes, in every way. Her body-servant. That's been my punishment. Woman, she calls me. I've had to serve her woman's body. Guard it, tend it, wash it, dress it. The time came soon enough when I could have wished she'd taken the knife to my parts after all. Instead of that, she's gelded me another way.

Damn you! I was born a man, with a man's hands, a man's desires. She makes me lift the clothes from her body, and each layer's warmer than the last. She makes me wash her skin and loosen her hair. And all the time she sits unmoved, as if it had been Erith's hands touching her flesh. I don't think she loves her own body, the way Margawse does. Cold as death my hands were that first night, and trembling. She never stirred when I touched her. I hadn't handled as many women as you might think. Only my wife, and what I did for the god. And that's not the same. Then I'd got strong drink inside me, and the drums were beating. I was the god. I wasn't for ordinary women.

At home, with the horns stripped off, I'd been a man again. Only then I'd dreamed too high. After Morgan's wedding, that day her green eyes looked straight into mine, I'd dreamed. I'd dance the god for the queen and be a full man for her too, whenever she wanted me, night or day. She's made me live with the corpse of that fancy, ever since.

When we'd finished, she laid herself on the bed, with her little grey cat curled close beside her. Luned and I drew the coverlet over her shoulders. We left her lying in that big bed.

I found out then where I had to sleep – stretched like a dog on the floor at the foot of the bed. I couldn't believe she meant it. I had cushions and blankets enough. It wasn't that. All night I could hear every breath Morgan drew. I could feel when she turned in her sleep. I could smell her. It's a scent like pine-forests, she has.

I couldn't sleep. I lay and shivered like the dog I felt. One thing I dreaded more than anything else: that Urien would come. I've had to endure it often enough since then. They put me outside the door while he's there, but it's not far enough I can't hear.

She spared me that, the first time. The night she heard that Arthur was alive, she slept alone.

21

Next morning I found myself huddled in a wagon with Luned, guarding Morgan's baggage on the road to Carlisle. You can imagine how that felt, trundling through the gates of Gwendoleu's town with all the crowd staring as we went by, where last time I'd been down there in the street on my own feet and I'd been the one staring at the fine folk riding past me.

When it came to the feast I crouched in the darkest corner of Gwendoleu's hall, trying to hide my woman's gown from the real men. I wasn't sorry then to be at a low table. I kept my head bent over my platter and tucked in my shaved chin, for all that I'd wrapped it up in linen. How long could I go on living like this? An old woman with a razor in her pocket. Frightened every hour of coming face-to-face with somebody who had known Teilo Smith. And there were plenty of them. Woman? She'd put that name on me. But it was the real women I was most afraid of.

I could hardly eat at that feast. I dreaded the night again.

Gwendoleu was hammering on the high table.

"Emrys! Where is Emrys Silver-Tongue? By God, he's been missing from my table once too often! What dog of a bard is it that's not here to sing when I feast the kings and queens of the North? I'll have his throat when I see him!"

I started at that name, and looked round sharp. I'd clean forgotten Merlyn had been Gwendoleu's bard. But he wasn't there. How could he be, with Morgan in the hall?

Margawse beckoned to her own bard, who jumped forward pretty smartly. Well, who wouldn't? There'd be rich pickings at a great feast like that for a poet who knew how to turn a compliment to kings and queens. It wasn't every day he'd get such a chance. This one was a ladies' man. He strolled that hall, peering into all the queens' faces and praising the beauty that he saw and the fine sons they'd given their lords, or would do soon. And many's the buckle and jewel they tossed him for it. It didn't do much for Gwendoleu's temper, though. He had no sons. And no queen either. She'd died in childbed. So he looked pretty darkly at those that had. He knew what folk were saying about young Urien.

But I couldn't be bothered with kings and queens just then. I had that other name to wrestle with. Emrys Silver-Tongue. Like a shadow in the street the day of Morgan's wedding. I wept then, and didn't care who saw me. The greatest enchanter this land has ever known. Soul-friend to Uther Pendragon in the old days, and to young Arthur now.

If only I'd met him just half an hour earlier. If only I hadn't lost my head when I saw that witch Morgan. If only I hadn't sent my power out to catch hers. I could have been Arthur's man now, instead of Morgan's woman. Smith to a greater king than Urien, maybe. Only by the time I saw Arthur I wasn't Smith. The lad hadn't recognised what I was. He'd shouted me out of his path. I couldn't mend the past, though I've groaned for what I've lost every night since. It had hung on such a small thing either way, like a sword balanced on an anvil. Just a few heartbeats. And I'd tumbled off on Morgan's side, with the women.

Gwendoleu was thumping the table. "No more women's songs. Can you not sing of war, man? Are all the bards in Britain gone soft? Is that why there's no red blood in our kings' veins these days? Get Emrys Silver-Tongue!"

One of his men came up and murmured in his ear.

"What's that you say? Silver-Tongue's gone off to join that whelp? How dare he leave my court without permission! That braggart boy Arthur, that thinks he's somebody because he's wet his new sword on a handful of Saxons? Emrys bids me join them! I'll string that Druid's harp with his own guts!"

Morgan was on her feet and was holding her throat.

"Emrys. What Druid? You called him Silver-Tongue. But ... Emrys *who*? Is that why I have never heard your bard play at any feast where I have been these past three years? No, he would not risk that! Emrys and Arthur. All this time so close to me. Emrys Merlyn!"

There was a noise ran round the hall at that.

"Merlyn?"

"That Druid that stole the Pendragon's son?"

"He was here!"

The messenger nodded. Gwendoleu looked so startled he couldn't speak for a bit. Then he crashed his fist down on the table.

"Impostor! False to one king before, and now to me. He calls the Men of the North to follow Arthur? To take our oath to his puppy? I'll see that chief dead who raises his sword to another banner than mine of Solway! Where's Urien of Rheged gone? Has that wee snake snapped out of his egg too to take the Red Dragon's side?"

He glared down the table. I think he could hardly see for drink. But Urien was a brave lad, I'll say that for him. He rose in his place and gave Gwendoleu back look for look. Men had their hands on their knives. I think most of the kings hardly knew which side to take.

Our chieftain spoke up like a man. "Urien of Rheged is here, and loyal kinsman to Gwendoleu. There is no quarrel I know of between Lyvennet and Carlisle."

"So who is this cub that Merlyn Silver-Tongue leaves my board for? What father does this upstart Arthur boast?"

"Sir," says the man, "we've heard only that Merlyn has fostered him these fourteen years. Folk are saying . . . he was fairy-got."

"Hell's balls! Damnation to you if you take me for an idiot!"

He spoke like a plain, blunt man that doesn't believe in the old ways. But he didn't fool me. Gwendoleu practised more than a bit of magic himself. He had reason to fear it more than most.

Bishop Curran was having a word to steady him. That wouldn't cool his temper. Gwendoleu never had much time for the Church. That was more Urien's style.

Margawse's husband, King Lot, leaned over to have a word in his ear. He was a black-browed man, with a twisted sort of smile. Well, if Gwendoleu had been angry before, he was madder now. He let out a screech that had brave men backing off from him. There was no telling which one he might hurl his goblet at.

"The Pendragon's lost son was named Arthur? And now here's an Arthur come, and Merlyn calls the kings of Britain to follow him! Is that what you're saying? Another Pendragon?"

Well, you can guess who he was looking so venomous at when he said that. Margawse, Lot's wife. She was step-daughter to the old Pendragon, wasn't she? Arthur's half-sister. And then at Morgan too.

"You nest of vipers! You litter of weasels! Have you false women been plotting this all these years behind my back? Did you come here to Carlisle to mock me? You'd like to strip Gwendoleu's power from him and give it to your little brother, wouldn't you? Yes, you'll call your husbands to join Arthur's pack! There'll be rich pickings for the whole family."

He was coming across the dais to them, none too steady. Lot was on his feet, and Urien too, and it was more than daggers their warriors were reaching for now.

It was the bishop that got in his path and stopped him. Old Curran. I didn't think he had it in him. I'd got him down for a place-server that would mind where his meat came from and who feathered his nest. He got Gwendoleu by the arm, though, and talked soft to him.

"Peace, your majesty, in the name of Christ. Would you dishonour your own hall? These ladies are queens and guests."

"Queens and witches! Get out!"

Those two gathered up their skirts and swept out of the hall. Margawse laughed at him as she went and picked up a plate of fowl and cakes and carried it off with her. She was bold, that one.

We had to follow, their husbands and all the rest of us. But at the door of the ladies' bower the men went another way from me. I had to pull myself up short not to go on with them.

Margawse settled herself on the cushions while Morgan paced up and down the room. She's fuller than Morgan. Softer-fleshed. She had four big sons already, and daughters too. Both those queens have green eyes, but they're not the same. Morgan's can be like winter ice. But Margawse's are warm and inviting. They tell you it's open house with her. She was licking chicken grease off her fingers.

"So! Merlyn was here in Carlisle these last three years, and you never knew it!"

"I sensed treachery. I could not put a name to what I knew. *You!*" She whipped round sudden on me. I nearly fainted when I saw what was in her eyes. I just cowered in the corner. She'd have the truth out of me now. I should have told her sooner.

But Margawse hadn't finished.

"What if our little brother can beat the Saxons? What if he does indeed free Britain from the foreigners? What will our husbands do? Is Gwendoleu right? Will they cry Arthur High King over all the Britons?"

Morgan's black hair looked like striking snakes, she whirled about so fast.

"Merlyn must not succeed! There shall not be another Uther in the land!"

"What then? Gorlois's three daughters, to bring his little princeling down? Or do you plan to keep all the fun to yourself?"

She leaned back against the cushions and broke out laughing. A sort of slow, lazy laughter, like a cuckoo in May. She's the only one I've ever met who dares to laugh at Morgan.

"Yes! I can see it in your face. Morgan's power matched against Merlyn's. Spells. Potions. And for what? Not to raise your husband Urien over my Lot and Elaine's Nentres? No. For Morgan's pride. You want the bards to sing you the greatest enchantress of all, even though they may blacken your name and gild the fame of poor dead Arthur afterwards. Oh, Morgan, Morgan! Will you never learn? Did you get nothing but magic from our mother? There are more ways than one of killing a cat. Leave the spells to Merlyn and the blades to Arthur. I tell you again, our power is *here*."

Margawse stroked her own body. Her hands caressed her gown round her breasts and thighs. I just had to crouch in my corner and moan to myself. She stretched herself out on the cushions and her eyes sparkled.

"What do you say, Morgan? A Saxon sword may save us the task in the next battle. But say it does not? Say they spit the little cub back at us. What then? A contest? Your power against mine to see which of us can bring Arthur down?"

"If I had been born a boy! Gorlois's son. Arthur would not have been needed then. I should have shown Uther's kind what kingship means."

"But you are not. And Gorlois was not a king. Be what you are, a woman. Do not despise it. Remember Mother. Was it Merlyn's power that brought Uther to Tintagel? Or was it Ygerne's? You should ask Elaine. She was there in the woods helping Mother make the charm that got our brother. And where were you?"

Her laughter filled the room. She had no shame. For herself, or for her mother.

This time Morgan hit her full across the face, before anybody could stop her.

"Ygerne is Arthur's mother! Not mine, since the night she lay with Father's murderer! You know where I was the day she cast the spell. I was hunting with Father. That was the last time we rode together."

She broke out sobbing. That was a terrible thing to me, to see Morgan in tears, as it might have been my own daughter. I don't know how it was, but it frightened me more than when she was angry. It was as if the world rocked off balance.

Margawse had jumped up quick. There was a great red mark across her face. But she watched her sister crying and just straightened her skirt and smiled.

"You see? You rode with the warriors, but the men couldn't save him. This must be women's work."

She drew out something from under the cushion.

"I found this in your chest in Lyvennet."

It was a bronze mirror, rare enough to make me gasp. There were chased settings for red enamel and a fine workmanship of serpents on its handle.

"The Christmas Arthur was born, Merlyn made me the gift of such a mirror. Did he give this to you?"

Morgan barely nodded.

"But you have not cared for it well. It is dented. Did you dash it on the floor when you heard who had given it?"

"I want no gift from him."

Margawse admired herself in the mirror.

"My face looks crooked in it, but I can still tell I am beautiful. So are you, Morgan. Look at yourself! Use what you are!"

"Never! I will not be like you!"

Morgan snatched the mirror off her sister and flung it clear through the window. There was a clang as it hit the paving outside. That hurt me as if it had been my own bones breaking, to treat good workmanship like that. Margawse shrugged and smiled and led her ladies off to bed.

Afterwards I went and fetched that mirror. It was too valuable to be left lying there. But I cried out when I picked it up. It had been dented before, but it was broken now. There were bits of red enamel scattered all over the stones. The polished side had cracked in half a dozen places. You couldn't have found your true self in it any more.

And still I hadn't told her what I knew.

22

I hadn't fooled her. Morgan got it out of me when Margawse had gone. Every last bit of it. Nimue's house. Merlyn. How they'd schooled Arthur. What I'd told Nimue. What I hadn't told her ... which wasn't much. Right down to the morning Arthur got his sword. You can be sure she made me tell her every last detail of that. I can see her now, leaning forward with her eyes huge in the candlelight. A magic sword that could beat every enemy he fought. A scabbard that would heal every wound he got.

"So, no man can bring him down. But Nimue has netted Merlyn in her lake."

She was mighty quiet after that, as if she'd gone deep inside herself. But she wasn't tired. Her face was as bright as if she'd never need to sleep again. It was a long while before she started questioning me again.

She bled me like a leech. It was going on dawn before she'd finished with me.

Next morning the men held their council. But I wouldn't have been allowed in there, even if I had been wearing breeches. That was for the kings and such. Should they join Arthur's banner or shouldn't they? Council! We could hear them yelling at each other right across the yard. When I used to take council with the wise about our own business it had been done grave and seemly. I saw to that. But these lords seem to think he has the best right who can shout loudest and hit hardest. They're bred for war. Even among their own kin there's fighting to see which of them will come out on top. Gwendoleu and Lot had plenty to say by the sound of it. Sometimes the shouting would go a bit quiet and Margawse would look at

Morgan with her sly grin. Maybe that was young Urien piping up to say what he thought, but then maybe it could have been the bishop too. They were all in it.

The two queens took themselves off for a walk round the red walls of Carlisle. We followed after them. Morgan had seen to it I had a sharp knife in my belt. She didn't trust Gwendoleu. There were guards following too. But those sisters wouldn't let any of us so close we could overhear what they were saying with their heads together. It was a bright morning. I remember the water round the town throwing a sort of silver light up into the sky. And Morgan still had a brightness about her too and a spring in her step, for all she'd hardly slept a wink that night.

We hadn't got halfway round before we could see there was a commotion in the street and a whole troop more were riding up to the gate. Margawse grabbed hold of her sister's arm.

"It's Elaine! And Nentres. Back from the south."

Queens or no, the two of them were practically running back to the palace. The kings came crowding out of the hall to welcome Nentres, and there was a fresh lot of horsemen to set the grooms scurrying and the steward shouting for food and beds. The rest of our young men hauled themselves up smartly and looked down their noses at the newcomers. You could see they'd travelled far and were too dirty and tired to show themselves off as they'd have liked. Yes, and the women were not much better. They took the cloaks off Elaine's maids as if they didn't want to spoil their own dresses with the dust.

I hardly got a look at King Nentres before he was gone with the men. But I had plenty of time to study Queen Elaine. She didn't jump down quick out of her chariot like her sisters would. She was fat, and that's not a thing you often see in highborn ladies. I don't mean curved, like Margawse, so you could dream of putting your arm round her and squeezing soft flesh. No, more like a spider. A big sack of a body a man wouldn't want to touch, let alone squeeze. And where Margawse's face was smooth, and dolled up with creams and paints, Elaine's was sagging into wrinkles, though she wasn't much more than a year older. I'd rather not know what she'd seen or done to age her so. I'd been frightened of Morgan from the start, and I had enough sense to see I'd need to step carefully with Margawse. But right from that first sight I had an idea that Elaine might be the most dangerous of the three.

After that we couldn't hear what was going on in the council hall, there was so much fussing among the women over Elaine. The sisters were peeling off her cloak and hood, and sending for food and wine and water to wash her. I brought the bowl and unlaced her shoes. As I washed the dust away with my big, cracked hands I could feel her watching me. I looked up and met her eyes. Not green, like her sisters'. Grey. That should have been cool and quiet, not so unsettling. But they were wise. And you know there's a world of peril in that word. She didn't say anything to me. She didn't need to. I saw she knew more of my secrets than I'd even told Morgan.

She'd brought her daughter with her. That was a solemn child. She stood behind her mother's chair and never spoke once, but sucked her thumb and watched us all. Morgan and Margawse started to interrupt each other, telling how Arthur had won his first scrap against the Saxons. How Merlyn had thrown off his disguise and come out into the open and how nobody had suspected he'd been here all the time. How their kings were in council now arguing over it. Should they throw in their lot with Arthur and help him to glory over the Saxons? Or should they turn their own spears against him before he got too great?

But Elaine had brought news of her own. "The kings of the south will join his banner."

"Not Mark of Tintagel?"

"Mark, no. Our cousin keeps to Cornwall. But Cador the Duke, and Geraint and many others. They will march east on Lindsey soon."

"To Lincoln? So far into the enemy's land? Following a child of fourteen?" Morgan put her hand to her throat as though something was choking her.

"We were not children at fourteen. Do not imagine he is."

"The kings of the south have more to fear than our lords. It is their soft cornlands the Saxons covet." That was Margawse. You could tell she'd be sorry if Lot didn't go to war.

"But why would they trust a boy, whose sword is hardly baptised, to lead them?"

Elaine pulled off her gloves and handed them to her maid, so all the rings on her fat fingers flashed. "You forget, this boy is Uther Pendragon's son. Do you recall the morning we first set our eyes on that man? First he struck the blow that killed our father. By night he charmed his way into our mother's bed. Next morning he stood on the hillside opposite Tintagel and laughed as she came over the causeway to be his queen, with Arthur already in her belly. Yet before an hour was out, I was laughing with him too, and so were you, Margawse, even with the tears for Father still wet on our cheeks. They say this boy has the glamour to be another Pendragon."

"I did not laugh," said Morgan, very low and fierce.

"No, you did not . . ." Elaine looked at her, thoughtful. "But if the magic of his smile is not enough, Arthur has other sorcery his father used. It was Merlyn who bewitched Uther and himself and Ulfin past Tintagel's nuns."

"He shall not bewitch me."

"I hear that Arthur does not know that story."

"That sets our husbands a pretty problem!" Margawse laughed. "Shall they tell the world that Arthur is the Pendragon's son and claim we are his sisters? Or would that strengthen his cause?"

Morgan hit her fist against her palm. "Why would Merlyn keep such a secret? Why does he not shout Arthur's blood from the ramparts?"

Luned spoke then. That startled me. She wasn't one to raise her voice. "Merlyn did not win every round, madam. Uther died by cunning, like his brother, great Ambrosius, before him. Both of them poisoned by witchcraft in their beds, not dying valiantly on the battlefield. We saw to that."

Margawse gave a little giggle after a bit. "You mean, maybe Merlyn thinks the male line he chose has an unlucky sound? Perhaps he fears to put a shadow into our little Arthur's mind."

"And other people's."

"Better a boy from nowhere, until victory is sure. An elfin prince, wielding his magic sword Caliburn. Undefeatable."

Well, they looked at Morgan queerly when she said that.

"Tell them, Woman."

So she made me go over it all again. I'd rather she'd done the talking herself. Those queens questioned me mightily about the sword and scabbard, you can be sure. Elaine kept her eyes on me for an uncomfortable long while after I'd done. I don't think she trusted which side I was on.

Margawse burst out laughing. "We could tell them the truth, couldn't we, Elaine? We were there, at Tintagel, when he was got. We were there in Bossiney the night Arthur was born. We were there at the feast in London when Uther fell in love with Mother. His Easter crown-wearing, after he'd risen to glory driving the Saxons out of York."

"Uther did not! He did not!" cried Morgan. "How could you misremember? Has Merlyn bewitched you too? It was Father's courage that saved York. Without him, Uther Pendragon would have been killed shamefully, like a badger in his hole."

"And if Uther had died before he saw Ygerne, he would not have killed Father. And Arthur would never have been born," said Elaine. "A curious deliverance."

They were all three pretty quiet at that, looking at each other and drumming their fine jewelled fingers. Elaine has a shrouded sort of face. I couldn't tell what she was thinking. Margawse was hot with excitement. She wanted this war. Her sort don't care what side their lord's on or if he falls or not, so long as it makes their blood run faster. There'll always be another man somewhere. Morgan, though, her face was pale and her eyes dark and staring – that surprised me. Urien was getting to be a fine young chief, but I hadn't thought she was as much in love with him as all that, to mind that he might be going into danger. Yet there was someone she feared for.

Well, horses gallop faster than men can talk. Before our kings had made up their minds what to do, Arthur was outside the walls of Lincoln. Then we got word that Cheldric the German had landed with his fleet and was on his way to raise the siege. The Men of the North wouldn't help Arthur then. They thought his luck was finished. We heard how some Saxon chief had disguised himself as a harper with one half of his face shaved and the other hairy, to make folk laugh, and had danced his way past Arthur's nose till his mates inside hauled him up the walls with the good news that help was coming. Lot and Nentres cheered over their wine-cups. That was one in the eye for that guiser Merlyn, you could see them thinking. Only I saw Urien eyeing the weapons hung on the walls. Poor lad. He'd never fought a proper battle. He'd his name to win yet. I could see he'd have dearly loved to ride to Arthur's aid then, only Gwendoleu said no.

Those British lads had to fall back from Lindsey. Morgan started singing the day she heard the news, as happy as a skylark. But tides turn. Arthur caught Cheldric and his Germans in a wood. He hadn't men enough of his own to pen them in. They say Merlyn charmed the trees to help them. His warriors chopped them down till they'd made a wall so thick the Saxons couldn't climb out. They had to buy their lives. It was Arthur's first war. He was scarcely fifteen years old yet, but he set a stern price. Those Saxons had to hand over everything they'd got with them. Gold, silver, weapons, armour, even the clothes off their backs. I've heard he drove them naked into their boats and sent them off across the cold sea to find their way home and never come back to Britain. I wish I'd been there to see it. But he kept hostages, youngsters from noble families, to see they kept their word. He wasn't green.

Well, our queens and their husbands had to move now, one way or the other. Arthur was riding back to the City of the Legions. He was a hero. We harnessed our horses and set out south to meet him. Would that family tag on to his cloak-end, now that he'd proved himself? Or would they cut him down for bragging himself too big? They were still arguing the toss amongst themselves. But they'd got the women with them, so it looked like peace.

When we got close we started to hear the stories.

Arthur was a Christian warlord with an open hand. He'd rescued the churches from the heathen and given a great pile of treasure to every man who fought for him, till he'd none left for himself.

Arthur was a fairy's child, come to save old Britain, and then he'd vanish under the hill till he was needed again.

Arthur was a devil's child, who raped women and stole what he wanted for his wars.

Our kings wouldn't humble themselves to go to his fort straight off. And anyway, it was the women of that family who had the true power. They decided one of those queens should go for them, to see how the land lay.

Morgan and Margawse were on their feet at the same time. Elaine never stirred.

"Oh, let me! Let me! I shall die if I don't see him soon!"

You can he sure that red-headed one was keen to do it. Morgan hardly got out more than a whisper.

"I will go."

But Margawse was the elder, and her husband was a bigger king than Urien in those days. She got her way.

You could see she couldn't wait to set her eyes on Arthur. She dressed herself in her finest green gown, with a yellow and purple mantle round her shoulders. She picked out a fine skewbald horse, white and red, and had a rich saddle put on it. She took her four growing sons behind her for squires, with little spears in their hands. With her red hair strung with jewels and her flesh sweet with perfumes and oils she looked like a fairy herself, riding off to Arthur's feast at the City of the Legions.

Morgan was in a foul temper, like a cat with fleas. She boxed Luned's ears and she cut me to the bone with cruel words for what I had been once and wasn't now. There was a goblin in her, and it grew worse as the day went on.

When Margawse's troop was just a cloud of dust on the road, she swung round and hissed at me. "Go after her! Watch everything she does, and bring word to me of what passes between her and Arthur. Miss nothing."

Once Merlyn had driven me to Morgan like that. Watch her! See what she does and bring me word. Now Morgan was sending me back to spy on him. I was nothing but a piece of jetsam to them, tossed backwards and forwards between his wind and her tide. I'd find no safe landing-place in that storm.

I had no choice. I got a mule. I was scared, all right. I never wanted to see Merlyn again. I muffled myself in cloak and hood, though it was blazing harvest-time. Lugh's feast. I must have looked an ugly shadow following behind those pretty laughing women in their bright dresses.

23

If I'd felt low before, dressed like a woman, I felt worse still when I saw where I'd come. The whole town of Caerleon was an armed camp. Arthur was no king. He hadn't got a proper palace anywhere yet. Soldiers called out as we passed. You'd think they'd never seen a woman before. You might not believe it, but I felt hotter at some of the things they shouted than those ladies in front of me seemed to. I squeezed up tight to the tail of their procession and got myself passed in through the gate with them. If Margawse saw I was there she didn't try to stop me.

It was one of those summer evenings when it seems as if the day never wants to go to bed. The sun had gone down but it was still light outside. There was a smell of horses and leather, and we had to push our way through a fair old crowd of soldiers to get to Arthur's hall. All of them grinning at Margawse and her troop.

He'd set himself up in one of the Roman fortresses. City of the Legions. He always liked that, did Arthur. The Roman uniform, and the badges, and the toga at night. Latin names: Arcturus, Imperator. Only he was never a Roman really, not underneath. Merlyn and Nimue had seen to that.

It wasn't his palace, but he'd made himself pretty much at home there. He'd set up his headquarters in one of their great stone buildings. The weeds had hardly started to pull it apart yet. Inside the hall there were lights beginning to sparkle and the smell of good roast meat to make you hungry. I could hear men laughing loud, sounding a bit drunk already, though it was early yet. They had music, and not just the one harper by the noise. There was a new name for the bards to praise now, and from all we'd heard Arthur was a generous leader. He'd give gold as fast as he got it, if he was in a good humour. Well, a warlord can, can't he? When his storehouse is empty his men take more from those who can't say no to them.

Still, it was their victory celebration. I couldn't grudge it to them. I'd have been the same. Well, I'd thought Gwendoleu's feast in Carlisle was a noisy affair. But the goings-on in Arthur's hall made that seem like Christian Lent! There was a great roar came out to greet us. Even Margawse checked for a moment.

I could see past her into the lamplight. Men. That's a short word to hurt so much. I recognised more than a few of them from Nimue's house. They'd been boys when I'd watched them ride off, but they were men all right now. Young men. Fighting men. And wild with victory over other men. Arthur was a big general now. He'd got warbands flocking to him. Older men, too. I saw the tales were true. They'd kept some Saxons with them. There was a row of strangers down one side of the hall. Yellow hair in plaits. Sick faces. They were the only ones that weren't stamping and cheering. Those had to be the hostages. Saxons? Those monsters with bloody axes I'd had nightmares about? This lot were just human beings, like you and me. They weren't very old, but then nor were most of them in that hall. Arthur's lads had got their manhood taking those hostages.

And what had I sunk to? Worse than when I'd known them before.

A dragging dress, with the hem fouled by the dung of their horses.

A white-haired head I hardly dared to lift, wrapped up in linen under my drooping hood. Woman!

I'd been Smith. Good smith's leathers, I'd had. With my own hands I'd sunk them in the bog. If only I'd been wearing them the day I met Arthur. If he could have felt the strength of my shoulder muscles, seen me swing a hammer. As fine a craftsman as ever struck spark from iron. The best. I'd had power in my hands. And what had these hands done to bring me so low? It still makes my insides curl every time I think of it. Fool. Fool! It was my own life I cut short when I grabbed that girl. It was Morgan made me do it!

Still, there was one thing those men didn't have, or not enough of it. Women. There were two girls, one with skin as black as peat, dancing in front of Arthur's table. Beads round their foreheads and hips and ankles, and not a lot else. That was making the men yell and stamp. There were serving-maids, but hardly a lady sitting at table. So it was nothing to the cheer that went up when Margawse swept into the hall. Well, who wouldn't cheer? She had her cloak thrown back from her white shoulders and her red hair falling free, and all her women behind her. These ladies smiled merrily, but I could see they were eyeing those warriors to tell how drunk they might be.

I wasn't a true woman, but I was more coward than those who were. I told myself those fighting-men would hardly cheer at the sight of me. I had to slink after the ladies all the same. Morgan had sent me to do it. I must have looked a queer sort of figure, creeping behind them like that.

I never reached the door. A hand gripped my wrist from behind, tight as an owl on a shrew. It turned me to the last light from the sunset. I was eye-to-eye with Merlyn. I don't know which of us got the bigger shock. He'd been suspicious, but I wasn't what he'd expected, I could see that. There was fear in both our faces, right enough, catching sight of each other like that. He knew me this time, no doubt about that. Merlyn could see keen as a hawk when he was clear of his little enchantress. He realised too late he should have known me before.

"It was you! White-Chin, the holy man!"

Two could play at that game. "Emrys Silver-Tongue? Gwendoleu's bard, is it? In Arthur's camp?"

"Use your wits, man. Merlyn takes many shapes, and good reason for them. If I fooled Gwendoleu it was for Britain's advantage. But you have worse to answer for. I knew Morgan was too close for safety, but I did not suspect she would place you in Nimue's house to spy. How long were you there?"

"A year, near enough. But I wasn't her spy. Never! I was running from her as hard as I could go."

He peered into my face, closer than I could bear to meet him. I think he was more puzzled than angry.

"Yes. I know why your smithy was empty. I might have fled to the forest myself if she had done that to me. But a year? At the heart of our secret. And Arthur survived."

"Damn you and Morgan! I didn't want anything to do with either of you."

"No? Whatever the truth, I am inclined to believe you think that true. Yet what you want is not what is. You were always marked for Morgan. Still, Arthur did live to take his sword, and now he is riding the road to victory. Two rounds so far to us. Who takes the third? You come from Morgan's camp tonight. You followed her here, even into the heart of Arthur's army.'

I nodded. I'd taken Morgan's service now. That's what he'd pressed me to do three years ago. Though there hadn't been a thought about Merlyn in my head when Morgan shaved me. But that wasn't exactly what he meant, saying it was Morgan I'd followed here. It wasn't her inside the hall. Wise though he was, he could still be fooled by a woman.

Merlyn had come late to the feast, keeping his own time as usual. The moment he'd guessed what was afoot he'd kept his back to the door, so he couldn't see what I did: red Margawse, with the candles flaming on her hair as she bent her knee to Arthur. She could do that very prettily. It was half mocking to make them both smile, and half as if she was offering herself to him as a sort of tribute. The Queen of Lothian, come to do him honour. And Arthur was laughing and raising her to her feet, leading her round to the high table. Sitting her down beside him, making everyone else move out of her way. Raising his drinking-horn to her. Not Morgan. Why should I tell Merlyn that? What had he ever done to help me?

Quick as a flash Merlyn called to one of his stewards. In his own way he was as much of a general as Arthur, though it was different weapons he feared. He still had his own face hidden from the hall.

"See the Pendragon eats and drinks nothing that hasn't been tasted. Warn Cei and Bedwyr to be on their guard. Tell them to have every one of the queen's women watched. Trust none of them."

He let go of my arm. I rubbed the place a bit. He was strong, was Merlyn, even if he did often go dressed like a poet or a fool.

He grinned a bit at that. "I'm sorry. But I do not take chances, with false women or real ones. Morgan was once a vicious child. I doubt that a girl-hood penned up in Tintagel nunnery has mellowed her. And it seems she has learned as much of magic there as of Christian saintliness. But she is long past a child now. Once she might have struck Arthur down with her knife before all his warband, and never mind if she died for it afterwards herself. Now I fear she has grown more subtle. Even so, I wonder why she has humbled herself to pay Arthur court. Morgan was always proud. I do not like it."

You could see he felt there was something here he hadn't put his finger on. There was a deal of questions he still needed answering. After all these years he didn't want to tangle with Morgan – for Morgan he thought it was in there – till he'd found out from me how the wind blew. And it was a cold thought to me that even a great man like him was afraid of her. He hadn't saved me from those three queens and I was sure he couldn't now. I was

Morgan's creature. So why should I tell him it wasn't Morgan there in the hall? He was a wise man, wasn't he, and a lot more than that? And I'd had my wisdom stolen away from me, that day he got me by the wrist. Let him find the truth out for himself, if he was so clever.

Instead I said, "Court, is it? That's mighty quick. I hadn't heard that they'd cried him a king yet."

He didn't like that.

"All the island of Britain shall be his kingdom before I've done. Arthur will prove himself emperor by deed as well as blood. When the kings gather, I shall proclaim the lad Ambrosius's nephew. Pendragon's son. His mother Ygerne was of the old royal house of the West. He has the true blood in his veins. And enough Saxon blood on his spear already to prove his right to any diadem. We'll clear the north of Picts and Scots next, all the barbarians who helped the enemy. There'll be a harvest of heads rolling in the heather. We'll take no hostages there. The Church will crown him. Next summer will see him High King over all the Britons."

"That'll be nice for you. Uther Pendragon's magician. Then sunk to Gwendoleu's minstrel. You'd be coming back up in the world as soul-friend to King Arthur of all Britain, wouldn't you? But where does that leave me? I was Teilo Smith. King in our craft. I had power. Till the black day I set eyes on you and Morgan of Cornwall. *Look* at me!"

Well, there was some pity in his eyes, but a sort of smugness with it, so I could have hit him.

"Too much power, Teilo. And still you aimed higher. It has broken stronger men than you."

"Not Emrys Merlyn?"

"I never lost my power. I hid it for a season. No one takes it away from me."

Oh no? I thought. Not even pretty Nimue, wheedling secrets out of both of us, while she's making a man out of Arthur and women out of us? I didn't say that, but he must have seen the look in my eyes. He shook his head.

"Man, I can see Morgan's made you suffer!"

Well, for the sake of that one word he called me, I gave up arguing and let him lead me off to a private room. He filled me with meat and ale while he questioned me about Morgan. We were there a long while. The daylight went and the stars came out and we could hear plenty of shouting and dancing from the hall. I hadn't talked man to man like that since Morgan took me in. He got far more out of me than I did from him. I was Morgan's servant. He saw I wasn't strong enough to be trusted.

We'd shared more than a jug or two when there was a sudden knocking at the door. His steward was there.

"Sir! Sir! I think you should come. It's Arthur, sir. He's been a long time out of the hall, with the red-haired queen. We thought no harm, after the victory. We could hardly stop him. The young lords have been so long without the company of their own sort of ladies. All her women seemed in such a pleasant humour, and Lord Bedwyr just laughs and won't let me knock at the chamber door . . ."

"The chamber door? With whom? *What* red-haired queen?" Merlyn flung round on me. "Who has come here tonight? You told me it was Black Morgan!"

"I said nothing of the sort. It was you who said that."

"*Not* Morgan? Then who . . .?" His face went white. He'd known that family too long not to see what it meant. "Not *Margawse*?"

I nodded. I enjoyed that. It did me good to see him dumbfounded for once.

"Oh, by all the gods! This is a black day's work you've to answer for." He buried his face in his hands. "Tell me the worst. How long have those two been gone?"

The steward was stuttering. "An . . . an hour, maybe. But the queen left her knife on the table and we tasted their wine. Lord Bedwyr is standing guard at the door. Wouldn't he have heard if there'd been any treachery?"

"Heard? Yes, and laughed to hear it, as I once laughed outside another bedchamber in Tintagel!"

Merlyn tore his hair and rushed out of the room.

The hall had gone quiet. The dancing was finished. Those boy-hostages had vanished. They'd be locked up safe somewhere for the night. There were drunk men sprawled over the tables in a mess of crumbs and beer. Half Margawse's women were still leaning on them, with their arms twined round their necks. Some were rolling in the straw with those who were still half-awake. A few more were sat whispering together in a corner. Margawse's sons were sleeping like babies. Even that sharp-eyed Cei was snoring, with his head on his arms. Merlyn rushed past them, knocking over tables as he ran, and out through a door at the back. I couldn't hear what he cursed at Bedwyr before he broke open the chamber door.

"What's all the fuss about?" Arthur's bodyguard asked. "A sweet lady like that, when the lad's won a great victory? Where's the harm in it? I wish I was general and set to be emperor, I don't mind telling you, if that's the way all queens come to pay their war-taxes!"

It had been a long time since I'd found anything to laugh about. "What's the harm? Well, here's the joke. That queen's his sister! Do you think the Church is going to crown him High King now? Let's see if Merlyn can keep *this* secret for another fourteen years!"

24

I'd gone to the City of the Legions as Morgan's spy, but it didn't need me to tell her the news. Margawse couldn't wait to do it herself. She came back rosy as a girl, and skipping like a lamb in spring, for all she was the mother of four sons and a powerful queen. It was the women's tents she went to first. She had to tell Elaine and Morgan before any king. She let her cloak slip off and threw herself down on the grass in front of her sisters, and never mind that her green skirts went riding up over her legs. Those white thighs. Redheads like her have skin like buttermilk. She threw back her head and smiled, very wide.

At first I thought Morgan wasn't going to speak to her. She had her mouth fastened up tight. But she couldn't help herself.

"What was he like? Is it really him? Is it our brother Arthur?"

She looked like a cat ready to spring and as hungry too. You could tell it in the sparkle of her green eyes, the way her body was crouched.

Before Margawse had time to answer, Lot and Urien and Nentres, with their chief lords, came rushing up from the horse-lines to hear her story. Margawse liked that even better. She'd rather have men listen to her than just her two sisters. She turned her smile on them.

"Arthur doesn't want to be a king!"

Lot wasn't going to swallow that. "Pendragon's son! Battle-chief of the Cymry against the Saxons? And not fancy himself as High King? What else could he want?"

"You forget. He has not been told yet that he is Uther's child. Nor I Ygerne's! And, for the rest, the title he fancies is Emperor. The Roman

Imperator. Leader of Battles. He is a boy of fifteen. War! That's all he cares about. War and glory. To be a hero in a Roman kilt and make the Cymry sing of him as long as the British tongue has bards."

"For that he must be High King. How else could such a warleader hold the whole island? He needs thousands of men. Garrisons along the coast, south and east. Legions in the north to keep the Picts beyond the Wall. Fast cavalry to drive back the Irish pirates from the west wherever they land. And then a mighty host to purge all Saxons, man, woman and child, from the soft belly of Britain. He needs horses. Corn for men and beasts. Forts. Ships. Gold to pay his warriors and mead to sweeten them. He cannot do all that with a pack of schoolboys galloping about like footloose brigands."

"Fight, yes. But he does not want to sit in the high chair of a council chamber, to listen for hours to old men wagging their beards at him. To have to bother with taxes, laws, justice. He says Merlyn must see to all that."

"Such power would please Merlyn very well," said Morgan.

As if she'd been standing beside me in Caerleon when he'd spoken to me.

"He shall not have that."

It's not often Elaine speaks. When she does, heads turn her way and there's a queer sort of quiet.

Lot wasn't finished though. "Merlyn or Arthur, it's all the same. He must have power to order what he wants from those who have it."

Margawse blushed like a girl and looked down at her hands. "Arthur does not need to order. He has other means of getting what he wants."

I got a quick look at King Lot when she said that. He had a face as black as a thundercloud that's going to ruin a harvest. He must have known what she was. He'd lived with her long enough. Gawain their son was almost as old as Arthur.

"Our brother must be High King," said Morgan.

"You of all people say that?" marvelled Margawse. "You wanted him dead!"

"No. I wished him never to have been born."

"Ygerne's son, and therefore he must be High King. Uther's son, and therefore a dead king. Is that what you want?" Nentres wasn't a man who said much, either. He wasn't hot and fierce like Lot. But when he spoke other men listened. You got the feeling that once Nentres had weighed a thing up it was as good as decided.

Lot laughed at that, very sharp and bitter. "So that's your game! I see it now. Crown Arthur Pendragon and then murder him. Then claim his diadem for the Pendragon's sister. And look which of our three queens is the eldest!"

Another man would have struck him for that, brother-in-law or no. But Nentres just smiled. There was a nasty while of silence. You could see them all turning the thought over in their heads.

Urien spoke up for himself. "I think we should take this adventure Arthur offers. Never mind if anyone's High King at the end of it. Britain is being eaten away by foreign rats. If we do not drive them back now they will soon be in Rheged and Lothian and Dumnonia. The north and west will fall like the south and east. If we do not join our swords to Arthur's now, all Christian Britain will fall under the axe of the pagans. Shall it be said of us that we stood by like cowards?"

The lords had started to cheer him. It was what they'd been hoping to hear. They'd sooner fight the Saxons than their own kind. But there were some queer sorts of grins when he finished. They had their bishops and churches. They went to the Offering on Sundays. But they couldn't help but know what nature their queens were. Those women didn't trouble to hide it. It wasn't a thing they were ashamed of.

But he'd said the right thing, that lad. It was what all men want. A sword in their hand at last and a call to battle. Urien got his way. Pretty soon they were off to their own side of the camp. It was men's talk now, battle-talk. Maybe there'd be war of a different sort afterwards, but there'd be plenty of Saxon blood to shed first.

When they'd gone, Margawse lay back on the grass and laughed, very long and merry.

"They would all fight against Arthur if they knew the rest of my story. But instead they will make him their king now!"

For the second time Elaine spoke, under the shade of an awning where she was sitting with her daughter.

"Our mother Ygerne would not match her power against less than the High King of Britain. Neither shall we. What we make, we can also destroy."

"Morgan is less particular where her power strikes. A nun. A black-smith. A husband still ink-stained from the schoolroom. The King of all Britain might be too high for her! Such a shame. Oh, Morgan! He's a pet of a boy to take with you under the blanket."

Margawse was heaving and writhing on the turf as if she was doing it again. You could see Morgan didn't believe it at first. Not though she must have known like the rest of us what her sister was. It came out like a screech.

"No! Margawse! You could not! Say you did not!"

I never thought I'd see Morgan shocked. She'd lived through much in her life already. Her father murdered and her mother seduced, if that's how it was, by the same man. Herself a noted Lady in the Old Religion. She's not a virgin. Oh no, Morgan's not a virgin. I should know. Haven't I had to lie with my head in my arms when Urien comes to bed her? Guarding the door, but close enough to hear them. Him serious. Too scared to speak at first. And her murmuring encouragement to him like a mother. But when he comes on her, panting and crying, then she goes silent. She never gasps or whimpers. You'd think she'd emptied herself before he came. I suppose it's a sort of kindness to him. How could a young man like that have lived if Morgan the Wise had really come to meet him?

But Margawse shocked her.

When she saw Morgan's face, Margawse opened her mouth and laughed. There wasn't any sound at first, then high and shrill. Luned and I grabbed at Morgan's arms. Queen or not, we could hardly hold her.

"You foul-arsed cat! *You!* And Arthur? You whore! A wife and queen. The mother of princes. Arthur's own *sister!*"

"Why not? The gods did it with their sisters. Call it a sacred marriage if it makes you feel better. We both enjoyed it. It was a contest, remember? My way against yours. My power, Morgan. Here! I said I would bring him down, not you, and so I have!"

We couldn't hold Morgan then. She tore herself free of us and hurled herself on Margawse. Those two queens wrestled together, rolling on the ground. We had to drag her off. There was damage done. Margawse had the worst of it, and she fell back gasping. But she was still laughing, with her red hair tumbled over her face.

"Oh, dear, Morgan! Arthur has gentler hands than you. Such a pretty little warrior. You should have felt the down of his beard between my breasts. And smelt the sweetness of his breath as he nibbled my neck."

Morgan stood and stared at her sister teasing her. And I got a fright. The tears were rolling down her face. She didn't make another sound. She didn't stir. She might have been turned to wood. But the tears were falling like great drops of blood.

Elaine's voice came out of the shadow then. It sounded as strained as if she'd been a very old woman on her death-bed. She must have reached a cruel long way into the future to see what she did. It cost her.

"Margawse is right. She carries Arthur's ruin in her belly. And wounds worse than that."

Somehow it didn't seem important then, what the men were deciding in their war-council. The battle that counted had already been fought some-where else.

Luned and I led Morgan back to her own tent. She said just three words.

"I have lost."

She lay on her bed and wept the rest of that day.

25

Morgan turned home for Rheged. She wouldn't stay and meet Arthur now, not though she'd been so hot to see him before. Back at Lyvennet, she dressed herself in black, with just a circle of gold on her head and not another jewel. For days on end she stood at the gate of her castle from morning to night, handing out medicines to anyone that would take them. There were plenty came. But some of them passed on by when they saw her. She looked so wild.

The men stopped, though.

After that, it was all news of war. Arthur hung those hostage boys. Well, he had to, didn't he? That two-faced Cheldric hadn't gone home at all. He'd doubled his ships about and landed back down at Totnes, in Dumnonia, where Morgan comes from. He reaped a grim harvest there, from all accounts. There were men beheaded, women raped, children drowned, beasts slaughtered and farms burned. And where was young Arthur while all this was going on? Up north of the Wall giving the Picts what for, so they'd learn not to attack good British folk while his back was turned fighting Saxons. So he had the length of the whole island to ride when he got the news.

But ride he did. They say that when he went into battle in the end he went berserk. He stormed up the hill at the head of his army with his golden dragon-helmet on his head and crying, "Christ fight for us! The Mother aid us!" and I'll leave you to guess just who he meant. Well, the Saxons fled, and he left Cador the Keen to finish them off. Cador was Duke in Dumnonia. It was his country. He'd seen the slaughter.

Arthur had left some unfinished business in Pictland. They'd got his friends holed up in Alclud and they'd likely have died if he hadn't got back when he did. I wish I could have been there to see it. I'd have given anything to have heard the clash of steel and know it was the edge I put on their weapons that was shearing through hair and bone. I'd have worked all night to mend their broken spears and patch a shield or breastplate for the next day's fighting. I could have helped Arthur win. He got the victory without me, though. He taught the Picts a proper lesson.

They say there's a loch there with sixty islands. Sixty streams flow into it and only one runs out. On every one of those sixty crags there's a fierce eagle that flies into the air and screams when disaster's coming.

I bet the skies were pretty noisy when Arthur's lads rode up that glen. They drove the savages out into the water till they clung to the rocks for dear life. Then our British boys built boats and went after them.

There were hundreds of Picts drowned or starved, or the loch monsters got them. He'd have finished the lot, just as they'd have finished the mates he'd left behind in Alclud if he hadn't got back in time to save them.

It wasn't warriors stopped his slaughter. It was Christian bishops and presbyters, dressed like Lent without their fine robes. A sorry procession of them, come to rescue his enemies from what they deserved. Nuns with their heads black with cinders. Pictish women barefoot, tearing their faces with their own claws. Even little children crying for their daddies, so I've heard.

Well, Arthur was young. He hadn't the stomach to say no to them. He let them keep their menfolk, what was left of them. He reckoned he could call it a victory, so long as those painted barbarians kept to the moors where they belonged and left us British the good lands either side of the Wall. The Church crowed they'd got the better of him, though. They're always the same. He saves their churches for them, yet the moment he acts like a man, they're down on him.

Urien rode with Arthur on that campaign. It made a man of him. He came back taller and harder about the body than when he rode out. And sterner in his face too. He'd dreamed of war. All lads do. But he'd seen what it meant now. He's never turned back from that day. When Arthur's trumpet calls, he's there at the front of our men. I don't wonder that Gwendoleu looked sour at him. His Solway warriors would have liked a chance to grease their swords like that. Lot and Nentres fought with Arthur too. But Gwendoleu stayed at home. He didn't trust Arthur.

And where was I while the men were fighting? Back in Lyvennet, in a dun full of women. Bit by bit the scorch-marks had flaked off my skin, though I've never quite lost the scars. The muscles I'd been so proud of had turned to soft fat. I still shaved a few white bristles off my chin every day. So there was only one thing left to mark that I was once a proper man.

I still have a man's feelings whimpering under this skirt. Hiding a rusty weapon, you might say. What good does it do me? She might as well have taken it with her razor, and left me in peace.

I was never easy. I still went bent to hide my face from guards and servants. Then there came one day when I tried to raise my head and pain caught me in the back. I knew then I'd always go stooped. I couldn't have swung a hammer after that. When Morgan broke my body, she broke my spirit too. I'll always be a lady's woman now, in a women's dun. Me, that was Teilo Smith.

There was another broken like me: Luned. Solemn as an owl, and nearly as wise too, for all she'd once been a nun. For the rest, Morgan had surrounded herself with pretty girls, as young and gay as ever Erith was. Yes, I mean you. Preen yourselves as much as you like. But it was only us two that she let close to her. If you didn't know better you might almost have called us her friends. The rest could have been swallows flitting round a rock that's cold and still. Except sometimes she'd go hunting after the boar and the wind would whip the colour into her cheeks and she'd be laughing like a young girl, till she got back.

Margawse came to visit us. Her belly was big now, with Arthur's child. And the eldest sister, Elaine the Fair. It always sends a shudder through me when they call her that.

Morgan had stayed slender and hard, like a young fir-tree. You'd never have thought she'd borne twins. And I had the measure of Red Margawse. Bright as a poppy in a cornfield, and as warm. If she'd been short of men, I think she'd have taken even my poor white head in her lap. She knew my secret. She wasn't above teasing me.

But Elaine was fat and pale, like a spider on a leaf. She never stirred out of doors if she could help it. She didn't ride out hunting with her sisters. You never saw her tapping her feet to the harping and dancing. She'd sit over a fire, everlastingly weaving strands of coloured wool and snipping the fringes with her scissors.

The war-host was back from Pictland. That winter it was Urien's turn to stand Arthur a feast. I'd never seen Morgan so fretful. She was all over the place, scolding the stewards to have everything right, as if they hadn't done it all a hundred times before.

Someone else rode through the gate just before Arthur's lot came in sight. A covered chariot. We'd none of us been told about that. A woman got out and helped another lady down, dressed in plain white. Morgan greeted the lady and kissed her, a little stiffly I thought. I couldn't hear what was said. She led her into the hall. I should have followed them straight away, but I didn't.

It wasn't just Arthur I was looking out for. It was a fine cold day, with just a hint of spring coming. It still hurt me to look down from that hilltop and see Way Bank, just a little cluster of thatch among the apple orchards. I'd worked there once. I'd been a man and a king. I'd had a wife and daughter. I'd been Smith. But Morgan had looked out from here and cursed me.

So I had to stand among women on the walls and watch fighting men ride up the hill. Arthur was at the head of them, dressed like a Roman general in his scarlet cloak. He was bare-headed. No need for his dragon-helmet here. He was among friends, wasn't he? And he had all his grinning warriors behind him.

Urien was waiting in the gate to greet him, all decked out in gold chains and best tunic, and practically the whole household was out in the yard. Only Morgan and her sisters hung back a long while in the hall, so I went in to see what was up. I didn't expect Elaine to stir till she had to, but it wasn't like the other two to hide themselves. Margawse was behind the door. She couldn't stop giggling. I guessed she was a bit embarrassed to face Arthur out in broad daylight, now he was a great general and not just a little lad out of nowhere. She'd enjoyed the joke, but she hadn't quite worked out how she was to tell him what had come of it.

Morgan was the strange one. She was the lady of the castle, and she can play the part of a queen better than any I know. She should have been at the gate beside Urien to greet her guest. But I found her sitting there, facing that lady in white, and neither of them saying a word to the other.

We heard the noise from the gate. Morgan threw up her head then and her eyes went wide. I saw her sisters were watching her, to see what she'd do.

"Arthur is here!" said Margawse.

"The son of Uther Pendragon, who killed Father," Elaine murmured.

All three of them looked at that other lady.

Morgan got up, very slowly, and drew herself up tall. She straightened her dress. She didn't seem bothered about the shouting outside. Luned brought her a mirror and she smoothed her hair and touched her face. Very beautiful she looked, that morning. It was a new gown she had on, yellow and crimson, like trees in autumn. At last she picked up a goblet that had been on the table beside her. She held her other hand out to the lady in white, and the two of them walked out into the light of day. There wasn't a hint of a smile on Morgan's face as she went past us.

I looked at Luned, and she at me. Neither of us had any idea what might be in Morgan's mind. This would be the first time she'd met her brother since that night at Tintagel when Merlyn snatched the baby out of her arms. We followed close after her.

Out in the yard it was a sight to warm the heart of any Briton, man or woman. A huge crowd of young men, warriors now. Sure of themselves, they looked, and bearing their new battle-scars proudly. All dressed up in fine peacetime harness with a load of jewellery. And Arthur at their head, jumping down from his horse beside Urien. I'd hardly have recognised him now. He had a full, curling moustache, and his brow was a bit furrowed and his jawline harder. But grinning like a hound as he saw Morgan coming to greet him. He didn't wait for her to cross the courtyard. He came striding to meet her with his arms held out. She stopped still, with the lady beside her. Standing behind her, I couldn't see her face, but Morgan did a thing I hadn't expected. She sank down on one knee before him and said in a quiet voice, but so clear the whole dun could hear her, "Greetings, Lord Arthur, son of Uther Pendragon and Ygerne."

That stopped him short, and a sort of buzz ran through the crowd. His eyes flew round to the lords behind him. You could see plain enough nobody had yet told him where he'd sprung from. But he had a quick mind. He wasn't slow to see what it meant.

"Lady! You are telling me I am the High King Uther's son? Can you prove this true? *Where is that devil Merlyn?'*

Morgan signed to the lady with her. That other had a small sweet voice, but loud enough for those nearest to hear.

"You have no need of Merlyn. I bore Uther a son, fifteen years ago last Midwinter. Merlyn stole him away when he was one week old. There are those here who can testify to you I am the Queen Ygerne. My own wise woman's blood tells me I have found my lost child."

The colour flamed in Arthur's face, and then he embraced his mother, only softer than he usually does with a woman. Still, that little lady was almost swallowed up in his arms. A great shout went up from the nobles crowding round. "Pendragon! Pendragon! Arthur of Britain! Arthur Pendragon!" And soon the whole army was crying that name. Whatever the lad had said before about being High King, you could see now that the fire was in his blood. He swung round on them all with that great grin he gives everybody, as though he knows they all love him. And they cheered him louder.

But Morgan hadn't finished. He turned to her and she held up her goblet to him.

"Morgan, daughter of Gorlois and Ygerne, offers Arthur her welcome."

I couldn't see Morgan's face, but I watched his. That great grin faded. The blood rose right up to his forehead, dark red under the gold. He didn't know what to say. As if he'd come face-to-face with something that had never happened to him before. It seemed a mighty long time to the rest of us that those two looked at each other, as though there was nobody else but them in the whole world.

Then he found his voice, and very deep and husky it sounded.

"Arthur Pendragon gives you his heartfelt thanks . . . Sister!"

Again that pause. He gave her a solemn bow. Like two actors in a play, they were.

Then he reached out his hand to take her cup. Their fingers almost met.

"Stop!"

A figure came hurtling across that courtyard towards them. Like a wildman, it was. Merlyn, in a black bearskin with a cudgel in his hand. With a roar that sounded more like a beast than a human he snatched the cup from between them. I thought he was going to dash it to the ground. Then he seemed to recollect himself and looked around. Well, you can bet the warriors are all crowding forward, hands to weapons. Luned's angry and Morgan is back on her feet. Merlyn picks on a page. He couldn't have been more than ten years old. And he holds Morgan's goblet to the boy's lips.

"Drink!"

The lad was terrified. You could see his round eyes over the lip of that goblet. He hadn't a notion what it was all about or why they had lighted on him. He swallowed a mouthful. I daresay it was the first time he'd ever tasted good wine. There was a long grim hush while we waited. Merlyn had put a thought into everybody's head that hadn't been there before. It blackened that day and many since. We saw the blood rush sudden to the boy's cheeks. He gagged a bit, and we thought he was going to fall. Then he gave a hiccup and started to grin at us all, wanting to know if he'd done it right, whatever it was for.

Well, a great roar of laughter went up from all those men. Arthur tossed down the wine. He gave Morgan back her cup, but the magic had gone. He hugged and kissed her, but no more than he'd have done any other lady. It was his mother he smiled at, and her hand he took. As Morgan led the way into her hall she turned such a look on Merlyn that it made me feel faint. I've never seen so much hatred pass between one human and another.

Merlyn was always a fool about women. She wouldn't have done it with her own hand. That's not how my Annis died.

But, then again, maybe he did know she'd put nothing in that wine. I wonder now if Merlyn might not have been cleverer than I took him for. He'd separated them properly.

Arthur had already had two surprises, but they weren't done yet. At the door of the hall Margawse was waiting to greet him. Arthur gave a start when he set eyes on her, and burst out into a peal of laughter, quite different from the way he'd checked at Morgan. "The red-haired Queen of Lothian! We meet again!" he grinned.

"This is Margawse, daughter of Gorlois. She is also your sister," says Morgan gravely.

Well, that stopped him laughing, all right. He looked down at Margawse's swollen belly and back at her wicked face. And then round pretty quick for Lot. He backed away from Morgan as if he thought her touch would burn him. He'd gone mighty pale, and his glance was going between those two sisters, as if they were kelpies risen out of a lake to eat him.

Morgan smiled, very coolly now. "And this too is your sister. Elaine, the eldest child of Ygerne and Gorlois."

I don't think Arthur even noticed Elaine.

Arthur and Morgan. That's how it's always been. Those two. Like sword-dancers, nipping in and out of the blades without ever touching.

26

Those queens had Arthur trapped before he'd hardly started. What's done can't be undone. Still, it was a brave week's feasting Urien gave him. There was dancing and sword-playing and hunting and hurly, games of war where the men could show off in front of the ladies. Arthur's warriors had a fine time of it, with all Morgan's and Margawse's ladies to flatter them. There wasn't one of Urien's men could shift Cei in single combat. And Bedwyr stepped a pretty figure in the reel. But Arthur had no joy at that feast. He flung himself into the hunting and wrestling as if he didn't care if he broke his neck. At table he threw back horn after horn of wine. You'd think he couldn't get drunk quickly enough. I saw his eyes going along the board to Margawse, staring at her body with that sick look in his face.

He'd gaze at Morgan too, often enough, and she would look back at him. Very long and grave they stared into each other's eyes, those two. They were always polite, but you'd think they were each accusing the other. Still, for the rest, I'd never seen Morgan take so much trouble to make herself look beautiful or put herself out so much to please men. From that day she changed. Almost reckless she was. She flirted with all his young warriors and made them welcome, almost as if she'd been Margawse. There was one in particular she'd call to sit near her. A thin stick of a young man, with hair as white as a Saxon. I can't think what she saw in him. Accolon, they called him.

She was sweet to all of them except Arthur. Since that first morning she couldn't manage a smile when she looked at him, though she clapped when he fought, harder than she did for her own husband. He showed her honour too. Well, she was his hostess, and his sister. He wouldn't let her shame him.

Margawse and Elaine were at her to decide what they should do next. But she wouldn't talk to them. It was only her mother Ygerne she'd meet in her room in secret. Not even Luned and I were allowed to know what passed between them. For the rest of the time she kept herself busy with her guests, and laughing merry as a lark, except when her eyes met Arthur's. It's a funny thing, though. She wouldn't let Urien in her bed all that week.

On the last day of the feast she made me do something that seemed odd to me. She gave me a parcel wrapped in a linen cloth.

"Take this to Merlyn. Tell him Morgan the Wise returns his gift. She will not use it."

It was heavy. I could feel hard metal through the wrappings. A handle of twisted branches fitting snugly to the fingers, and a smooth round plate. I guessed near enough what it was. A lady's mirror. It hadn't been my sort of work. I was for horse-harness, fire-irons, tools. Manly stuff. But I'd been a noted craftsman in those parts. If ladies had something broken that they treasured and there was no gold- or silversmith by, they might bring it to Teilo's smithy at Way Bank and smile at me to make it whole again. I know rare work when I feel it. It woke a kind of hunger in me.

I found Merlyn in his sleeping-stall, though it was broad daylight. I hadn't wanted to go, but I felt a bit better when I saw that magician hunched on his bed with his knees tucked up to his chin and a scowl on his face. He'd spent a deal of time sulking indoors since that first morning. He was getting it good and strong from both sides. Morgan and her sisters had fairly bested him. Margawse could hardly stop herself laughing in his face. And Arthur couldn't look at him without shouting and swearing, for keeping a secret past its time. So I didn't expect I'd be a welcome visitor.

I said my message, just as she told me, and held out the package. He gave a great sort of sigh, so I felt a bit sorry for him. He knew what it was too, and he sat for a long time just looking at it without opening the wrappings. At last he shot me a look full in the eyes, and he could see I was greedy for a sight of it. He untwisted the cloth and I must have given a bit of a gasp, for I remembered now when I'd seen that same mirror before. It had been a beauty once. All coiling serpents on the handle and vines and peacocks engraved on the back-plate, and the other side polished bronze, so you could see your face clear in it. Or should have done. Morgan had broken it. She'd flung it from her so hard, when Margawse had taunted her, the handle had bent. The plate was so buckled and cracked now that the loveliest face in the world would have looked crooked in it. I was a craftsman. I felt as if I'd been damaged myself.

"She will not use it," I repeated.

"Is that phase over so quickly? Must she go straight from the virgin to the hag? And we lose Britain's summer?"

He pulled a face like a goblin, and his head sank between his shoulders. He had his hand deep in his pocket.

"Then give her this!" I'd never heard him sound so vicious. He was usually a merry sort of man.

He had it ready. He must have foreseen. It was a little silver box decorated with dragons and horses. But I knew that wasn't the real gift. There was something inside it that rattled. I took it to Morgan. I don't know how it was, it was only a small thing, that you could fit in the palm of one hand. But it felt heavy, heavier than you can imagine, so that by the time I got back to Morgan's room I could hardly bear the weight of it.

There was only Luned with her. When I told her Merlyn had sent her another gift, Morgan didn't move or say a word. I put it down on her lap, very carefully, so my hands wouldn't touch her. She sat and stared at it for a fair old time. Then, with just the tips of her fingers, she opened the lid. It wasn't much. The sort of present any gentleman might give to a lady. A pair of silver scissors, shaped like the beak of a heron. You'd have thought she'd have done like any other lady would, picked them up and tried them, cut something, even if it was only empty air. But Morgan just sat very still, looking down at them for a long, long while. And then she closed the lid.

27

Even fat spiders stir out of their hole when the fly touches the web. Margawse's time came. We were all of us gathered there in her castle at Din Eidyn, north of the Wall. Elaine, Morgan, their women, me. When the red queen's first pains started you can guess what I was afraid of. How far would Morgan push her cruel joke on me? If joke it was. I looked at the curtain hanging in front of Margawse's bedchamber, and Margawse herself holding her hands over the belly where Arthur's child was pushing, and I felt mighty queer. There's some magic even I never pretended to.

I needn't have worried. After a bit the pains came so hard that Margawse cried out. It was Elaine got up from the corner of the fireplace where she'd been sitting. She waved her hand to three of her own women and they helped Margawse in with them through the curtain. Morgan took one step after them, but Elaine drew the curtain in her face. I'd never have thought Morgan would stand for that, not with the fierce high pride she had. Then I saw the look in her eyes. Stricken, I'd call it, as if she'd just had news of a death. But there was nothing said by either of those sisters.

I was left outside, and Morgan and Luned as well. This wasn't their work. They weren't welcome at a childbirth, for all Morgan had the name of a great healer. There was something here I couldn't quite put my finger on. You felt these two still carried something of the convent with them from Tintagel. They'd both borne babies, but that didn't count, somehow. You might have thought they were still virgins.

It was Margawse you'd look to for hot blood and birthing. She could

159

hardly stop sons springing out of her hole. Four fine wee warriors in the making already, and folk hardly bothered to count her daughters.

And Elaine? Well, she was only a year older than Margawse, and she had a wide, soft lap to nurse babies on. But sometimes she'd look older even than a great-grandmother. I had a nasty sort of feeling, catching sight of her eyes then, as if I'd only to lean over just a little bit further and I'd be falling down a bottomless well. Hundreds and hundreds of years, going back into darkness, all those women, generation before generation, back to the very first One. That's what I thought I was seeing when I looked at her. I've seen old stone things like her. Those big hips and breasts. That flat face that sees nothing or everything. I kept away from them. They weren't my magic. They wanted more blood than I knew how to give.

It was going on evening when the women went inside the curtain. May Eve. There were the proper things done in the castle courtyard that night, but we had different magic on our minds. Taking out, not putting in. Even so, it still hurt me not to be dancing the god. When the sun went down there was a queer sort of hush outside. Not a cloud anywhere, and the sky so pale it was almost white. Up on the hilltops I knew the bonfires would be standing ready. May Eve, Beltaine. They kept the feast a fine old way in Margawse's land. The Christian bishops had little say up here. This wasn't Roman country like Rheged. When the stars pricked out we could hear the drums begin to beat.

When we'd worked our own spells, Morgan went to stand in the doorway and breathe the cool air. I noticed her hands kept clenching on her skirt and then she'd have to force herself to open them wide, as women must do for the birthing.

But we had a long time to wait. In the middle of the night we saw the fires leaping up on all the crags around us. Before long Margawse's folk came charging back, banging drums and blowing whistles. They danced into the yard, waving torches and singing, "Summer is come in today!"

I thought the baby was being born then. We heard a great cry from the queen's bedchamber. But when we swung round expecting to see someone bursting through the curtain to tell us, it hung still. We turned back to the yard, and I saw a sight that made me suck in my breath. They were dancing the Horse. I'd been the Stag myself. It cuts me to the quick to see another tribe make magic stronger than mine, anyplace. Still, I'd seen Horses before. Morgan had brought hers from Cornwall. When it swings close to us, with its tall hat on its head and its tarred skirts, that's a thing to make men skip and the women scream. All the same, the people love that Horse. A childless woman won't run so far the black skirt can't cover her, and we all weep when the Horse dies before it rises again.

This was a Horse of a kind I hadn't seen before, and it scared me rigid, with the torchlight flaring on its great bony head. They'd taken a real horse's skull, and if I was you I wouldn't ask how that creature met its end. They'd buried it deep, till the worms had picked the flesh from the white bone. Then they'd mounted it on a pole and put two great red eyes of glass in the holes of its skull. That god was nodding high over our heads to the beat of drums and the shriek of pipes.

Morgan bowed to her.

And still Margawse screamed inside that chamber.

Dawn came, and there were more fires as they burned the gorse and drove out the spirits from the dun with rattles and horns. You never heard such a din. Then the young ones brought in the maypole, fresh cut and strung with leaves and flowers. A weapon to open up any woman, that was! But still we waited.

There was the old battle. The King and Queen of Summer and all their people. Both of them young, virgins, they have to be, and dressed in the prettiest coloured clothes all hung with flowers. And then the Queen and King of Winter, all in dull greys and browns, trimmed with fur. They looked hefty fighters, both of them. Under those skirts She was a man, like me. It's the same every May Day. You know what it's like. The Summer fights the Winter, and the Summer wins. Their side have a feast, out of doors in the sunshine, with dancing round the maypole, and the Winter's beaten and those folk have to eat their feast shut up in a dark barn, till their turn comes round again. That's how it's always played. The fight's a real old set-to, mind you. It's expected. The lads enjoy themselves giving knock for knock as hard as they can, and the lasses can lay about them too. But we know who'll win. The Summer has to. If it didn't, if one year we didn't make the magic strong enough . . . It makes my mind go dark to think about what might follow.

Well, that year I thought the worst had happened. The Queen of Winter, in her crown of holly, went driving against the little King of Summer, and down he went, that boy in his white gown and his cloak of green and gold. He must have slipped on the sappy grass. There was a great roar as the Winter folk closed round him. And through it I heard three screams higher than all the rest. Morgan's beside me, crying out in terror. Margawse's, as though she'd been split in two. And Elaine's. I swear that hers was triumph.

A moment after, we forgot the battle outside, because the curtain rattled.

"It is done!" said Elaine's voice.

She was standing there holding a little bundle in her arms. She had such a smile on her face as she showed it to us, and suddenly I saw why they called her Elaine the Fair. She'd been a beautiful young woman not so long since.

I hadn't thought a newborn baby would be that small. It wasn't like either of its parents. Dark red skin, and puckered, with black eyelashes closed on its cheeks. Morgan stroked its face with her finger. She still looked pretty shaken.

"Look on him well and know him," Elaine said.

"Arthur's son," says Morgan, very low.

"Ours."

We didn't get long to look at him. Elaine carried him back inside the curtain to his mother.

Outside, it looked as if they'd sorted the battle out all right. The little King was on his feet again. The Summer folk were cheering him. I couldn't see a sign of the Winter people anywhere.

28

'I will take the baby," said Morgan.

They were all three agreed on that. Margawse had crafted their weapon; now Morgan would guard it. Lot might have his suspicions, but Arthur knew. There were some pretty powerful spells spoken over that boy before those three parted. I put my voice to the rest, though I didn't think it would do the poor little chap much good. Morgan had robbed me of my power.

All those long, jolting miles back to Lyvennet I held the wee fellow on my knee in the chariot. Morgan was never a motherly sort of woman, but she fed that baby from her own breast when he cried. It gave me a queer sort of shiver to see that: Arthur's son sucking from Morgan's teat. She let her hair fall forward like a curtain so we couldn't see her face. It mixed with the baby's black hair till you couldn't tell one from the other. He might have been her own bairn. But when he'd finished sucking her, she'd pass him to one of us.

Luned seemed afraid to touch him, so it was mostly me he fell to.

What's done can't be undone. That didn't stop Merlyn from trying, though.

Arthur was off east with his army that summer, winning more battles and growing a bigger duke all the time. He'd got all the common people cheering for him. They love a battle-hero. It's only when he needs their taxes they start to grumble. We knew he'd be back before the end of summer, and Merlyn with him. They'd have a different score to settle when they got the news from Din Eidyn. They couldn't leave it here. Merlyn had used his craft to get Uther's son. Now Margawse had used

163

hers to make Arthur's. He wouldn't let that rest. He couldn't have that boy grow up to spoil things for Arthur.

I thought Morgan meant to hide the child. Get a couple she trusted to bring him up as their own, till the lad was grown and could learn who his father was. I'd thought of a name or two that I knew for wise folk.

Well, I'd been a workman. Noble by skill, but I'd needed to go craftily. Smile and nod at the gentry, and do what you have to behind their back. That was how I was used to thinking.

I should have known Morgan wasn't like that. She's highborn. Wasn't she the daughter of Gorlois, who went to his death and would have taken his wife with him if he'd had his way, sooner than give Uther Pendragon what he wanted? Our black queen walked the ramparts, nursing that boy in her arms, and looking south almost as if she was willing his father to come.

He made for Din Eidyn first, and I bet Margawse laughed in his face. When we heard he was hunting the child in Lothian, Morgan made her plans. She knew we'd be next. She was ready when he came.

Arthur rode up the hill into Lyvennet with Merlyn beside him and a troop of his warriors behind. They hadn't come for a feast this time. They looked grim. We weren't sure then how much his men had been told about what was up. He'd try to keep the worst secret. I saw the way they fingered their weapons and the shifty air they had as they looked over their shoulders. They weren't sure they'd get much help from honest steel. I reckoned he'd sold them a story about witchcraft. They didn't know how to fight it.

Urien greeted Arthur a sight more stiffly this time and had the grooms look to the horses. He must have half-guessed what was going to happen. He'd been with Arthur in battle. Morgan hadn't. She couldn't have carried through with it if she'd known, could she?

Well, Arthur hadn't taken two steps towards the hall before he heard the noise. It was worse than pig-sticking time. I don't wonder the lad looked startled. He didn't know what it meant, straight off. But Merlyn did. I watched that enchanter's face change. If he'd looked sour before, he was furious now. First Margawse had cheated them, and now Morgan. He stormed into the hall, even if he did push Arthur in front of him for form's sake. He knew what they'd find.

Morgan was facing him on the dais before the high table. She was as white as death, but she had her loveliest smile ready for Arthur. She had stood her women all around the hall. And in the straw in the middle, all swaddled up and yelling and trying to kick, there were babies. Scores of them. May-born, all of them, only a few weeks old. She'd gathered every baby in her land the same age as Arthur's son. Highborn, lowborn, crafts-women's bairns or slaves. Well, May Day babies are supposed to be lucky, aren't they? Their mothers expected to take those children home richer than they went. There were more than a few mites had been brought in who looked newer than they should have been. Morgan had seen them all washed and fed and wrapped in clean linen with the same rich shawl around them, so you couldn't tell one from another.

I sometimes wonder what would have happened if she'd won. Would all those babies have got back to their right mothers? There could have been some queer crossings made that day. Slaves for nobles. Baptised Christians for first-vowed pagans. It's hard to tell them apart when they're that small.

His boy was there with all the rest. Morgan's not a cheat. She had her chin mighty high in the air as she smiled at Arthur.

He didn't bother with polite greetings. "Get these women out!"

She looked a bit dangerous then, but she didn't stop smiling.

"The women are my witnesses."

Arthur fairly leaped up on to the dais. I moved in quick, but then I stopped. It was my job to protect her, but I was miles out of my depth here. He got her by the arm. He couldn't bawl at her, though you could see he felt like it. He couldn't tell the whole world what was wrong. She'd got that weapon over him.

I saw Urien come in at the back, with Cei and Bedwyr.

But Arthur had a weapon of his own. He leaned over Morgan. He had his arm round her waist now. He was kissing her mouth.

"Give me my son!" he murmured, so that those others couldn't hear him.

The roses came in her cheeks and her eyes flashed a bit greener.

"It is your sister Margawse who gave you a child, not I!" she whispered.

He drew her closer then and his fingers were stroking the hair on the back of her neck.

"Morgan, Morgan! Why do you hold yourself so stiff? *Which is he?*'

She couldn't speak. He smiled at her very lovingly with his blue eyes, like a little boy that's used to getting what he wants.

"Come on, now. Let us be friends. Where is the harm? Would you keep the son from his father?"

"Your child is safe with me." She was looking him straight in the eye, though she could hardly stand.

Arthur turned to Merlyn for help. I think he hoped the old magician could scry the boy out, like a dowser testing till the hazel-stick jumps. Well, who's to say? Perhaps if he'd kept his head, he could have done. But he couldn't hold still. He strode up and down the hall while Arthur waited. He was hopping over babies; peering into their faces till they screamed, and mad as hell because Morgan was mocking them. There was such a racket from the bairns crying, and the smell they were making in the straw, you couldn't think. I never thought such scraps of flesh could have made such a din. All mouth they seemed. My Mair was such a sweet peaceful baby. We only ever had the one.

Merlyn got back from stamping all round the hall.

"Have you found him?" shouted Arthur.

"How can I tell? All babies look the same to me."

They say Merlyn was married once, before he went wild in the woods. I couldn't imagine it.

Arthur and Morgan were still locked together and murmuring now like a couple of wasps.

"I am asking you to hand my son to me."

"You could not recognise your sister. Now it seems you do not know your own child."

"Bitch!" cried Arthur. And he struck her across the face.

Merlyn snapped his fingers. Before we knew where we were, there was a hall full of armed men. Arthur drew his sword. Morgan gasped and some of the women screamed. Well, Urien yelled and his guards came charging in after Arthur's. They took one look at the Pendragon with Caliburn in his hand, and Morgan with his mark on her cheek, and the blood started to run. It's a funny thing. Folk here are afraid of Morgan, but they love her too in a queer sort of way. She's healed many, when no one else could. They haven't suffered by her as I have. But there weren't enough of them. Arthur's warriors had Urien's men back against the wall in no time. This was work the lads understood. Their teeth were flashing as bright as their blades now. But they weren't expecting what came next.

"Pick up those babies," Merlyn ordered them.

That shook them. A lot of them were too young to be family men. But some of them were. And the rest had little brothers, sisters. They looked to Arthur for a lead. He nodded his head.

Cei moved first. He was always a hard man.

"Do not, for shame!" Urien cried out. Arthur was his hero, but Morgan was his lady. He didn't want to bloody his sword in this quarrel. You could see that.

"Urien, for your honour. You swore loyalty to me!" said Arthur.

"You pledged your love to me," Morgan came back at him.

Urien looked from one to the other. King of Rheged he might be, but in those days he was still a young warrior, who'd not long proved himself in front of his hero. He was in love with Arthur, like the rest of us, or with his dream of him. Or maybe he feared what would happen to the children.

"Give Arthur what he wants," he ordered his wife.

"I will not," she told him. "My father denied Uther Pendragon. So I defy his son."

"What have our fathers to do with this? Take up the children," Arthur told his men. "Do what Merlyn says."

I think every woman in the hall shrieked then, except Morgan. She went white to the lips but she stood her ground. She must have thought he was trying her, to see how soon she'd break. She couldn't have known he meant to kill all those little babies and still kept silent, could she? Those two gazed so hard at each other it was like that first time in the yard. You'd have thought there was nobody in the hall but them, for all the howling. There wasn't either of them would give in to the other.

"Carry them outside and put them in a wagon," Arthur said.

He never turned to watch them do it. He only stared at Morgan. And she at him.

Cei took the first one in his arms, and then the rest bent to it. When she saw what was happening, Morgan let out one awful wail, but that was all. Arthur turned his back on her and jumped down off the dais.

The other women shrilled louder and started to fling themselves on the swords. It would have made your stomach turn over to hear them. Some of those babies had been born here in our castle. Half of Arthur's warriors kept them penned in behind a fence of blades. I think they were glad enough to keep their backs turned on what their mates were doing. Merlyn was in charge now. I don't think any of the rest of us believed Arthur would go through with it, not on either side. I knew when they got to Arthur's boy. Morgan's face didn't move a muscle. She wouldn't give him away.

They started to carry the babies out. Morgan called after him then, very hoarse and broken.

"Do not do this, Arthur. For your soul's sake."

A queer thing, that, for a pagan like her to say.

He didn't turn. He just strode out following Merlyn into the daylight. She came to herself then and screamed such curses after him as should have shrivelled the flesh on his bones. Urien's men couldn't look her in the eye.

Morgan paid those parents the honour-price in gold afterwards. It couldn't stop the keening that day, though. After she'd turned the women out of the hall it seemed mighty quiet, like a death-chamber.

"Follow him," Morgan ordered me. It was hardly more than a whisper she could get out.

I got a mule and went after them. I had a long ride. Merlyn didn't trust her, even then. They went through Rheged and into Gwendoleu's land, all the way to the Solway, searching out every cottage to see if there were more May babies yet. They piled them all in their wagon, with the mothers howling and weeping after them. They didn't butcher the children there and then. They hadn't got the stomach for it and they wouldn't dishonour good steel. I heard later that Arthur had spun them a yarn about a nightmare he'd had. At a May Day feast his hall took fire and a beam fell out of the roof and pinned him by the legs. It was threatening to burn him to death. He'd woken up screaming and sweating. That crafty Merlyn joined in then and told them what it meant. Or as much of it as he thought fit for them to know. That beam was an enemy born on May Day to bring Arthur to ruin. If they wanted to keep their hope of glory they had to find it and tear it out before the fire took hold.

Gwendoleu didn't try and stop them either. It wasn't love for Arthur with him. I think he'd lived close enough to those three sisters to guess pretty near the truth. Arthur was one Pendragon too many for him already. Another son to that line wouldn't suit him.

They got to the Solway Firth with a wagon full of babies. They seized a boat. I couldn't have stopped them. One humpbacked woman against Merlyn and a war-troop. Even if I'd had my old power, what spells could I have done, if Morgan's own curses hadn't been enough to halt them? I just had to watch.

They were a deal of time loading those poor little bairns into the ship. They took trouble over it. They didn't just throw them in, any old how. They were too soft-hearted for that. They laid them out in rows and settled them as comfortably as they could, and never mind if it was their last voyage. Near on a hundred of them there were, and quieter now. The little mites had worn themselves out with crying. His men pushed the boat down the mud to the water's edge. Merlyn tapped Arthur's shoulder. He'd got the child. He had to finish it. It was Arthur's hand gave the last push and sent it spinning a bit out into the current.

She's a quiet river, the Esk. She doesn't fret and foam. There was a sort of silver light over the water-meadows. A flock of seagulls started to circle over the boat. Their screams were so loud we couldn't hear any more crying. The boat dwindled down the tideway. I saw the first gull dive and I looked away.

Bedwyr laughed then, just a little light sound. And that broke the charm. All those young men began shouting and joking and slapping each other on the back as if they'd won a famous victory. They'd done the job and they hadn't had to get blood on their swords to shame them. Only Arthur couldn't raise a smile, and Merlyn was still muttering and making signs with his hands. He hadn't lost his power yet, as I had mine. But it was wasted effort in the end. He should have known. Those three sisters had forged their weapon to bring Arthur down. He couldn't alter it. His spells would turn back on him.

I had to go home and tell Morgan. She stared at me with big eyes, like a little girl whose puppy has been taken by wolves.

"Arthur . . . has killed . . . them . . . *all?*"

I nodded.

She gave a great yell of grief and tore her dress and pulled at her hair and clawed her face. And all her women did the same. All over the north there were mothers howling, in Margawse's land, and in Elaine's. He didn't stop at Rheged. None of the kings dared say no to him. He'd stirred up too hot a war with the Saxons. They couldn't break with Arthur now till it was won.

Well, if the women cursed Arthur they cursed Merlyn more. Nobles, slaves, Christians, wise. Men damned him behind his back too. Young men that had lost their firstborn sons. Grandfathers. Uncles. Merlyn was done for from that day. It didn't need Nimue to finish him off. In time they could forgive their hero Arthur, as long as he went on winning battles, anyrate. It was easier to blame Merlyn. This wasn't warrior's work, it had the mark of magic on it, you could hear them telling each other.

Only Morgan went to the stone circle. She threw herself down on the ground and wept her heart out and beat the stones.

"I hate Arthur! I hate him!"

Then she knelt up and stared at Luned and me, very still.

"Was it because of me? Did I do this? Morgan the Healer! Do I destroy everyone I touch?"

Well, what could the pair of us say to her?

29

Well, if the Church had been stiff with Arthur before, they really came down on him for that. They called a great synod. Their bishops and abbots, some of them women too, came from all over the land. Those Christian folk think themselves somebody because they can hark back to cities with big names like Rome and Constantinople and Jerusalem. They think it's their empire still. They rate their word above a king's.

Arthur listened to them, though. He had a taste for Rome. He fancied the legions and the emperor's diadem. He followed their religion too.

Those long-faced bishops heaped a penance on him. Said those children had angels in Heaven weeping for them. He walked barefoot from Bath to their oldest church in Glastonbury. He kept vigil and fasted a day and a night there. He gave away every last scrap of gold and jewels he had left to pay the honour-price of those children. Their parents got rich, after all. They had it from both sides. They say he paid for his own son's blood with horses. I wasn't there to see Margawse's face when she got her quittance.

But when all's said and done, I don't reckon Arthur was truly sorry for what he did. He'd had to get rid of the boy, hadn't he? If he was made to do penance to wipe his slate clean, he'd pay the price. He'd got what he wanted. It's a bitter war these two sides are fighting, brother and sisters. We haven't seen the last of it, by a long way.

From the time Arthur took the baby, things changed. It had seemed like a dance before, with those sisters and Arthur, bowing and curtseying as they stepped their reel round him. The pipes were playing a lament now.

But Morgan had other tunes in mind. She called me to join her circle. I tell you, I was as scared then as the first time I'd been summoned as a green lad. I couldn't feel any power still. I knew the danger I might be putting myself in. But Morgan had named me, and I had to go.

I joined my hands with the rest. I sang the words. I moved my body with the ring. I couldn't think why she wanted me. I couldn't give her what she needed unless she gave me back my power.

When Arthur had finished his fast, the church decided he'd settled the score. Dubric, top bishop of the land, laid his hands on his head and forgave him. Well, those Christians need Arthur as much as he needs them, don't they? Their priests are flesh and blood, like their congregations. They bleed the same as their Hung-Up Man when the heathen turn nasty. Arthur's the only one they can look to to save them.

And so he did. It was like summertime after that. The whole country was coming to life and flowering again. We had hope at last. We thought we'd found a leader who could throw out the Saxons. Everywhere I went following Urien and Morgan it was the same story. Men with a shine in their eyes, quicker to get a leg across a horse than a woman these days. Little kings forgetting to quarrel with their neighbours because they'd bigger fish to fry now. Brothers, we felt like, wherever we rode. Brothers . . .! I couldn't go. I couldn't fettle one horse for Arthur's cavalry. Morgan and her sisters were on the losing side. I'd sunk with them.

Merlyn never did penance. Even the bishops didn't have the nerve to order that. It told against him, though. Folk forgave Arthur afterwards, with his blue eyes and his golden curls and his magic sword to wave over his head. He and his brave lads galloped the land from end to end. They stirred up blood that had run cold and slow too long. And those that never saw him in the flesh fell in love with him as hard as those that had. They had their dream of him. The young Pendragon, that had only seen sixteen summers, who had hammered both Saxons and Picts.

It left Merlyn stranded, though. It was him folk put the blame on for the children.

But if there's one thing you can guarantee will soften the coldest heart, it's a royal wedding. The whole world loves a lover. That was a stroke of genius on Merlyn's part to turn the tide for Arthur.

There was a fort down in Cornwall, Celliwig, that Arthur was mighty fond of. He still had his army headquarters in the City of the Legions. And he had plenty of business in the north, sweetening men like Gwendoleu and Lot to make sure they kept off the Picts. But it was down in Dumnonia he found her, fostered at Duke Cador the Keen's court: Gwenhyvar. When it came to women, that family always seemed to turn to the south-west. The orchards of Dumnonia grow a rare apple.

It worked, that plan of theirs, Arthur's and Merlyn's. They were canny generals, both of them. As soon as they announced the wedding, the Council of Britain cried Arthur High King. There'd be a double coronation on their marriage day, for him and her. It was little Gwenhyvar's blood that settled it. That was a famous line of kings she brought with her from the west. Better than any wedding gift. They needed that if Arthur's sons should ever want to be kings. His own birth was still a bit too cloudy for some folk. There was only Merlyn's word for it, and Ygerne's. And the Church wasn't too happy about either of them. But you couldn't argue with Gwenhyvar's history. She could trace kings back to Roman times, and further.

Morgan, Margawse, Elaine, they all got a summons to his wedding. I didn't think they'd go, not after what he'd done. Morgan looked black when she got the news. She rode out hunting that day and so reckless, by all accounts, it's a wonder she didn't kill herself. Her star was waning fast now. Her twins were growing. She wasn't a soft-faced girl, like Gwenhyvar. She'd lost Arthur's son that she'd nursed at her own breast. There'd been wreckage washed up from that ship. A few little scraps of flesh and bone the gulls had left. Arthur was going to he High King.

But I was wrong. Morgan couldn't have wanted to dance at his wedding, but she did. And where she went I had to follow. I stood behind her in the church at the City of the Legions, and I'd even become enough of an old biddy to feel pleased that I'd got a new blue gown to wear, and a fresh white veil for my head. But then I heard the trumpets sounding for the bride's procession, and I looked round and saw the nobles standing on the church steps – Arthur, the Bishop Dubric, and other kings and priests round them – and I couldn't stop myself thinking of another wedding procession years ago. Me, standing in a windy street, dressed like a man, to get my first sight of Morgan as a bride. And then Merlyn coming.

This was another city and a different queen. I couldn't get a sight of her with the noblemen crowding round to lift her down from her chariot. Then the trumpets rang out again and the choir burst into singing and all the deacons and presbyters and bishops in their finest cloaks came swinging up the nave in a cloud of incense. Arthur was leading his bride, and every head was turned round to stare. I still remember the shock I had when I first clapped eyes on Gwenhyvar. She was lovely enough. It wasn't that. She didn't have power.

I heard a little catch of breath in front of me, so I knew that Morgan had seen it too. We looked at each other, Morgan, Luned, me. And then across at Margawse and Elaine. There was the same thought in all our faces. I hadn't guessed till then how strong we might still be, those three sisters with their wise women gathered round them, yes, and even me, now she'd let me in. I couldn't think why Merlyn had let Arthur pick this little lass for his queen, blood-line or not. He must have been too sure that we were beaten.

She was . . . pretty. Yes, that's the word for Gwenhyvar. Pretty as any girl I've ever seen, I'll grant her that. All dolled up in sky-blue and stiff cloth-of-gold and hung thick with jewels. I called to mind how Morgan had looked in her plain white dress with fresh flowers on her head, and her hair falling like a raven's wing round her white neck. She'd been beautiful that day; she still was. And flaming red Margawse. There was fire in those sisters, mountains, oceans, ages of beauty. Gwenhyvar's might last for a few days. She was smiling round at us all as if this was the best day of her life. I even felt a bit sorry for her. She'd got what she wanted. A king that would go down in legend. A lusty lover. Wealth for the taking, if he could go on winning battles. And everybody calling her the most beautiful woman in the land, because she was Arthur's queen now. He led her past Gorlois's three daughters. And there wasn't a flicker of fear in her eyes when she smiled at them. Nobody had told her. She didn't know what she was walking into.

I looked round when they'd passed, and got a start that made me wonder if I was seeing things. Merlyn, dressed up like a lord, slipping in at the back of the congregation, and Nimue flashing her silk and coral beside him. That took the cockiness out of me, and I went a bit cold. It was the first time I'd set eyes on the Lady since she drove me out from her lake. And Emrys Merlyn? In a Christian church?

30

It was Arthur's sisters prepared his marriage bed. They were the highest ladies in the land now. It's a wonder Merlyn didn't think of that. I know what kind of charms they laid between the sheets. I helped them do it. It would be a marvel if that coupling ever bore fruit. After it was ready, Margawse and Elaine and all their ladies went off to join the feast. Morgan wasn't in any hurry. She stood there stroking the place where Arthur was going to lie. It looked as if she was willing something more than we'd done yet. Then she gripped the end of the bed. I could see she was having a struggle with herself over something. Well, in the end she turned on her heel and followed after the rest.

That was a feast and a half! You'll never see a handsomer young couple. Gwenhyvar with that long silver-fair hair, cool as a waterfall, and her cheeks bright with wine and as soft as rose-petals. Hardly old enough to be wedded. And him! He had everything falling in his lap now. When he looked at Gwenhyvar he fairly shone like the sun. He'd been lucky in war, and now it looked as if he'd be lucky in bed too, and both of them with golden crowns on their heads. Everybody was feasting and dancing, and there were so many fresh young lasses about that the men were trying not to make drunken pigs of themselves too early. Even Bishop Dubric was laughing with Cei. It seemed like old wounds were healing at last.

Old wounds were healing. All of a sudden a lump of meat jumped up my throat so I was almost sick with excitement. Back there in Gwenhyvar's bedchamber, when my hands were stroking her sheets, and Arthur's, while my voice was chanting the charm with all the others, I had felt it. Yes, *felt* it! The burning in my hands. Magic flowing down my veins. No, not flowing. I was running ahead too fast. But trickling, anyway. Yes, I could say that. Real power. Nothing like what I'd been used to before. Oh, no. But still power. Like the first green shoot of spring that you see poking up through the snow. It was coming back to me.

It wasn't just the beer putting a flush on my face then and making my eyes sparkle. Years fell off me. And better than that. I could feel myself sitting up straighter, squaring my shoulders, lifting my head more like a man. I looked up the long hall, through the smoke of the fire and the steam of the dishes, and I saw Morgan's face looking at me, like the moon through cloud, with her hair black as night round it. Only it wasn't cold and distant. It swam closer as I stared. And it was a warm woman's face, not a proud queen's. Her mouth curved in a smile then and her eyes shone green, sweet as they'd never been for me before. It was only a moment across that crowded hall, but Morgan smiled at me as though I was a man again.

It was gone almost before I'd seen it. She turned to call out some pretty compliment to Arthur and lift her cup. And somebody reached across my face to grab a hunk of bread.

I sat drunk, or bewitched, trying to take in what had happened. My power was coming back. Morgan had smiled at me.

I could have warned Arthur that night. I could have told Merlyn what those queens were doing. I kept quiet. For the sake of the smile in Morgan's eyes. For the first tingle of power in my blood. Not even for the promise, just the hope, that there might be something more to come.

There was one who didn't need warning, though. When we got back to Gwenhyvar's room, Nimue was there before us, and from the look she gave us I don't doubt she'd been busy undoing a bit of what we'd done.

There was the usual lot of laughing and bawdy jokes when the ladies seized Gwenhyvar and carried her off to her bridal chamber, and we left a lot more horseplay behind us as Arthur made out he was trying to follow her. His mates held him back and they were acting out a fair old set-to. He'd have to wait till he was sent for. I'd dearly have loved to have stayed in that hall with the men and joined in the fun. Down a few more beakers with the rest of them before the queens sent word his bride was ready for him. I hadn't felt so much like a man for years. But it was too soon for that. I still had the disguise of a woman, though I'd hotter blood underneath tonight. I'd have to stick with that side a bit longer.

Only when I saw that smile on Nimue's face I nearly changed my mind. If I could have left the lot of them and run back to my blacksmith's forge then it would have been enough for me. Those women could keep the magic. I'd drop it all. Horns, Smith. Just to be like any common man. But I'd learned my lesson too late. I wonder whether, if back at the beginning I'd been willing to hand over some of my power to her, Morgan might have let me keep what I had. Well, that was long past. I was in with them too deep now.

It was funny. I'd seen so many women in their nightclothes by then it didn't stir me like it might have done seeing Gwenhyvar lying on fine linen sheets, with that white-gold hair brushed out around her and a loose thin gown embroidered with gold that it wouldn't take a man like Arthur a moment to pull off. There were little lamps, but not too close and not too many, and armfuls of flowers and bundles of corn everywhere you looked, so the air was sweet with the scent of them. Only you wouldn't have slept easily if you'd looked too closely at some of them. She was very young, that little lass. Years younger than Morgan had been on her own wedding night. Probably more of a child than Morgan of Cornwall ever was, if half what Luned told me about her is true. Very pleased with herself, Gwenhyvar looked, lying there in that big bed with all of us fussing round her to make her beautiful. Still, a bit frightened too. And she had reason to be, more than she knew of. It was a dark family she was marrying into. Well, she came from Dumnonia. She should have listened to the bards.

They sent us to fetch him. It was my hands that grabbed Arthur's sleeve and helped to haul him away from the wine-cups. You can be sure he came willingly. He wasn't shy. Arthur was no virgin, as we well knew. Cei and Bedwyr were struggling to keep close, but there was such a press of ladies in the corridor they got separated from him. This was women's business.

But Arthur had to stop when he got to the bedchamber door. All three of his sisters were standing there, barring his way. Morgan, Margawse, Elaine. Flashing their smiles and taunting him, they were, even Elaine. Nimue was there with them too, and some of her maidens. Gwenhyvar hadn't brought enough of her own people with her to put up a struggle. It was his own sisters he'd have to fight his way past to get at her. He had to do it right.

Well, there was a fair old tussle, with him laughing and wrestling the women at the same time and all of us joining in and pretending to haul him back. Some of Arthur's lads came up and took us from behind. It was sweeter armfuls than me they went for. You should have heard the squealing.

Then, all of a sudden, it was over and Arthur was inside the door. He slammed it behind him, and the women hammered on it, but it didn't open, of course. It all went quiet then, and we looked at each other and put our dresses straight. The sisters stopped laughing.

I looked back down the corridor. Merlyn was standing by the corner rubbing his hands. He caught my eye over the rest and he took a step nearer, as though I was one of his own people. I stared him full in the face. I wasn't laughing either now. Merlyn couldn't give me back anything I wanted. It was Morgan who'd broken me. She was the one who would have to make me whole. Merlyn was never a healer.

When I looked back, Nimue was watching both of us.

The men went back then to join the singing in the hall, all except Cei and Bedwyr. Feast or not, those two were wearing swords. But we women stayed and listened. Morgan was leaning against the door as if she was guarding it, only she had her eyes closed. We didn't have long to wait. There was just a little cry, and then a man's laugh. Next thing, there was Arthur in the doorway waving a bloodied sheet on the end of Caliburn. Bedwyr snatched it off him and tore back to the hall with it and we could hear all the men cheering. I looked round for Morgan. She wasn't grinning like the rest. She was pressed against the door where Arthur had been. It was shut fast again now. She was shaking. And Merlyn was back at the end of the corridor. He smiled at her then, a very powerful smile, as if he'd done something very clever.

Well, after that, there was nothing left for the rest of us to do but to go back and join the feast.

I've never seen Morgan drink so much, or dance so wildly. She had the men shouting and clapping her. I caught Margawse looking at Elaine as if the two of them couldn't believe what they were seeing.

I couldn't either. Well, you know what it's like when a feast's nearly over, and the bards have run out of songs and we've all drunk more than we should have done. There's plenty of corners in the straw that'll take two, and it was a warm night for those that would rather be private outside. It was a wedding feast, after all.

That's when it hits me hardest.

Still, it shook me more than anything else that had happened that night when I saw Morgan get up from the wine-cups and pull Accolon by the hand. That lank-haired youth from Arthur's own warband. She could hardly stagger to the door, but he put his hand round her waist and held her steady. Before they disappeared into the night, she had both her arms round his neck. That scared me properly. I looked round for Luned, but she'd gone off to see to Morgan's children. There was only me. I was her guard-dog. That's what she'd collared me for. As close to her in everything she did as a breastplate. I had to follow.

I turned round at the door. Urien had half-risen off the bench. He wasn't as drunk as some of them. I thought he was starting to come after us. But he just sank back down on his seat and put his head in his hands.

When I got outside I had an awful moment. I feared I'd lost them in the dark. But they couldn't walk straight, either of them. And they weren't troubling to keep quiet. Morgan was singing. She's not one to hide what she's doing under a cloak. They took the path down to the river. There's willow trees there, and long, soft grass.

31

I watched them do it. And I saw her safe back to bed afterwards. I thought she'd sleep then. But every time I opened my eyes I saw by starlight her long white hands clenched round a knot of the sheet.

I don't know when it was I woke, but it felt like the very deadest part of night, everything so quiet I thought it had snowed, though it was summertime. I don't wonder those old Romans went to so much trouble to heat their palaces in winter. There's something unnatural to me about lying in a house of stone, all straight-sided with every corner squared off. No curves to it. No crumbly clay or ragged ends of thatch. They've used the dead bones of the earth, not the living flesh of her. I felt a chill come over me as I sat up.

Then I saw what it was had roused me. Morgan's little daughter, Morfudd. She was tugging at her mother's hand. I went colder still when I thought that it might have been someone worse beside the bed. I was supposed to be the queen's watchdog.

Morfudd was whispering, "Mam, come on! Come and see."

I saw Morgan stand up, and she might have been sleepwalking. She had that slow but driven look about her. Well, of course, I feared worse than that, that it was her spirit I was watching, and I might find her body still lying in her bed. But the sheets were empty behind her, and hardly rumpled. She'd lain very still, no matter what she felt.

Morfudd dragged her over to Elaine's bed. I heard Morgan draw in her breath sharp, and I saw why. Then she was making for the door, quicker now. I had to follow where she led. She picked her way through the room outside. It was full of sleeping women and children. Luned was lying there, beside little Owain. We had to step over them both. Morgan put her finger to her lips and signed to Morfudd she'd got to stay behind. She didn't look back at me, but I'll bet she knew I was there.

The torches had burned out in the corridor, and there wasn't so much starlight. She seemed to know which way to go. There was a long porchway opening on a courtyard, then a dark passage. It led straight back to Gwenhyvar's bedchamber, and Arthur's. She had no weapon in her hand. I remember noticing that.

Suddenly she stopped short and pressed herself into an alcove, deep in the shadow. I did the same, though I'd wrapped myself in a darker robe than hers. Someone was coming away from Arthur's bedroom. There was a last torch still guttering down there. I could just about make the guards out. Some guards! Cei and Bedwyr, slumped asleep against the wall. A little heap of Gwenhyvar's women in the antechamber, with their arms flung across each other. Even Arthur's dog was sprawled out and snoring. And one woman, stepping slowly past them all towards us. Heavy but silent. No tiptoeing maiden, this one. No slender lady. Big, like a mountain. With spreading hips and breasts hanging over her waist. But moving quiet and dainty as a cat. Elaine, for sure. She had her cloak wrapped close about her and she was clutching something in the folds of it to her breasts.

She turned before she reached us, round the porch to the other side of the yard. She'd vanished like a huge moth into the dark.

Morgan stood still so long then, I began to fear she'd turned to stone, like another Roman statue. But then she moved on, and she was hurrying more than before, and not so certain either. Nobody stirred in the anteroom, not even if we touched them. I was mighty scared stepping past Cei and seeing the naked weapon in his hand. At the bedroom door Morgan hesitated a long while. I think she had to force herself to raise the latch and swing it open.

Some of the lamps were still burning softly here. The air was full of the sweet scent of flowers. Arthur and Gwenhyvar had their faces turned to each other, his arm thrown over her breasts and a big grin on his face. They were fast asleep. Close by his other hand was a naked sword, with the scabbard dropped on the skin rug below it.

When Morgan saw that, she gave a start. She stepped up to the bed and she raised that heavy sword as if she couldn't help herself. I didn't know what she meant to do, or how I could stop her. She held it lifted in both hands over the couple. Then she ran her finger along the blade, as if she was testing it. I've done the same thing myself with a weapon hundreds of times. She studied the hilt, and felt the jewels on the guard, and the knots and coils of it. I'd seen Caliburn close up once before, in Nimue's house. I knew it was magic workmanship. But Morgan didn't seem satisfied, somehow. She had it poised in both hands again, as though she was weighing it. She must have felt me watching. There wasn't a flicker of surprise in her face when she turned round and handed me the sword.

I almost dropped it. Caliburn! Arthur's sword, that he'd got his manhood from Nimue with and all his victories since. A man's weapon, that Nimue wouldn't let me touch. But when Morgan offers you something, you don't refuse. I took it from her, and the years fell off me. I was a smith again, and I had the armourer's craft. That sword was heavy, and fine workmanship. A good edge to the blade. The right weight and balance. Handsomely jewelled. But . . . that was all. The old true power I'd felt in my blood that evening didn't quicken to it. This wasn't magic. It couldn't be Caliburn. The same look, but not the same feel. Morgan sighed, just a little gasp of sound. She knew it already.

"I have come too late. She was here before me."

"What does it mean?" I whispered.

"Hurt."

She took the false sword back from me. She stood holding it over the marriage bed where Arthur was lying with Gwenhyvar in his arms.

Arthur stirred a bit and rubbed his cheek against Gwenhyvar. I saw that sword shiver in Morgan's hands.

Only, all of a sudden, there was a loud wail.

"Mammy! No! No! Don't do it!"

It sounded shocking through that palace where everybody was sleeping.

Well, I whipped round as fast as if I'd been stung by a hornet, and there was Morgan's little son, Owain, behind us with his big round eyes and not a stitch on him. Luned came running in after him. When she saw what was going on she looked terrified.

Well, Owain's cry was just like cockcrow, or a hunting-horn. It shattered the spell those sisters had put on everybody. Ladies, sentries, Arthur, Gwenhyvar – they were all awake and shouting or swearing, and there was Morgan with that great sword in her hands standing by Arthur's bed and staring down at Owain.

Then she flung it away from her. It would have hit Gwenhyvar if Arthur hadn't caught it. I'd snatched up Owain and tried to cover his mouth, but it was far too late for that. There were weapons out on either side of the door. All that saved us then was the clutter of women rushing this way and that and trying to make out what was happening.

Arthur was kicking off the sheets. Morgan had started for the door. She'd got nothing to protect her. She snatched up the scabbard from the rug and held it out in front of her and shouted one word. The mob in the doorway parted like a cleft stick. We were out of the anteroom and then racing across the courtyard into the dark. There was chaos all round us. Torches flaring up. Men yelling. Women calling out to know what was wrong. And nobody sure what had started it. Except Arthur. We heard him shout, "Seize Morgan! Merlyn was right! She would have killed me with my own sword on my wedding night!"

We met Urien running to meet us. He hadn't heard Arthur rightly. Not then. I threw Owain to him. This was no night for children. We'd lost one boy already.

There was still one hope. Morgan's own people will die for her. One smile can make them hers for life, never mind the healing. I should know. They had horses ready almost before she gave the order. We leaped astride. There must have been twenty of us, men and women. I don't know how many of the guards got killed before the gates were opened and we were galloping for dear life and the north.

They pressed us hard. Arthur's men were battle-hardened and their horses were trained for speed and strength. They ran us down in an old wet wood, where the trees had fallen hundreds of years since and others had sprung up out of the carcasses, and even those were hung with long beards of moss. It was coming on morning, and a mist was creeping up out of the bogs and pools between the boulders. Morgan made us dismount. We turned the horses loose and drove them away. Some of the beasts tried to follow us but they soon backed off in terror when they saw where she was leading us. We went right down into the black bog. Morgan spoke a great charm over us. It turned us to stone. We stood still and lifeless, with our hooded heads rising up out of the mud like rocks. There was black water sucking all round us. Horrible serpents slithering over our legs, but we couldn't move. The mist kept shifting to and fro so we couldn't see anything clear. Then Arthur's troop came splashing and shouting down to the edge of the water. They'd followed our tracks this far. But their horses whinnied in fright once their hooves started to sink.

"How wide is this mere? What lies on the other side?" I heard Cei calling to Urien.

Yes. He was with them. Even her husband was hunting her now. None of them knew how to follow her. Our horses were scattered all over the wood. We stayed in the water, like kelpies, listening.

They picked out some hoofmarks further up and moved on, searching. When their noise had died we heard a bittern booming. A pair of grey herons landed on the water. Then the mist started fraying. I thought we were done for then. I was sure he would have left a sentry behind, but we were alone.

We caught a few of the horses. The rest of our party we left to follow us on foot. It was a long journey. But not as long by hundreds of miles as the distance that was fixed now between Morgan and Arthur.

We daren't stop, even in Rheged. All the way into Lothian Morgan carried Arthur's scabbard held close against her.

32

Morgan fled to Din Eidyn. Margawse and Elaine joined her there. It was women's business now. Their men didn't know the half of what had been done.

We didn't meet in the palace. What we had now was too secret for that. There was a cave in the hillside, with a spring running outside it and hazel trees hanging over the mouth. Inside there was a great slab of rock cut for a table. It had been well used. Margawse lit a fire on it.

There were nine of us.

Elaine laid Caliburn down on the stone. We didn't need telling this was the real one. I'd sometimes wondered if Arthur did take it into battle, or if it was just for show. I'd thought maybe just owning it would be enough to get him victory. I was wrong. There was enough of that cold north light to see the stains where the blood had been cleaned off. There were nicks on its edge. That sword had seen hard service. He'd used it.

Elaine said, "Our brother has won his last victory."

Morgan had her head bowed, staring at Arthur's weapon. Then she lifted her eyes slowly and looked hard at her sister.

"You would stop him here? With a line drawn across Britain? The north and west for the Cymry, the south and east to the Saxons?"

"Dumnonia is safe, and so are Rheged, Garlot, Lothian. The road to London is still ours. Why should we care what happens to the rest?"

"Britain must always be a woman divided? Her heart given to one king? Her womb to another?"

"Arthur is already too strong. Merlyn's foster-son! The Church has

185

crowned him with their power as well. And now he has Gwenhyvar's royal blood."

Morgan bowed her head again.

Margawse had kept pretty silent, for her, up till now.

"Well, Morgan? Elaine has brought Caliburn. The greatest talisman Arthur had. Where is your boasting now? What weapon will you raise against Arthur?"

"I have it already."

Morgan signed to me and I gave her the scabbard I had been holding all this time. Only, at the last moment I didn't want to let go of it. There was such a comfort coming off that blackened wood, even through the thickness of cloth that was wrapped round it. I didn't doubt Nimue had spoken the truth. I don't know where she'd got it from. Caliburn was a marvel, but this had an older look by far. As if the sword had been meant to serve the scabbard, and not the other way round.

Morgan didn't want to give it up either. I could see it cost her an effort to lay it by the sword.

Those other two queens sucked in their breath. Morgan hadn't told them.

Elaine smiled, a bit coolly. It had taken some of the shine off her deed. And Margawse raised her eyebrows.

"A strange prize for Morgan the Healer! Elaine has taken his power to wound. But you have robbed him of healing."

She knew that already. She'd wept when she came to next morning and realised what she was holding. She'd flown at me as if it was my fault. But she'd kept it with her, hadn't she?

All this time, Morgan's hand was still on the scabbard, as though she couldn't hand it over even yet. Then she opened her fingers and stepped back quick.

"Arthur is no longer a god. The barriers are down. He can be defeated and hurt like any other man." She was pretty vicious the way she turned on Margawse. "Well, sister? And what blow will you strike?"

She shouldn't have said that. Margawse flashed back at her.

"How dare you ask that? I showed my weapon before either of you. I opened my womb to Arthur. I bore his son, the baby he killed, who was my vengeance for our father. Elaine was right to strip away his power to wound. And I will never let you give him back his healing."

Well, that was a shock. I'd always seen Margawse laughing. The whole world was a joke to her, and men the biggest laugh. I hadn't thought till then she could be hurt.

That was a black day for Britain when Arthur took those children and pushed them down the Solway. It changed a lot. Though it didn't alter as much as he thought it had at the time. I sometimes wonder what would have happened if he'd handed those sisters the victory. Owned the boy for his son. Their child and his. But he had Caliburn then, and his crown to win. He wasn't going to let himself be defeated, was he? By a pack of women.

It was Elaine caught our eyes then. She was leaning forward over the table. Her hands were gripping it in pain and her breath was coming short like a woman in labour.

"No! Starboard! Starboard! The rock!"

We all looked at each other, scared. You can have lived all your life with the power, used it often enough yourself, and still it *is* power. You never get used to it. You wouldn't last long if you did. It can shake the strongest when it comes unasked and it's naked and screaming in the room with you. Elaine's voice rose into a high screech, like seagulls yelping. It had gone past words now. We heard a baby crying out in terror. It was gulping. Gasping for air. Then a little sob, and silence. None of us dared move. The queen's eyes were squeezed shut on her fat cheeks and her mouth slack and dribbling.

"Get a bowl," Margawse whispered to two of her women.

One of them fetched a basin of water from the spring. They didn't need to be told what else. Dried herbs from the back of the cave, crumbled to a powder and sprinkled over. The pot boiled quickly over the fire and more stuff was added. I recognised some of it. There was a scum that eddied and sank, and the steam coiled off it. I was breathing heavy fumes and beginning to feel a bit strange myself. Morgan pulled up a stool and lowered her sister to sit on it. Elaine's eyes opened, blue in the creases of fat, and she stared down into the pot. It was a long, long time she looked and said nothing.

Margawse couldn't hold herself in any longer. "What is it? Tell us! What can you scry?"

"A house by the tideway . . . A rat in a fishing-creel . . . A coracle."

We waited.

"A stone in a field, that the ravens light on. The bonfire lit for Midsummer Night. People dancing."

"Yes! Yes!"

"A baby boy at a woman's breast."

Her head sagged forward. Luned moved quick and took the bowl off the table. Elaine was snoring now. We let her rest. She'd done her part.

"I will find him," Morgan said quietly. "Rivers do not flow on for ever. I shall find that stone, that house. The sword was meant to go into its own scabbard."

She looked at Margawse when she said that, very sadly. It struck me then that those two are more alike than you'd think.

Only Margawse wasn't sad. She'd changed entirely. She seized hold of Caliburn. The jewels were back in her eyes and the gold in her hair. She was laughing again.

"You see? Did I not sheathe Arthur well? The boy's alive! We have him trapped!"

She would have grabbed the scabbard and joined them both together, but Morgan snatched it back.

"No! Not like that! Not by guile and treachery. It was meant to be done openly, freely, by his choice and hers. The sword married to the scabbard and the world made whole."

Margawse laughed at her bitterly then.

"You still hope that? Poor innocent little Morgan! Still galloping after the men and hoping they'll notice you. You have learned nothing, have you?"

"And you have much to unlearn."

They were like a pair of swordsmen with their guards locked in each other's, that can't get free. Then Morgan twisted round and signalled to Luned and me it was time to go.

Margawse looked a bit frightened. "Morgan! If you find my baby you won't tell the world straight away, will you? That he is my son by Arthur? Not yet. If Lot found out . . ."

We all knew her husband had shut his eyes for pride's sake these many years. It hadn't sweetened him. He might still kill her if she gave him the proof.

"I promise you, I shall guard Arthur's child as dearly as if I had mothered him."

I shan't tell you how those three hid that sword and scabbard. They set a fearsome watch over it.

When it was done, Morgan sent word to Urien she was coming

home. She was too proud to run away. All the same, we didn't know what to expect.

Arthur was waiting for her. He had men of war camped outside her walls. She only checked for a few moments when we rode clear of the forest and had our first sight of them.

"Lyvennet has a royal guest, and I not there to do him honour."

The colour was burning in her cheeks and she kicked her horse on. There was a queer sort of hush as she rode through their camp up to her own gate. The yard was full of warriors staring at her.

I wondered what would happen when she walked into the hall. Would Arthur order his men to seize her, in her own castle? Would her husband stand by and watch?

Arthur was by the fire, facing the door. From the look in his eyes, I fancy he wasn't too sure what to do, himself. If he'd seen one flicker of guilt on her face, he might have got up his nerve and given his men the order. But she wouldn't make it that easy for him. She'd grown up in a hard school. Ten years shut up in a nunnery, because she'd once stolen him away and might have drowned him, but didn't. What had she done worse now by holding a sword over his marriage bed and not letting it fall? She walked up that long hall towards him, with her hands held out in greeting, and smiling at him sweeter than ever she'd done when they were supposed to be friends.

"Welcome, brother! Morgan of Rheged is grieved that she was not here to offer you her cup a second time."

He was so surprised he even let her kiss him. She acted a sight freer with men nowadays. Urien looked grimmer than either of that pair. He'd got his men behind him this time, fully armed. Arthur came to and pushed her away from him. There was hot blood in his cheeks, more than in hers.

"You used sorcery on my guards. You tried to kill me, your brother and your king!"

"All my life I have suffered that accusation. For a man so threatened, Arthur is very much alive."

"I am your anointed ruler. The sword that Nimue gave me would not serve your evil purpose and turn to strike me."

He should have seen the start she gave. It was plain enough to me. She was staring at her brother's thigh. He was wearing it now. That jewelled sword I'd held in my hand that looked like Caliburn and wasn't. And something else had changed. It hung in a magnificent scabbard now. Gold filigree studded with seven kinds of jewels, not a thing of battered wood and bound with cracked silver. I was like a dog with two bones. I didn't know which way to turn. I'd been a smith. That was a scabbard fit for a king. Any man would be proud of it. But I'd felt the power of healing in the other one.

"What is that you wear at your side?" she asked, quite steady.

Arthur patted it. "My sweetheart, Caliburn. What else?"

"And has Caliburn brought you victory this summer'

"You know we have not taken the field yet."

"But I see you no longer wear the scabbard."

"I have a new one. The glory of Rome may have left this island but we still have craftsmen who know how to arm a king."

"Where is the old one?"

He shrugged. "Lost sight of in the mayhem you left behind you. It will have turned up by the time I get back to Caerleon."

"Do you value so lightly the gifts of the Lady? What does Merlyn say about its loss?"

She couldn't seem to take her eyes off his false weapon.

Arthur cleared his throat. He was looking angry again, and a mite uncomfortable. "Merlyn has left my court."

"Left you! When?"

"On my wedding night, while we feasted."

"Then, Nimue?"

"They went together, it seems."

"They thought I threatened you with both sword and sorcery, and they left you? Now I understand!"

"I do not fear your spells! I am a Christian king now. I have better guardians."

Morgan raised her eyes to her brother. She'd turned pale. "So Merlyn does not know the scabbard is missing? Or that Caliburn was . . . saved?"

"Merlyn's time is past. He has served his purpose. I had no need of sorcerer's help that night."

"Ungrateful! When, without him, you would not be here?"

"What do you mean? Caliburn was a truer friend. Your own son cried out against you and made you drop it. Even the little children accuse you, sister."

Well, I thought she'd choke.

"Little children! You dare say that . . . to me!"

If he'd been red before, he turned nearly purple then.

"I have served penance for that, haven't I? The parents have had their gold. What else could I do? That May Day child threatened my life and, with it, Britain's safety. It was a necessity."

"Necessity!" she screamed at him. "Is that what Merlyn said? The blood that must always be shed? The *necessity* for which my father died and you were got by magic?"

"There was no magic! I am Uther Pendragon's son and a crowned Christian king. Merlyn was my foster-father, but no more than that. All the magic my father needed was a brave sword and a loving heart."

She fell back a step. It's not often you see Morgan taken by surprise. Even Luned gasped out loud, and she was never one to voice her mind in public.

"Has Merlyn never told you?"

"Told me what? The old story? How my father desired Ygerne? The blood of kings from both sides, meeting in me to save this island? How Uther slew Gorlois in fair fight? How he married our mother and gave her the son that your father had denied her? And that is why you sisters hate me!"

Morgan cried out at him.

"Did Merlyn not tell you that the Pendragon tricked our mother? That while my father lay wounded Uther took on his features by sorcery? That three of them charmed their way into Tintagel? Uther, Ulfin and Merlyn? That when she lay in his arms Ygerne believed it was Gorlois who was entering her? That you were falsely got?"

You could see he hadn't heard the full story. Like a smack in the face, it was. All his young man's pride in swords and spears and a handsome body melting away into mist and magic. He looked round to someone for help. His friends were nearly all his age. Cei, Bedwyr, Accolon. How could they tell him the truth?

It was Luned's voice settled it. Clear. Cold. Hard. The only time I heard her raise it in front of men without first being spoken to.

"Ask my Lord Ulfin what was done in Tintagel."

Yes, the old warrior was there, hiding his face at the back of the crowd. Uther Pendragon's boyhood friend. His skin looked as grey as his hair. He must have been twice the age of those ruddy-faced lads round Arthur. But he looked older even than that. Too much magic. I knew the signs. Aye, I should, shouldn't I? Arthur ordered him to come forward. Pride wouldn't let him have it told in secret.

"You were my father's comrade and bodyguard. You have sworn that same oath to me, his son. *Tell us, on your honour, and my father's, how I was got.'*

Ulfin wasn't enjoying this.

"Sire, we besieged Dimiliock. Gorlois broke out to fight us and Uther struck him down with his own hand. When we saw he could not live long we let his men carry him inside the walls. Then Merlyn put a charm on us. Uther took on the form of Gorlois; Merlyn, Britael; I became Jordan. We passed Tintagel's gate-porter at dead of night, pleading extremity of need. He let us keep our arms. The abbess herself, for friendship of Gorlois, welcomed us in. Merlyn and I brought the king to Ygerne's bed and stood guard outside. In the morning Gorlois was dead and his widow was carrying the Pendragon's son."

Well, Arthur's face might have been on fire as he looked back to Morgan. Neither of them lowered their eyes. I'll give him that. She smiled a bit.

"You see, brother?"

He swallowed, as if he had a job to speak.

"I did not know. It was not honourably done. You have been wronged."

Now that might sound like Morgan's victory to you. Only if she'd been a man she'd have known she'd lost him for sure then. He might have forgiven her a sword-wound to the flesh, but she'd hit his pride.

She didn't see it. She held out her hand to him, very grave and sweetly.

"Do you understand now what lies between us that must be healed?"

"That is long past. My father, your mother. I was only the baby." He'd got that winning smile back on his face again as he put his hand up towards hers. "Can you not forgive me, sister? What more do you want?"

"I think you know."

"I do not. Why draw this sword over my bed to kill me?"

"If I had intended to kill, I should have done it. Gwenhyvar would have been dead before either of you woke."

"*Gwenhyvar* dead? Why?" He dropped his hand.

She'd given herself away. I felt a lurch in my stomach, as though the rest of us were water that had run out through a hole in a tub, and left those two. I'd seen his face.

She laughed and tried to turn it aside.

"Why? To make the Pendragon suffer loss, as Gorlois's daughters have mourned since that night in Tintagel! What else should I mean?"

But it was too late. I reckon he hardly knew what he was saying. "I warn you, do not touch Gwenhyvar! By God, I'd turn this sword against you then."

"As you turned it on my women here in this hall, the day you took the children?"

"Can you never have done with that?"

"Can you still not see the wound that waits to be healed?"

"Healing is your job. Fighting is mine. Take the scabbard and leave the sword to me!"

"Did Merlyn teach you that?"

"Merlyn is gone, damn you!"

Arthur flung himself out of Lyvennet and back to Gwenhyvar.

33

Funny how clothes can make a difference to the way you feel. Morgan's always been proud, and she's a beautiful woman. She'd look a queen, and lovely, in a piece of sack. But even your richest jewel takes on more fire in a proper goldsmith's setting. It was still the dark colours she favoured, but the cloth was the best you could buy now. Rich green, like wet moss. Blue as deep as your shadow on a frosty morning. Or a dark strong red. But all thick embroidered. She has an eye for good workmanship. And jewels! She'd come to us dressed simple as a nun in her fresh flowers. But now she'd take all the stones Urien cared to heap on her. It was as if she couldn't have the man she wanted, so she was out to dazzle all the others. Except those moons when we danced barefoot and naked on the earth that made us. Yes, even me now; so she could call me Woman every other hour, but then she owned I wasn't.

It's a thing you may not have expected, but I'd come to take a pride in my own clothes too. We were a queer bodyguard she'd chosen: Luned, thrown out of an abbey, a clever nun that was fool enough to bear a baby; and me, chased out of the world of men for fancying myself wiser than Morgan of Tintagel. But we were hers; we were queen's women. She couldn't help our faces, but she wouldn't be shamed by our bodies. We had good gowns, like these, the best stuff, and fine white linen for our heads.

So I wasn't too pleased when she told me to slip off my good striped dress and put on a worn old gown of brown that looked as if somebody had cleaned out the hencoop in it. Still, I saw the sense of it, and the patched old shoes and the otterskin bag. I took a staff in my hand as if I'd trudged miles. I didn't need to walk, though. We took her chariot. Morgan drove, with

Luned sitting beside her. She has a way with horses, with any animal, come to that. She has that little grey cat, with the scars on its side where the hair's never grown back properly, and she'll sit for hours with it on her knee, crooning to it. Have you seen the guard dogs in the yard cringe when she passes? Soft as puppies. They wag their tails and flatten their ears and look up at her, all pleading-like, and she'll stroke their heads and murmur something to every one of them.

I showed her the spot where Arthur had pushed those poor little mites down into the water. There's tales enough told of that now. I'm not surprised folk are afraid of the place. A cold stretch of grass and mud. The wind comes whistling over. In the evening they say you can hear the screaming of babies snatched from their mothers and floating out to their deaths, and feel their little tears falling on you like rain.

She stood alone at the edge of the water for a good while. Then we skirted the marshes and went on downstream, working the south side first. At every farm and shed and hut she stopped the chariot, a good way off and sent me forward. She knew how I could act the part of a wise woman. The hardest part was seeing the women's faces when I asked.

"I have charms to sell, dearie. Medicine for a year-old baby. Do you have such a one? Give him this cordial every new moon while you're weaning him, and he'll grow up strong and handsome as a prince."

There were a few that showed interest. Mothers who were carrying their bairns on their arms and showing them off proudly to anyone who'd look. But they weren't afraid. Theirs were too young to be him. It was the other women, the ones that slammed the door in my face and cursed me. Some, mostly the young ones, burst into tears. It had been their first, you see. The men growled at me too, and told me to hold my tongue. I got no payment from them, not so much as a piece of bread.

We came to the sea and stood on the sands watching the white horses come running towards us from the Isle of Man. Next day we tried the north shore.

I think she knew. I reckon she could have taken us straight to the place if she'd wanted. Perhaps she was afraid the gods were playing games with her. She wanted to find that boy too much. I don't say Elaine could have told her wrong; the seeing's always true, but sometimes it doesn't mean what you think it does. If she was going to lose the child she'd set her heart on a second time, then she'd put off the hour. Or maybe it was like when you've got a plate of mushrooms in front of you, and you keep the biggest and juiciest one till the last.

We knew the stone, as we know every holy marker in all our land, and Gwendoleu's. A round rock in the grass by the firth, all on its own as if it had fallen out of the sky. The Stone of Mabon, the Son of Modron the Mother. It seemed like an omen, that. There was a house nearby, a lonely place. And a shed beside, with a man mending a net, and a coracle pulled up on the turf. I gave him the time of day, though it always chokes me a bit, seeing a craftsman at his trade. I went on to the house and he gave a loud whistle after me. It was a clean sort of place, a few beasts and fowls well cared for and making a crooning chatter as I passed them by. I didn't need to knock at the door. There was a woman sitting under an apple-tree with her back to me, rocking a bit with something on her knee. She looked round and saw a stranger. She couldn't have heard her husband whistle. Her face changed, and she gave a little cry and darted into the house, quick as a startled bird into the bushes. She came out again pulling the front of her dress straight and smiling at me as if nothing had happened.

"Good day, granny. What can I do for you?"

I said my piece and I thought she caught her breath a bit, though she laughed to cover it.

"I've no child so small, thank God. It's a wonder you come peddling such wares in these parts. Are you a wise woman, and yet don't know what happened here last summer? How many other houses have you asked at?"

She was shrewder than I'd bargained for. Plenty of women had cursed me but nobody else had challenged me straight out. Grief's like an empty belly. It won't let you think about anything but yourself. This woman wasn't grieving.

"Death goes and life comes. You can't stop what will be. There'll be a baby again where there were empty arms last summer." And I looked her full in the eyes and nodded, so she knew I was on her side and not Arthur's.

She was still careful. "That's true. Sit down and drink a cup of milk. How much would you want for such a cordial? Could it really keep the child safe ... if I were to have another ... against sickness and wizardry?"

"It could. And I have one besides with power to shield him even from the king himself." My eyes never left her face.

I saw her colour. It wasn't guilt. It wasn't even fear. She was angry. She had older children. They'd come looking round the corner to see the visitor. She'd shooed them back to work. They looked well grown and sensible enough to keep her secret. And now she was nursing another woman's baby where her own had sucked. He had to be her foster-child.

"You think they would come back? Those red ravagers! Were there not enough drowned bairns on the sands to satisfy them?"

"Arthur has done penance for it. That arrow's shot. But you're right. The danger's not past."

"Folk say it was really Merlyn's doing. He'll have a longer memory than the young one."

"Arthur's flown south. And Merlyn's gone mighty quiet, so I've heard. He's not been seen in a long while."

"Good riddance, I'd say!"

I drank the milk, and made her a present of the cordial. We hadn't cheated. It was strong stuff, the best magic we could brew. We wanted the child's safety as much as she did. She held the flask to her chest, but she was looking a bit doubtful now, scared, as if she might have given away more than she should.

"Bless me, mother," she said. "We live in bad times."

"For you, the good times are just beginning," I promised.

I brought Morgan to her, wrapped in a great black cloak and hood that hid her finery. That gave the fisherman's wife a shock, when she found who it was. But she was equal to it. Her name was Fencha. The two of them talked, woman to woman. Morgan might be a queen, but she was still Morgan the Healer. Everybody knew that, even in Solway. The woman trusted her, and Morgan trusted Fencha. She had milk enough, and no suckling of her own, or coming either.

She fetched her husband in. I liked the man. He wasn't a talker. He'd found the baby on the sand, and worse things than him they'd had to bury. They'd both been agreed on what she'd done. We'd give them payment. Not gold; that might make the neighbours" tongues wag. Good cloth. A pair of cows. A bigger boat. And the promise of more in return for their caring and silence. Morgan could trust him. Still, she made him turn pale when she warned him what she'd do if he proved her wrong.

Fencha had asked us in when she found it was a queen she had to deal with, and she'd sat Morgan in the best chair. There was a blanket hanging to hide the bed, and no sign of the boy. When her husband had gone back to his work she still didn't open that curtain. She was a careful woman, Fencha, and he was a quiet baby. In the end, Morgan had to lower her pride and ask.

"May I see him?"

Just for a moment, I thought the woman was going to say no. She seemed to think she had power, even over Morgan. But she beckoned us through the curtain. I noticed, though, she picked the boy up off the bed and held him cradled in her arms, as if he was hers, and not three-quarters blood to our queen. Morgan's sister's child, by her half-brother.

He wasn't a handsome baby. Too red in the face, and a bit puckered, just as if he was frowning. Straight black hair and dark eyes. He stared up at Morgan with a knowing look. She held out her finger and his little fist gripped round it. The blood rushed to her face and her free hand went quick to her heart. She didn't say anything for a while.

Fencha softened a bit when she saw that and put him in Morgan's arms.

The queen lifted a gold chain from her neck and slipped it over the baby's head. It had a pendant like a horse's head. She'd brought it from Cornwall. It looked a big heavy thing, lying on his tiny chest. She took a silver phial out of the bag on her girdle and made smears of oil over the boy's brow and eyes and mouth and hands and heart. It left a golden stain on his skin, with just a thread of red in it. I knew why. It hadn't come from any flower or root, but it meant life. Luned and I said what has to be said as she made the five marks.

"You are mine now," she murmured, very low. "Your name is Modred."

34

War. And for the first time Arthur was beaten. So he wasn't a fairy prince. He was Uther's son. Human, like the rest of us. It wasn't much of a setback. He didn't lose too many men. But the wind changed.

Gwendoleu had never been for him. Merlyn had sung songs in his ears that had kept him sweet for some time after, but that summer he went back to the Ravens. He made a deal with the Saxons. Lot did too. We could guess why. Margawse and Arthur hadn't kept their secret as close as they thought they had. Lot hadn't got proof of it, but he knew. He'd have his revenge.

It cost him his life, and more kings with him. Margawse wailed as if she'd been in love with him all these years, after all. She made her sons swear they'd be revenged.

Urien always stayed loyal to Arthur. It cut a split in that family. There were others wounded by the end of that summer, fighting Saxons. Urien, and that young Accolon that Morgan got drunk with the night of Arthur's wedding, and Arthur himself. They'd taken them all by ship to Cornwall to be healed.

Morgan had a haunted look when she got the news.

"And not to me?"

"There are nuns near Celliwig that have a name for healing. They came from Tintagel, they say."

She didn't answer that straight off.

"Is Merlyn with them?" she asked.

"He is not."

"It is nothing," said Morgan. "Merlyn was always a man that walked by himself. In Cornwall he was always in and out of Uther's hall; here at midnight, gone by cockcrow, changing his shape with every season. We are not rid of him yet."

Yet there was never a man came north to Rheged but she asked, "Is Arthur healed?" And then, "Has Merlyn returned?"

And always the answer was no.

The Saxons pushed their border out a good long way that year.

Morgan went to Din Eidyn, though it was an early winter and bitter weather for travelling. I didn't hear the scrap, but she came away with what she went for: Arthur's sword and scabbard. She wouldn't tell any of us what she wanted them for.

"It must be ended," was all she'd say.

It was warmer going south, but wet roads for riding. We took a boat down the Severn. When we reached salt water we cast about till we could hire a bigger ship. It cost her. It was long past sailing weather. It was the first time I'd gone out to sea, and I thought it would be the last. The cliffs got higher, and the waves were almost as big, in spite of all the spells we made to hold them. We were creeping along the coast from port to port, and as likely as not holed up for days on end till the wind dropped. Most of the time I was scared silly. But Morgan seemed as if she was at home on that sea. Well, she was born by it. It's a grim coast, is Kernow. Narrow harbours like knife-wounds, and too many rocks offshore for my liking. I thought she was bringing us to our deaths.

Luned showed me Tintagel as we sailed past. It was an abbey once, but it's a stern fortress now, under King Mark, and better suited to it, to my way of thinking. You could see by their faces that Morgan hadn't forgotten how she'd been kept prisoner there, or Luned how she'd been a learned nun.

It made Luned spiteful. I'd never heard her speak so bold to Morgan. "Is it your brother's death we are bringing, or your husband's? Which of those would make you a bigger queen?"

"Beware! Do not presume too far. Remember Annis."

That shut her up.

My wife, dead of witchcraft, or from the poison I'd brewed.

We landed at Padstow. But we didn't ride straight to Arthur's court. Morgan had other business first. There was an old wise woman who'd been her nurse and kept a strong circle. They were a long time talking. There were spells made that night that changed the course of Britain.

Then we took the pack-road south to Celliwig. This wasn't a Roman place. No stone turrets and paved streets here. This was boulders, earth, wood, thatch. I felt more at home.

Morgan rode up to the gatehouse. She'd brought both sword and scabbard with her.

"Tell my brother: Morgan the Healer is here and would see him."

They ought to have recognised her before she spoke. At a name like that they should have waved her through the gate and shown her proper respect. She was the king's sister and the greatest healer in the land. Her own husband was lying here. They didn't. The sentries crossed their spears in front of us. They didn't trust her. It seemed those two couldn't ever forgive each other for what had been done. A lot of things had changed that year, but not the heart of it. We were left standing out in the cold wind. The first snow-clouds of winter were piling up over the moors too, a nasty yellow-grey. It's a pretty enough place to come hunting in the summer, Celliwig, but it struck mighty desolate that December morning.

It was Cei came to the gate. Arthur's a great one for courtesy, I'll give him that. It was the chief steward among his warriors he sent. Only Cei was never a man for sweet talk. He said what he'd been sent to say, bluntly.

"King Arthur will not see you, lady. You are not welcome at his court. Your husband has proved himself a loyal friend. But you sisters he will not trust or forgive again, ever. He knows now you have taken his sword, and the war has turned against us."

The colour came to her cheek then. Arthur forgive his sisters, when he'd tried to kill the boy? His sister's son, a bond more sacred than your own child! Though, it *was* his own child too, wasn't it? That was the trouble. And will be, till one or the other of them dies. Still, that was rich from him, knowing their family history as well.

I thought she'd whip out with some stream of scorn that would blister Cei's face. Or wheel her horse round in a sudden temper and gallop off from his dun, and never mind who she rode down on her way. But Morgan always surprises you.

She bent over the horse's neck to Cei, and let her breasts hang clear of her cloak. Her black hair tumbled down, so her face smiled out at him through it. That touch of pink in her cheeks, and her green eyes sweet and dancing. She made her voice like honey.

"Lord Cei, you are my brother's oldest friend. Arthur lies in great danger, but not from his sisters, though we have been greatly wronged. Let me through that I may bring him healing."

"He does not need your witches" spells to keep him safe. If magic were needed, we have Nimue."

"Nimue! They have returned? She and Merlyn!"

"The enchanter, no. The Lady came alone."

"So long without Merlyn? Battles lost. The king hurt. And she comes back alone?"

"Merlyn was never one to stay pinned down."

"Friend, you have a traitor in your camp. I must talk with my brother."

Cei had a soldier's face. Wooden. I think his brain was wooden too. "I have my orders. You must leave this fort. It would shame the king as well as yourself if we had to remove you by force. But I will do it if you are still here one hour from now."

I saw her hands tighten on the reins. The horse caught her mood. He threw up his head. She sat up straight and kept her seat while he pranced and side-stepped. I caught the bridle and soothed him down, like a smith needs to often enough.

It cost her some effort to keep her voice soft and winning. "At least warn him, Cei, as you love him. Tell him not to trust his Lady . . ."

"There are only two ladies of consequence here. Queen Gwenhyvar. You would surely not accuse her! And the Lady Nimue, his foster-mother, who trained us all to fight and gave Arthur his sword."

"Will she heal Arthur now? Both the king and the land?"

"He has the nuns for that. This was war, woman! Warriors bleed. We will avenge his wound a hundred times next year."

He turned on his heel and strode off across the yard. She hissed things after him that ought to have made him stumble. But he marched on with his back as stiff as a broom pole. Arthur wouldn't let her in.

She hadn't come all this way for nothing, though. When Morgan gets an idea in her head she won't be thwarted. Early next morning she sent me into the forest. I was lying in wait at sunrise when the king's court came out hunting, though not the king himself.

I could have done with the stout boots I wore when I was a smith. They give women finer ones in queen's palaces, to make your feet look smaller. I could feel the earth through the soles, frozen hard. I hadn't thought till I heard them coming how I'd get him on his own out of all that troop of lords and ladies and the rest. I needn't have worried. Morgan must have had a word in his horse's ear. She's got the skill. She wouldn't have needed to go near the stables to do that. Just a whisper from outside.

Sure enough, I was listening to the horns and peering out of the bushes to see who was riding up front, when there was bit of a crashing through the holly trees behind me. Accolon, on a black gelding. No one else near him. For all the years I've practised magic it still gives me a shiver when a thing falls out pat, like that.

He had a nasty scar across his neck, and he looked whiter still than before. But he could sit a horse again, and Arthur couldn't.

He didn't seem as surprised as he should have done when he recognised me. I took him to Morgan. The queen was leaning against the trunk of an ash. That's a sacred tree to us, of peace and rebirth. She had wrapped herself in a great cloak of fur, mixed grey and black. There were badger-pelts in amongst it. The hood was over her head in the cold and Morgan's little face looked out from it, white as a snowdrop. She smiled at Accolon. She could have bewitched any man. The two of them fell to hugging and kissing like a couple of sweethearts before they're married.

I'm not sure if I should tell you what happened next. I didn't understand it, and nor did Luned. Accolon wasn't one of the wise. He wasn't the king it was meant for. He hadn't the right to take it.

She drew the sword out from under her cloak. The true one, Caliburn. In its own black scabbard. She handed it to him very solemn and looked up at his face.

"You know what to do?"

As if it was something they'd already agreed between the pair of them.

He nodded, and raised the scabbard up and kissed it, with her hands still holding it. I could guess how that would feel wholesome against his wound. She let go of it.

"It shall be done by nightfall."

He hadn't taken three steps across the clearing towards his horse when a shout stopped him.

"Hold there!"

Nimue, on a mulberry roan, with a bright red hunting cloak blowing out around her.

"His sword!" she cried. Then she checked. She'd caught sight of Morgan leaning against the ash tree, watching her. Nimue doesn't change colour as easily as Morgan does. It's just that sharp edge on her pretty sparkle that warns you she means danger. "So it is *you*! You stole Caliburn from Arthur, and the scabbard with it."

"Arthur has lost more than that. And not by my doing."

"And just what would that mean?"

The Lady wasn't so bold now, seeing the four of us round her. She feared Morgan. She tried not to show it, but we could see.

"Where is Merlyn? What have you done with him?"

That was a mistake on Morgan's part. Yes, you're right, I did look over my shoulder when I said that. It's not often I'd dare say she hadn't been wise. But she was allowing that Nimue had a deal of power now, even over Merlyn. The Lady smiled. She has a brilliant smile. There's more of the daffodil about her than the snowdrop.

"I, responsible for the enchanter Merlyn? You sisters could never overcome him yourselves, and yet you believe I have?" You could see she was enjoying that.

It was plain to us that Morgan was having a hard job holding herself in. She'd suffered under Emrys Merlyn, all right. She'd lost her father through him, when she was eight years old. She'd seen her mother charmed away to Uther Pendragon. She'd spent ten years shut up in Tintagel because Merlyn feared her. He'd struck a chasm between her and Arthur. And there'd been nothing she could do to stop him.

And now here was Nimue, taunting her that she'd got power over the greatest sorcerer in the land. The Lady of the Lake. Just a pretty little flirt of a witch, you'd think, to look at her. Only I knew better.

"Where is Merlyn now?"

"Shall we say he is . . . resting?"

"Where?"

"You do not need to know that."

"*Where?*"

"U . . . under a rock. I will not tell you which!"

"How did he get there? Why did he go under this . . . *rock?*"

"Of his own free will . . . after I coaxed him. He wearied me with his attentions. He was always such a lascivious old man."

"You coveted Merlyn's power."

Nimue shot such a look at me then, it made me shudder. She knew I'd talked.

"I never took from him anything he did not willingly give me. You are too bitter. I offered him love and I got what I asked. You have learned that lesson too late. I am as great an enchanter as you three sisters now. Greater. But you were right in one thing. That power that Merlyn had belongs in a woman's hands. Mine, not yours. I am Nimue, Lady of the Lake. I raised Arthur. I shielded him from you. I armed him with sword and scabbard. He is mine. Not yours, not Merlyn's, not the Church's."

They were fighting over the lad like dogs over a bone.

"I see it all. You have chained Merlyn with sleep, deep underground, have you not? How long will you keep him prisoner? He is your prisoner, isn't he? When will you free him? What price have you set?"

Nimue gave a little pouting smile, but didn't answer.

Morgan stared at her, waiting, and then she screamed. I've never heard anything like it. Worse than when Arthur took Modred. It was such a desperate sound it shook a shower of snow from the trees and sent the crows up cawing into the air.

"You cannot do it! You made the great spell of binding, and you did not learn how to unloose it! Merlyn is trapped for ever, isn't he? There is no one, no one, who could break that now, except Merlyn himself, and he is sleeping. *Aah! Aah!* He will not come back to guard Arthur ever again!"

"Does that grieve you so much? I should not have thought it." The Lady sounded a bit sour and a lot less sure of herself.

"Grieve me? Did you never think of Arthur? Can you not see what you have done?"

"Arthur will recover. What has Merlyn to do with him now? He is made king."

"Do you still not know? Can you not feel? The world in balance. Sword and scabbard. It was always Merlyn and Morgan. Male and female. The left and right. And you have broken that! You thought you could take his place! Nimue, Lady of the Lake, to stand against Morgan. To hold the centre steady and keep Arthur on the pivot from destruction. To know the land whole. Fool! Fool! You deserve worse than death!"

Nimue was scared, all right. She had her hand out of her cloak, pointing at Morgan. Accolon leaped forward. He drew that sword out of its scabbard so fast I swear there were flames shooting out of the serpents' jaws. I don't know what would have happened, but there were two great shouts. Morgan's and Nimue's. He dropped them both in the snow, sword and scabbard. Morgan hadn't buckled the belt on him. His horse took off, like a stag leaping over a thicket. Poor old Accolon let out a yell and hung on for dear life. He didn't get far. A branch of an elm tree caught him across the throat and swept him clear off the saddle.

Next moment, Nimue's roan was off the other way. She was a good rider. She leaned down as she galloped and scooped her hand through the snow. Morgan dashed forward to stop her. The pair of them dived for Arthur's arms. I thought the horse's hooves would go clear through Morgan's hand. Then Nimue caught the weapon by the hilt. Caliburn. And she waved her treasure over her head to let us know.

She disappeared in a whirlwind of dead leaves and powdered snow. Morgan leaned back against the tree, clutching the scabbard. She was whiter still and shaking.

"The scabbard is worth ten times the sword. She knows that, and yet she chose the sword. Now Arthur has the blade, and I its sheath. And still they have not come together."

She looked down at what she was holding.

"Empty! The beam begins to slip," she said. "What waits at the bottom of the shaft into which we are falling? Tell me, Luned, Woman? If I pull Arthur over to my side at last, what will that mean? Will the end be darkness for us all?"

At last she pushed herself away from the tree of healing and went to Accolon, where he hung from the elm tree. Too late for any magic to help him. His neck was broken. The tears rolled down her cheek. She turned her back on him and walked away.

35

Arthur got better without his scabbard. The prayers of those nuns must have had power. Urien came home as well.

After he got Caliburn back things went better for Arthur. He won the great battle at Mount Badon that fixed a line across Britain between Cymry and Saxon. It's held ever since. No more than that. The land's split in two. Ours and theirs. I thought that might have seen the end of a different war, and a truce patched up between brother and sisters. But there was worse coming.

Morgan's not beaten easily. She made one last try. I'm not sure to this day what she intended.

Morgan called her sisters to Rheged. I wish I didn't have to talk about this. It makes me sick remembering it, even now. It could have been me, you see. I wonder it wasn't. There have been moments when I've wondered if that was what Morgan meant all along. She'd have her revenge on me. Morgan the Healer? She'd cursed my Annis to death, hadn't she? In a fit of fury; just because I'd done for Erith? Luned told me it might have been the poison I left behind in the bowl at the smithy. But I won't have that. She never forgets, Morgan. If I'd been Arthur, I wouldn't have trusted her either.

It was an errand we'd been on many times, Luned and me. There'd been an early frost, but the ground had thawed, and there were still berries and toadstools for the taking. I'd grown to fear the forest. My kingdom once. Where I used to walk respectful, but with the tread of a man who has a right to be there. Where I'd danced with the horns. Where I'd . . . Well, there's been nothing of that since I took the skirt. Not like it used to be. I'm only the Man-Woman in the dance now, not the god. Morgan had given a bit of power back to me, but not too much. She's kept the real strength in her own hands. She's got me trapped. A half-thing. The man in the skirt. Only enough magic to be useful to her.

I'd done a sacrilege in this forest. I'd spilt the power. I could see the trees watching me. The twigs were stirring on the ends of their branches as if they were itching to get me. I stuck close to Luned, though I knew she couldn't have helped me. She didn't like that. She was still scared of me. I could see she hadn't forgotten Erith either.

But it was the things we'd come for she feared more. The herbs of power. Roots, fruit, fungus. She had a sharp brain. She knew what she was looking for and where to find it. But when she hit upon it she never looked as if she was pleased to see it, no matter how rare it might be. You could tell she had to force herself to reach out her hand and take hold of it. She always wore gloves. Well, you have to be careful. Still, she needn't have shaken and paled the way she always did. There's healing in some of those poisons, if you use them right.

You can never be sure with Morgan whether she's sent you out to stock her herb-room or if she's planning something special. Often you find the things she asks of you, and then you just dry and powder them, or stew them in water and store them away. She keeps far more than Nimue. And she has more knowledge of how to use them. But then Nimue isn't known for a healer, is she? You don't find a rabble of poor and sick at her gate asking for help. Nimue's a warrior woman. What she wants is the power from them.

There's nothing good or evil in the plants themselves. Mind you, it isn't all leaves and berries in Morgan's store-room. There are things there that once had another sort of life, and some of those I wouldn't know how to call on for good. Still, they're nothing by themselves. It's how the wise woman uses them.

So I had a shock when I got back. Morgan called me to her. And it wasn't herbs she wanted from me this time. She had gold and silver and copper laid out on a table. I couldn't believe it. She started coaxing me to try a different sort of magic. My old craft. The sort you do with metal and hammer and file. She'd have seen the fire in my eyes too, when I heard what she wanted. She smiled very winningly, the way she can when she needs something off you. That should have warned me. I'd seen that smile before, and I've never been a free man since. She wouldn't let me go too far, though. I had to keep my skirt, even then. She's crippled my manhood for the rest of my life. I'll never be Smith swinging hammer on iron again.

Only she had these softer metals she wanted to win things from. She needed me. This wasn't women's magic. And she laid her hand on my arm very sweetly and made me feel more than half a man for a bit. She wouldn't tell me what it was for. Miles of precious wire she made me get ready, drawing it out with fire and tongs, and every bit of it pulled with a strong spell of holding. I wasn't a whitesmith. It was delicate work. I sweated over it.

At the same time the women were getting heaps of silk threads ready, dyed to her own liking.

Elaine and Margawse arrived at the end of November for Advent Sunday. Urien's always kept the Christian calendar. Our castle was full of Margawse's big sons, fighting all over the place and making a racket. I wondered if Morgan would take Margawse to see her last baby, at the fisherman's house. But that was one secret she kept even from the boy's own mother. Modred was safe with her.

I'd never seen Morgan look so gay as she did that feast-day. She fairly sparkled. Years fell off her. She was like a little girl that's planning a wonderful surprise for somebody she loves best. For days before, she'd been working beside us. She moved so quickly her hair fell loose and untidy and her mouth was open as if she was out of breath. There were roses in her cheeks and her eyes shone prettier than I'd seen them do for a long time. But there were times between when she'd suddenly change. She couldn't bear to stay indoors then. She'd walk the ramparts in the wind with her fists clenched and her eyes burning and her breath coming short. We daren't go near her.

Luned and I couldn't think what she was up to.

But we found out. It was Sunday, after the meal at midday. Elaine had gone to lie down. She was looking old before her time. She'd only had the one daughter, but they said it had robbed her of her strength. I think, myself, it's more likely the seeing did it. She moved herself slow and heavy. I wasn't sorry when she was out of the way. She's a brooding sort of woman that sees too much. I never feel comfortable when she's in the room. But Margawse was there, restless as ever and always nosy about what was going on.

Morgan sent two maids, and they came back with a length of cloth. Beautiful stuff it was, velvet, royal purple. I'd never seen cloth so rich and soft, both for feel and colour. I'd no idea she had it. I couldn't guess where she'd got it from or what it had cost her. Luned whispered to me it had come from Venice. I was none the wiser. I've never had book-learning like she had. All I know of the world is Britain, and that's enough for me. We rolled the cloth out in front of Morgan. There was plenty of it.

Margawse gasped for pleasure, and clapped her hands together.

"It's gorgeous, Morgan! What are you going to do with it? Is it for a new gown? Oh, I'm wild with envy! Is there not enough for two of us? I will give you my pair of black chariot-horses, my ruby necklace. You could have had my husband if he was still alive!"

She'd got over Lot. She went off into peals of laughter, running as if she was going to throw her arms round Morgan and wheedle her.

Something stopped her. Morgan wasn't in the mood for games now. She wasn't a little girl any more. We could all see that. She was standing over that rolled-out velvet with her eyelids closed. Her hands were knotted together and her lips whispering. We listened, but none of us could make out what she was saying. I don't know if she was casting a spell or saying a Christian prayer.

Then she sat down in her great carved chair, without speaking to us. She stared at the cloth, spread out before her like a big dark lake. She had a box at her side, where she kept her sewing things. We watched her open it in silence. Even Margawse didn't make a sound. Morgan fingered the things, a bit reluctant, taking her time. It seemed as though she had to make up her mind to something. Thimbles, needles, a teasing brush. All rich stuff. Gold, silver, ivory. At last she found the thing she was looking for.

She took it out and laid it in her lap. A pair of silver scissors. Shaped like a heron, with a beak that could open into two sharp blades and then close on the thread and snap it. I recognised them. I'd brought them to her, years ago. Merlyn's gift. In all the time I'd served her I'd never seen her use them. Queer, seeing them again now he'd gone, like a ghost from beyond. She nursed those scissors, turning them over in her hands, as though she was still having a struggle to decide.

Next moment she was a different woman. She sprang up and threw us a flashing smile.

And away she went, down on her hands and knees before us, with those shiny scissors snapping and ripping into her costly cloth. It made us gasp. She was working so fast. She didn't stop to measure or work out where to turn. But the shears seemed to know their own job. Before our eyes the shape fell into place. A wide full mantle, big enough to grace a grown man's shoulders. No king in the land wouldn't laugh to get such a gift.

Then she jumped to her feet and cried out as if Margawse had just put her question.

"There! It is a royal mantle, but neither for you nor for me. This is going to be my peace-offering to Arthur. A gift of the heart, costly enough to mend the hurt between us, if he will have it so. Is it not splendid cloth? A fitting colour for the Emperor of the Britons? And this is only the start. It shall be more magnificent yet, by far. I shall embroider designs upon it with gold and silver thread. I mean to use every art of needlework they taught me in Tintagel. There will never have been a cloak like this for richness, or for labour of love. I shall line it with silk and crust it with jewels, though it empty Urien's treasury to do it. Arthur thinks I have stolen what was his. Then let him have this for recompense!"

Her voice caught there on a kind of sob, or she might have been laughing.

Next day we started the Advent fast. Morgan's made no secret to the Church of where she leans, but she keeps their seasons too. She's still Urien's queen. It's a strange thing, but while she's in their chapel she whispers the prayers as if she means them, and takes their food. Like a wild filly running with a herd of tame horses. I think she's never entirely forgotten Tintagel.

For a month we all fasted and worked on that cloak. I didn't sew. I've never managed to bend my big fingers round that sort of work. But I had charge of the gold and silver wire, cutting and twisting it in fantastic shapes, so the women could lay them on the border and whip them into place with coloured silks. Morgan made me put a charm of power in every turn. And the jewels! Rubies, coral, lapis lazuli, amethyst. I'd never had such a hoard of stuff to work with in my life. It was my hand over all of it. That border grew like a serpent, getting fatter every day. It took on the shape of a dragon with ruby eyes, opening its great jaws at the throat. It was a feast for the eyes, when our bellies were empty.

We got to the week before Christmas. Arthur always keeps that feast at Carlisle, and a merry one too. The kings of the north had swung back to him since Lot died, though Gwendoleu mostly sulked in his hillfort upriver. Urien looked likely to get Carlisle off him before long.

Morgan's great cloak was all but finished. There was just the lining of gold silk to stitch into place.

The day before Christmas Eve Morgan went suddenly tired. As though her labour was over and the life had gone out of her. The ladies crowded round their handiwork and they couldn't stop chattering and squealing over it.

"The cost!"

"Its true worth is not in the jewels. Any king can buy gems if he is rich enough. But who else in the world could have offered him art to equal this?"

"Such skill!"

"Such devotion."

"Such craft."

Morgan sent them away. She went into her bedchamber and Margawse and Elaine went with her. They were a long time murmuring together behind the curtain.

They'd left the mantle spread out in the sunny-room and the light was falling in through the windows and making the jewels sparkle. Luned and I stayed guarding it. Morgan's little grey cat was eyeing it too. I could see he had ideas of making a bed on it, and I went to shoo him away. He growled at me, and kept on prowling round the edges.

Margawse came out of Morgan's room. She swung the curtain open, so we could see Morgan sitting on her bed beside Elaine.

"I'm going for a ride. It's too quiet here for me!"

She went out and called to her ladies, but I don't doubt she'd be hoping for men's company before she got to the stables. She'd been cooped up long enough with a crowd of women.

It wasn't long before Elaine followed. She drew the curtain shut behind her, but not before I'd had a glimpse of Morgan lying down now with her eyes shut.

There was nobody else left in the outer room but myself and Luned. Elaine gave orders. There wasn't anything special about the way she spoke them. She might have been telling her steward what to get ready for supper. It was just the things she asked for. We knew them, better than most of the wise in Britain, Luned and me. They were the most powerful things we'd got for Morgan's store-room. The sort she hardly ever used. We must have looked at each other pretty oddly. Elaine didn't threaten or coax us. She speaks slow and soft. I've never heard her raise her voice. But we went and fetched them. When she asks, folk don't argue. Besides, those three had been closeted together long enough. This must be Morgan's plan too, and Margawse's. I thought I was beginning to see it now.

She hardly had to tell us what she wanted done. We'd half-guessed already. It was powerful stuff. And the three of us to add our voices over it, though it was odd she didn't rouse Morgan.

But it didn't stop there. I found out then why she hadn't summoned her own women. It was me she needed. She hadn't brought that smith with her that had copied Caliburn. She got me to do the metalwork, bending the ends of all those little silver wires so they stuck through the cloth on the inside. Like a bush of little thorns, with charms as sharp. It was Luned she gave the job of painting them with what we'd brewed. That was cruel. Even though the nun wore stout leather gloves, you could see her hands were shaking. We'd lit the lamps, and the wind off the Pennines was making the flames flicker. It was a wonder she didn't prick herself then and make her own fears come true. It took her a long time.

She was given worse work still after that. All afternoon she sat and sewed the gold silk lining over what we'd done. She had to take the gloves off for that, you see. One little slip would have sent that spell into her own blood. She never stitched so careful.

And all the time we were doing it, Morgan was lying asleep, stiff and straight on her bed as if she was dead.

36

You can't get back what's once been smashed. But you can hurt yourself with working over it. I couldn't ride to Carlisle now without recalling the last time I'd walked there while I was still Teilo Smith. A sweet May day with the river winding away on my left and the blue sky smiling. And me in my leather tunic with my hands still black from handling iron. You might think I rode prouder now, in a queen's chariot. But I didn't. I'd had everything I wanted before. I stood on my own two feet, and danced on them too. Only I'd been too much of a greedy fool to see it. Well, I'd turned Queen Morgan's head, all right, and I'd got what I asked for.

Christmas Eve. Luned and me riding to King Arthur's court at Carlisle to give him a present from his sister Morgan.

Morgan wasn't invited. Not though she lived so close. She was out of favour now.

You can be sure there was another thing I was thinking of. Morgan would have her revenge. She wouldn't force poison on him, like I'd done with Erith. She didn't need to. She'd kill him with her spell. A love-gift! He'd take it. He couldn't refuse it once he'd seen it. He'd put her cloak round him. He'd die for vanity and greed, like his father Uther should have done when he took Ygerne all those years ago in Cornwall.

Morgan would work her spell from a distance, like she had with Annis. And that cruel death must have been her doing, mustn't it, not my carelessness?

She'd seen us off from the yard as pretty as a girl in love with her first sweetheart. Her cheeks were pink with the cold, and you could tell she was excited by the sparkle in her eyes. She lifted up the cloak to us so eager it made Luned cry out for fear. But it was parcelled up well. We'd folded it so you could only see the purple velvet on the outside and a bit of that fabulous embroidery on the hem. There wasn't a bit of her treacherous lining showing, nor any of those wicked points of wire sticking through. And now the whole of it was wrapped in a deerskin bag to keep it from harm – and us. It was lying on the seat in front of me, beside the driver. I couldn't take my eyes off it, and nor could Luned. She was shaking, and not just with the cold, though it was raw weather. We both knew we'd need to be out of that palace pretty smart before our High King put on his purple. Morgan couldn't have helped but see the danger she was putting us into.

Margawse had waved us off too. She'd have liked to ride with us, impudent as she was. She didn't care that Arthur had hated the sight of her since she'd mothered his son. Just once I'd seen how bitter she was under the surface. Just that once. This morning you'd have thought from the way she laughed she'd have bedded him again if she got the chance. But she hadn't forgiven him.

Elaine doesn't stir out of doors unless she has to. She doesn't smile much either. She stood in the doorway, like a spider poking out of a crack, while Morgan passed that cloak to us. Then she went inside and shut the door behind her.

Morgan caught my hand. It's not a thing she often did, though she's bolder with men now than she was at first.

"Tell Arthur . . . Tell him, while he holds the sword, Morgan keeps the scabbard. Tell him the two were made for each other. If he would sheathe his weapon, I will bring the cover for it."

She blushed when she said it, very deep and rosy.

"Tell him this mantle is the earnest of my faith. The most precious thing I could devise. Its cost is not in wealth of cloth and jewels, but in the gifts of hand and brain and eye that have been spent to make it. Such devotion cannot be bought. Nor can it buy his . . ." She had to break off. There was a word struggling to get to the surface, and a depth of cold and anger it needed to come through. ". . . love," she whispered.

She stepped back then and waved, and we trotted out of the gate with the horses" breath smoking in the winter air.

Sometimes I've puzzled over that. Could she really have meant it? What would have happened if Arthur had taken what she offered him and given her what she asked him on his side? But no. The magic of power I put in that metal at the first couldn't have held out against the curse I'd laid on it at the last. It couldn't have turned out any different.

It was a chill grey morning. The sort that makes the trees look black and the sky dirty. There was a hard frost on the road that made the wheels slip pretty often, but it wasn't so bad we couldn't travel. I'd been hoping we'd find there were snowdrifts or floods across the way and be forced to turn back. I didn't want this errand.

When we got to Carlisle those red walls seemed the only colour in a grim world. They let us through the city gate but stopped us at the king's palace. We said our piece, and they took our present through but made us wait behind. I wasn't sorry. I wanted to be out of there, and the quicker the better. But there were soldiers all round us. Luned hadn't told them all Morgan's message. How could she? That was for Arthur's ears only. Her Woman to his Man. We waited a long time till we saw the royal party come out of the church and in by a different door. Presently Bedwyr came to fetch us. Very gallant he acted to Luned, and even to me, though neither of us were noble ladies. Maybe he was teasing us.

It was warm in the hall they took us into. A grand place, it still seemed to me, with marble couches covered in bright rugs and cushions. A log fire leaping in the hearth but something more than that. The floor itself was warm as we walked over it. Well, you're used to it. I wasn't. There was a throng of lords and ladies gathered round the fire. And they looked glad of it too, after their prayers. Advent's a long fast, and it gives you all the sharper an appetite for Christmas. Bishop Curran was there among them. And Gwenhyvar, of course. She looked small and pale. Her clothes seemed too stiff and grand for such a slip of a girl. Not pregnant either, yet, by the look of her. It was Lady Nimue standing at Arthur's right hand, as if she was his rightful queen and not Gwenhyvar. Arthur himself was in front of the fire dressed in a white wool toga with a border of gold. He was drinking a goblet of hot wine and he looked ready for it.

They'd unwrapped the cloak from the deerskin, but no more. It was lying just as we'd folded it, bound up with a golden cord, in the middle of their fine patterned floor.

"This looks a royal piece of work my sister has sent me."

"Purple for mourning? Would she keep us in Lent?" asked Curran. "Gold is the colour for Christmas."

"Cheer up, man! Purple for empire. The Virgin's pains will soon be ended. The feast of the King is coming!" Arthur waved his goblet at us. "My apologies, ladies, that I kept you waiting in the cold. You will drink a cup of wine with us to make amends?"

I wouldn't say no to that. I needed courage from somewhere. I could see Luned's hand was shaking. I wanted to kick her for a dangerous fool.

They talked politely while we drank our wine, asking after Prince Owain and Princess Morfudd and the big sons of Margawse. There was one son he didn't think he had to worry about.

"Well!" said Arthur, the moment our cups were empty. "Will you not show us what my sister has sent?"

Morgan was right. She didn't need to force him. He'd seen enough already to tempt him. He could hardly take his eyes off it.

We couldn't put off the moment then, though Luned tried. She stammered out Morgan's message. I thought Arthur's cheeks might have got a bit redder as he listened. But his eye was still on the mantle. I don't think he properly took in what Morgan had said. And what did it matter anyway? In a little while his sword was going to be sheathed for good.

I undid the cord. Very carefully, you can be sure, and one of us on each side, we spread the mantle out across the floor. I felt I'd never seen it properly myself till then. They have more windows in this Roman hall than we did in Lyvennet. The lords and ladies crowded round it and marvelled over it. And well they might.

It was a cloak fit for an emperor. Rich purple, laced with gold at the throat. The dragon fairly danced around its border, with silver scales and jewels for eyes and spots and claws. I've never ceased to wonder how women in a cold bare convent could learn to embroider so gloriously as that. Where do they get their visions from? I'd never seen a mantle to touch it for richness. And nor had Arthur.

He swung round to Gwenhyvar, and you could see his man's pride in the grin he gave her. He cut a handsome figure as it was, and he'd dazzle any woman in that cloak, or man either.

"Well, my sweetheart? Will you not think your husband a finer fellow when he is robed in this? It seems I have won my last battle. Mount Badon was nothing to this. Morgan the Wise owns my right at last and offers me the purple."

He couldn't have heard. He hadn't listened to what she was really offering him. Or what she wanted in return from him.

"Oh, yes, yes!" cries Gwenhyvar. And she claps her hands and jumps up and down. "Put it on, Arthur. Now! Let us see you in it. You must wear it to the Great Offering on Christmas Day before all the people. Oh, do you think Morgan would make another cloak like this for me too?"

Arthur signed to two boys, and they ran forward to pick it up. I held my breath then, but they had hold of it by the hem. We hadn't tampered with that. It was mighty heavy and it trailed on the floor. Two lords moved to help them lift it up to Arthur's shoulders. Custennin of Cornwall was one and Gereint the other.

"Wait!" cried Nimue.

I'd known she was watching me all along. I'd hoped she'd think the sweat on my face was from the heat of the fire and the wine. I hadn't let my hands shake. I've handled strong magic before now. I've killed with it. But she was wise. She could see things under the surface. She could smell power in the room. She knew something was afoot. I stared her straight in the eye.

She looked from me to Luned. That nun was a fool. She was white and near to fainting. She hardly tried to hide it.

Nimue fastened on her like a weasel with a leveret.

"This mantle comes from Morgan's hand. Your sisters were always treacherous. Gorlois's daughter speaks you fair, but she has never loved you. Why should she want to send you such a gift as this? You, Uther Pendragon's son?"

"Because she is my sister. Because we share the same mother's blood. Merlyn is no longer here to divide us. I am Arthur, and not Uther. It was never me that Morgan hated. Why should she not be reconciled to me?"

"Then let us put your sister to the test. We will see how well Morgan loves you."

To the lords, "Put the mantle on Morgan's woman first."

I thought she meant me. I don't know why she didn't. Did she remember holding my hand in her fairy palace by the lake? It was Luned she pointed to.

The nun screamed. "No! No! It's a man's cloak. It's too fine for me. I'm only a serving-woman. Not even a lady. The cloak is not for me. Not for me!"

She tried to break away, but Custennin caught her from behind. They laid the cloak on her. She tried to catch it by the collar and hold it off her.

She knows its power, I told myself. That may still save her. If her hands are steady. If her gown is thick enough. If she holds just the purple, and lets it touch, ever so lightly on her shoulders . . .

But how could her hands be steady, knowing what she knew? She couldn't manage. It was too big and heavy, too weighed down with gold and silver and jewels. It fell over her, from her throat down to her feet, and the hem sprawled on the floor. She was swamped under all that purple.

She didn't speak then. She didn't stir one fingernail. You could tell she was holding her breath, as if standing as still as death could save her from it. I knew it couldn't. I could almost feel the weight of it, pressing against her back and her breasts, driving the bare points of wire into her flesh.

Arthur's court didn't feel it, though. They don't know yet how the magic was done. They've never learned the secret. Nimue held out her hand to keep them back. I could tell by her breathing she knew how close we'd come. All they could do was wait and watch.

Then Luned screamed again. It wasn't fear this time. It was pain. Her face began to swell. She turned black, like a monster. Her lips went blue. Her eyes were bloodshot, bulging out of her head, and there was a horrible froth foaming through her teeth. She crashed to the floor and writhed there, yelling and groaning. Our silver dragon coiled and thrashed around her. I came to my senses then and dashed for the door, while everyone was busy shouting and staring. But half a dozen of the men caught me. They held me so I couldn't clap my hands over my ears. I had the horror of a lifetime to live through again. I didn't want to listen to a woman dying in agony like that a second time, but they made me.

Well, Gwenhyvar wasn't the only one white now. I'd never seen Arthur so angry, and he'd had reason enough before. I was sure he'd kill me too. And it flashed on me then why Morgan had fooled him so easily. I reckon he'd wanted to believe it was true, that she really loved him, that those two could heal the breach between them. He'd wanted to think it had all been Merlyn's fault, and now there was nothing to keep them apart.

Well, if he had, that was all over now. He soon got a grip of himself. Bedwyr had his dagger at my throat, but Arthur ordered him to let me go. I couldn't believe it at first, till I saw what he was going to make me do. I was the one who had to pick Luned up, all twisted round in Morgan's mantle, with that terrible face poking out. I had to carry her by myself. None of them was going to help me. They didn't dare to touch her now.

It was a mighty long way across the yard, and the whole palace gone silent as the grave with the shock of it. I could feel the hate. I laid her in the chariot and I wondered that I was still alive myself. A thousand spikes I'd cursed, and not one had pricked me. I brought her body back to Lyvennet.

When Morgan saw the nun's black face she shrieked and tore her hair out. Don't think it was just Luned she was wailing for. She'd lost someone a sight dearer than that. I think she might have been happier if he'd been dead.

She threw herself on her knees in front of me and grabbed my hand. Morgan the Wise, kneeling to me!

"Tell me I did not do it! Tell me this was not my work! I meant it for love! Who am I, Smith? Tell me I am Morgan the Healer, not Morgan the Destroyer!"

I couldn't help her. It had very nearly been Arthur. And all those three must have agreed upon it, mustn't they?

37

The sword won't ever go into its scabbard now. That day won't come when brother and sister will be one. I don't know if it could ever have happened, or what that would have meant. But their chance has gone. They'd stepped a queer sort of dance before, but the music's finished now. There's been silence between those families a long while. He wouldn't even let his sisters' children come to his court till he'd cooled down. Only Morgan's husband Urien. He'd always been loyal.

It was Nimue saved Arthur's life. At least she was wise enough for that. But it set a gap between brother and sister deeper and darker than Merlyn ever drove. It'll never be healed.

Morgan knew it. Next day she took her chariot. There was no one else with us; she made me drive. She let me take a weapon. There was something more precious she kept on her own knee. It was the middle of winter and the snow was lying on the hills. It had been a morning like this when I'd seen Arthur get his sword.

When I saw where we were going, there was a knot went tight in my bowels. We passed Way Bank. There was smoke coming out of my cottage, but the forge was cold. Mair doesn't live there now. I've never heard where she went. We drove by without stopping.

It was a short road beyond that to the Long Lake. But that still wasn't far enough for Morgan. There was a chapel by the water and the priest was ringing his bell for the Christmas Offering. We carried on all along the shore, deeper into the hills yet. The track started to climb and it got rough going. We tethered the horses and went up on foot. Morgan led the way. She hadn't spoken all morning. There was another higher lake. Just a small one, this time. I never saw a blacker water. I got a glimpse of Helvellyn through a gap in the fells. It brought the ravens screaming in my head again and set me shuddering, like that time the hermit found me lost on the mountain. We were both of us close to madness again that day.

Morgan walked down through the reeds to the edge of the water. She didn't seem to notice the ice cracking and the black mud oozing round her feet, or the wind catching her hair and whipping it across her face. She was holding Arthur's scabbard in both hands, just as she'd nursed it to her all through the journey. I was aching to touch it. I knew how she'd be feeling the warmth of it through her palms. It was the only thing she had left now to comfort her. Such an old black battered thing it looked. Arthur never valued it as he had the sword, for all both wise women had warned him it was worth more than the sword.

But it wasn't him that was wounded now. That's still to come.

Morgan took a long, deep breath. She needed to summon every bit of strength she had to do it. Then she hurled the scabbard away from her. It wasn't a good throw. The thing shot up into the air, then did a crooked twist and dropped not far off us. It didn't matter. That little black lake was deep past seeing.

I saw the splash where it fell. I tried to keep my eyes on it. But it didn't sink slowly. We couldn't watch it fade from sight for the last time and say goodbye to it. One moment she had that scabbard in her hand, and then it was gone.

She stood there staring at the ripples. And long after they'd gone I had to rouse her. And still she never spoke a word.

She's only hurt herself. She can't have back what she's thrown away, any more than I can. And there'll be many another hurt before it's done.

The Christmas hymns were ringing out when we got back. She went into the chapel. I stayed outside. When she came out she was a different woman. The way she danced with Urien that night you'd never have guessed how much she'd lost.

But there was another weapon she'd kept hidden.

When Margawse and Elaine had gone home after the New Year, she sent me to the fisherman's hut by Mabon's Stone. Modred was weaned now. I paid Fencha handsomely and I brought him back with me.

The boy stood in front of Morgan. She had her twins on either side of her. She looked down at his dark little face for a long time. Then she hugged him to her so fiercely I feared she'd crush him. Modred yelled. She came to herself and gave him back to me.

"Guard him as you would my life."

And to Owain and Morfudd, "This is your brother."

Morgan's never met Arthur again, till now. But she's bred his son. All these years she's sat by the fire, nursing little Modred on her lap and crooning songs in his ear. Or walked with him on the ramparts at sunset, spinning him tales of old battles lost, while he looks up at her with his little eyes wide. She's taken him riding under the oak trees, and they've hunted more than deer. She's taught him well.

The king's friends don't come to her hall, though Arthur's let his nephews into his warband since. So how would he know that Morgan's foster-child was born on May Day in a year when all those babies should have died? Urien's kept quiet about it. He's too honest a Christian to think a little chap like Modred could mean anyone harm. She hasn't told him who the boy's mother is, or how he was fathered.

Fourteen now, and he's a handsome lad, for all he was such a scowling baby. Urien's taking him to Arthur's court today.

It's strange: Modred was Margawse's son, but he's growing more like Morgan with every day.

Lightning Source UK Ltd.
Milton Keynes UK
21 March 2011

169613UK00002BB/90/A